THE STAMPEDERS

THE STAMPEDERS

James B. Hendryx

GUNSMOKE

First published in the UK by Hammond

This hardback edition 2013
by AudioGO Ltd
by arrangement with
Golden West Literary Agency

ISBN 978 1 471 32133 7

British Library Cataloguing in Publication Data available.

Printed and bound in Great Britain by
MPG Books Group Limited

James B. Hendryx was born in Sauk Center, Minnesota. He attended the University of Minnesota and his early career was in journalism. Later he found work as a cowboy in Montana and work as a construction foreman. It was during this time that he began what would prove to be an extremely rewarding career as an author of Western fiction. His earliest books are set in Montana, but soon the location changes to the Northwestern regions of the Dominion of Canada and occasionally Alaska. *Downey of the Mounted* (Putnam, 1926) featured what became his first popular character creation, Corporal Cameron Downey of the Royal Northwest Mounted Police. At a time when other writers were writing Western fiction set in the American West, Hendryx created what was to be virtually a sub-genre, stories set in Canada with vivid local colour and distinctive Canadian dialogue. His books appealed not only to American readers but to Canadian and English readers throughout the British Commonwealth. To maximize his income from his fiction, Hendryx would publish most of his fiction first in magazines. In "Justice on Halfaday" in *Short Stories* (8/23/31), Corporal Downey was joined by another character, Black John Smith, who would become equally popular. Halfaday Creek was located on the Yukon/Alaska border, and this location would expand the variety of characters in Hendryx's fiction. Often he would put several of his short novels first published in magazines into book-length adventures, unified by the Halfaday setting and Black John Smith. Typical of these were *Outlaws of Halfaday Creek* (Doubleday, 1935) and *Badmen on Halfaday Creek* (Doubleday, 1950). Jarrolds published early titles in British editions, as later did Hammond. Hendryx depicted Canada with a notable police force, effective English law in the courts, and a belief that the rule of law prevails even in remote, wild regions. This is frequently in dramatic contrast to the cynicism regarding law enforcement in American Western fiction. Hendryx's Northwestern fiction over his long career certainly remains an impressive literary achievement.

CONTENTS

CONTENTS

I

The Deserter

The sea was calm. The whaler *Cormorant* rode at anchor, rising and falling lazily on the long, gentle swell of Norton Sound. The sky was heavily overcast, and in the intense blackness, punctuated only by the riding light high on the mast and the sickly pin points of light that glowed in the windows of the trading post at St. Michael a quarter of a mile away, Tilford Carter paced the deck, keeping his solitary watch. He paused and leaned against the rail. There was a tense set to his lips as his eyes fixed on the tiny lights. Dully to his ears came the monotonous surge of the swell as it broke against the shore. The ship had dropped anchor two days before to take on additional stores for the summer's venture into the Arctic.

"It's now or never," he muttered grimly, and shuddered slightly in the chill night air. "I heard the captain tell the mate that we'd pull out at daylight. And this is the last settlement we'll touch till fall." Slipping a hand into his pocket, young Carter fingered the little roll of bills he had that afternoon sewed in an oiled-silk wrapping. Withdrawing the hand, he gave a reassuring tug at the life belt he had strapped on under his pea jacket. "I may not make it, but drowning would be better than spending the summer on this stinking ship, with a damned sadist for a captain, and a brutal drunken mate, and a crew that was scooped up out of the gutters of Seattle. And I signed on for romance and adventure! Romance and adventure—hell! If I had Herman Melville here I'd wring his neck. I wish I'd never read *Moby Dick!*"

Stepping aft, he slipped a coil of rope from beneath the canvas cover of a boat, secured one end to the rail, and tossed the coil overboard. Slipping out of his pea jacket, he placed a hand on the rail, then whirled sharply at the sound of a rasping voice close to his ear. "Goin' someplace?" There was a slight grating sound as the speaker slid back the tin slide of an oil-dark lantern to reveal the face of the captain, whose yellowed snaggy teeth were bared in a sneering grin. "Figgerin' on desertin' ship, eh? It's ben tried afore now. But me—I know all the tricks. I got ways of findin' out. I got eyes in the fo'c'sle, an' when one of the boys tells me he sees you sewin' yer money up waterproof, I know'd what was comin'. I've handled uppity guys like you. Don't like 'em—no more'n the rest of the crew does. An' Mr. Jackson, the mate—he hates 'em worst of all. You'll find that out tomorrer when he starts in on yer bare back with his cat-o'-nine-tails. The crew'll be there to watch—good lesson fer 'em—in case they'd git notions of their own. I'll be there too, so you don't need to worry none—I'll stop him short of cuttin' you plumb in two. You signed on, an' I gotta git a summer's work outa you."

The words stung young Carter to fury. The next instant his fist crashed against the captain's outthrust jaw. Again he struck, and again, and the captain collapsed, pitching forward on his face. The dark lantern rolled along the deck, flaring smokily. Stooping, Carter picked it up and hurled it overboard, and again the world was plunged into blackness. Hastily removing his boots, Carter climbed over the rail, grasped the rope, and with a glance toward the tiny shore lights lowered himself hand over hand into the sea. The water was cold. He gasped as submergence in the icy water seemed to drive the very air from his lungs. Then he struck out, his eyes on the tiny pin points of light.

The cold water numbed his muscles—seemed to numb his very brain—and it was only by intense concentration that he drove the muscles of his arms and legs in long, powerful strokes. On and on he swam, his eyes on the little lights that never seemed to get any nearer. He changed from side stroke to breast stroke. He rolled over and swam on his back. And only then, as his eyes caught the gleam of the ship's riding light, did he realize that he was making headway—the riding light seemed as far away as the lights from the trading-post windows.

Doggedly he drove his numbed muscles. Each stroke became a conscious effort. He wasn't tired. The water no longer seemed cold. A delicious lassitude obsessed him. It seemed that he had been swimming for hours. The stroke slowed, and slowly his eyelids closed. The next instant he was strangling—coughing sea water from his lungs. His numbed brain again functioned, and he struck out, driving his muscles to their work. The trading lights seemed near now—almost within arm's reach—and in his ears the surge of the surf boomed loudly. Cautiously he lowered his feet. They struck bottom, but as he tried to stand his knees collapsed and he pitched forward, holding his breath as his body was lifted on a swell and tossed onto the mud amid a cascade of foaming water. Another swell broke over him, and driving his numbed muscles to their utmost effort, he crawled weakly out of reach of the breaking surf.

Til Carter never knew how long he lay there in the mud. It may have been minutes or hours before consciousness returned in the realization of a deadly chill—a chill that struck to his very bones. Gradually his brain cleared, and tentatively he moved his arms—his legs. He rose to his hands and knees, tried to stand, but his knees buckled under him and he sprawled in the mud. Again he tried, and again. On the third attempt he staggered a few steps and brought up against a pole that supported one end of a fish-drying wire. Grasping the pole with both hands, he managed to stand erect. He stamped his feet, slowly at first, then faster, as feeling returned to them. Releasing his grip with one hand, he thrashed his arm against his body. Changing hands, he repeated the performance with his other arm until finally the numbness was gone and he seemed to feel the blood coursing through his veins.

Still grasping the pole, he turned toward the trading post, only to encounter the Stygian blackness of the night. Far out over the water he could see the riding light at the masthead of the *Cormorant*. It looked to be miles away. "I'm lucky to be here," he muttered. "Damned lucky."

The trader had evidently doused his lights and gone to bed. Til thought of making his way through the darkness and awakening him. But what would happen? The trader was probably a friend of Captain Baggs. At least he was a business acquaintance. He had sold him certain stores. What would he do if a deserter from Baggs's ship should wake him up in the middle of the night and seek asylum? Til realized that he was not only a deserter but that he had assaulted a captain on his own ship. He knew that the law in such case made and provided was stern and unrelenting. But it wasn't the law he feared. Knowing Baggs for the vindictive sadist that he was, and the drunken mate Jackson, he realized that between the two of them, once he was returned to the *Cormorant*, his life wouldn't be worth a plugged nickel. And he knew that at the first break of dawn a boat would put off from the ship, under orders to bring him back. He glanced about, and an ominous graying in the east told him that dawn was not far off.

Releasing his grasp on the pole, he turned his back to the sea and walked inland. In the slowly increasing light he passed several shacks but kept on walking. At the end of a half hour the door of a shack situated on a rise a short distance back from the bank of one of the numerous sloughs that crisscross the delta country opened and a man stepped out. He was a short, thickset man with a wide, flat face, and he stood regarding him stolidly.

Til greeted him. "Hello! How's the chance to go in your house and dry out?"

The man blinked. "Who you?"

"Carter's my name—Til Carter. I'm wet and cold. I'd like to get dry."

The man continued to stare. "Me Kootlak," he stated.

Til smiled. "I'm glad to meet you."

The man returned the smile as his eyes scanned the surface of the slough, then turned seaward and fixed upon the distant *Cormorant*. "You com' off ship?" he asked.

Til hesitated, vainly casting about in his mind for some reasonable excuse for appearing at daylight, drenched to the skin, but could find none. "Yes," he answered. "In the night. I swam ashore."

Til thought he caught a gleam of approval in the dark eyes as Kootlak said: "Long swim. Mooch col'."

Til nodded. "Yes, that's why I'd like to get warm."

"You no like on ship—ron 'way?" the man asked.

Again Til Carter found himself groping for a reasonable excuse, and again he failed to produce one. "Yes," he answered. "I ran away."

The smile widened on the Eskimo's face. "Me, I'm no lak dat ship neider. Cap Baggs son-de-beetch. I sail wit heem las' sommer. Som'tam I'm lak I'm steek de harpoon een hees guts."

Til Carter laughed aloud as the tension on his nerves suddenly relaxed. "God be with you, brother!" he exclaimed fervidly, and thrust out his hand. "I hope that sometime you'll get the chance to do it! I knocked hell out of him last

13

night just before I left. I expect he'll have a crew in here hunting for me before long."

The Eskimo grasped the outthrust hand in a firm grip. "Cap Baggs—heem no fin'. Heem t'ink you no git to lan'. You git drownded. Come een de house. You git dry. De 'oman she mak' you som' grub."

II

Two Sourdoughs Connive

The steamer *Arctic*, chugging down the Yukon, swung
shoreward in answer to a signal and picked up Gordon
Bettles at Old Station, seventeen miles below the mouth of
the Tanana. As he picked his way down the muddy bank
and stepped onto the plank Bettles was vociferously greeted
by Jack McQuesten, a sourdough from Fortymile. "Damn
your old hide! Where you headin'? An' don't try to tell me
yer doin' all right down here! This middle-river country's
no good—an' never will be. Come on up to Fortymile! By
God, there's the comin' country! A man can pan out better'n wages jest snipin' the bars, an' quite a few of the boys
has made real strikes."

As the boat got under way the two sourdoughs moved
forward on deck and squatted on their packsacks. Bettles
filled his pipe. "Yer right about this middle-river country,
Jack," he agreed. "She ain't worth a damn. Got anything on
yer hip? I ain't had a drink since God knows when."

Reaching into his packsack, McQuesten drew out a bottle
and handed it to the other. "Go easy on it. That's all I've
got, an' she's about half gone. Got it off'n Hooch Albert at

Rampart. Wouldn't let me have but the one bottle, an' soaked me an ounce for it. Tastes like he made it out of coal oil an' chewin' tobacco—but it's got a wallop, at that. Albert claims there's goin' to be a big celebration down to Nulato the Fourth, an' he can git two ounces a bottle down there."

Bettles drew the cork, raised the bottle to his lips, and took a couple of liberal swallows. Gagging slightly, he made a wry face and handed the bottle back. "Yer givin' Albert all the best of it when you claim he made it out of coal oil an' chewin' tobacco. Damnedest-tastin' stuff I ever drank. Might taste better, though, after it begins to take holt."

McQuesten grinned. "Yeah, an' by that time it'll all be gone. An' that's another reason you ort to come up to Forty-mile. Bergman's got a good saloon up there. There don't no one bother him. The Mounted's got more sense than these damn U.S. marshals. But you didn't say where yer headin'."

"I'm goin' to St. Michael first. Then I figured I'd make another try on the Koyukuk."

"The Koyukuk! Cripes—I thought you'd got a bellyful of the Koyukuk. You put in two, three years up there an' never done no good."

"Al Mayo stopped by the other day an' he says there's some new strikes ben made above where I was."

"There's a camp named after you up there, ain't there?"

"Yeah, fellow name of Kemper's got a tradin' post there. It's where I first located at the foot of a big rapids about five hundred miles up the river. I didn't do so bad the first year. But she kind of petered out on me. There's a hell of a lot of country up there, an' quite a bit of gold's come out of it. I've still got faith in it. That's the reason I'm hittin' for St. Michael. There's an Eskimo down there name of Kootlak. He used to be up on the Koyukuk when I was. He knows the country. Lived up on the Jim River. The Jim runs into the Koyukuk about a hundred miles above Bettles. He's a damn good man. I figure he might like to go back there."

McQuesten shrugged. "Well, gold's where you find it. You might make a strike up there. I like the Fortymile country best. The Koyukuk's too far north. The season's too short an' it's too damn cold."

"Gettin' soft, eh?" Bettles grinned.

"Soft—hell! What I claim, what's the use in kihootin' off into a Godforsakin country like that when there's plenty of gold on the Fortymile? A man can put in more time on the Fortymile than he can on the Koyukuk, an' do it more comfortable. An' besides, we've got a saloon. Anyway, you can get up there a damn sight easier an' quicker than you used to."

"How do you mean—easier an' quicker?"

"Fellow name of Fred Martin's built a steamboat at Nulato to run the Koyukuk. Figures to make two trips a year—mebbe three. He's goin' to make his first start right after the celebration at Nulato on the Fourth. Heard about it in Rampart."

"An', by God, I'll be on that first run!" Bettles exclaimed. "An' Kootlak, too, if I can persuade him."

"I'm wishin' you luck," McQuesten said, "but I'm bettin' you'll be showin' up at Fortymile inside of two years. To hell with that north country!"

The *Arctic* pulled in at Nulato, and while she wooded up Bettles inspected the newly built steamboat and engaged passage for two on her maiden voyage up the Koyukuk. On a friendly tip from the trader he also purchased a bottle of hooch from a character who went by the name of Dog Face Nolan.

Back on the *Arctic*, the two sourdoughs resumed their seats and Bettles passed McQuesten the bottle. Taking a liberal swallow, he smacked his lips and handed the bottle back. "Tastes a little better'n Albert's," he admitted. "But mebbe it ain't got the wallop."

"Well, hell—a man can't expect everything," Bettles replied as he sampled the liquor and returned the cork.

"I was jest thinkin'," McQuesten said, "that mebbe the *Bear* will be at St. Michael when you git there."

"She might be. She's generally about the first boat in in the spring. You figurin' I might persuade Cap Heally to run me up the Koyukuk in the *Bear?*"

McQuesten grinned. "No. But, by God, if anyone could run her up the Koyukuk, Cap Heally could. I was thinkin' of Doc McCall."

"Somethin' ailin' you?"

"Yeah. It's that celebration at Nulato on the Fourth. You can't pull off no decent celebration without likker—an' it looks like all we're goin' to git is a choice between that God-awful-tastin' stuff of Hooch Albert's an' this here weakish concoction of Dog Face Nolan's—both of which I don't like neither one. You know Doc McCall a damn sight better'n I do. An' you know he's always collectin' native stuff—stone knives, an' axes, an' scrapers, an' lamps, besides petrified mammoth teeth, an' chunks of mammoth ivory, an' native skulls, an' the like of that. On top of all that, he saves specimens of queer fish, an' bugs, an' things."

Bettles frowned. "Well, s'pose he does? What of it? I shore as hell don't want to drink no likker made out of fish an' bugs!"

"Like this—in order to save them bugs an' fish an' things he's got to pickle 'em—pickle 'em in alcohol. I was wonderin' if you couldn't figure some way to trade him out of some alcohol. The boys up to Nulato would shore appreciate some good likker to celebrate on. We could mix it half an' half with water."

"By cripes, Jack, maybe you've got somethin' there!" Bettles exclaimed. "Shore I know about Doc collectin' all them things. Fact is I've got a partly fossilized mammoth tooth in my pack for him right now—an' a skull, an' a couple of slate spearheads. I was goin' to leave 'em with Nelson, the trader, to give to Doc when the *Bear* showed up."

"Yeah, but that stuff ain't no good fer what we want,"

McQuesten objected. "You don't have to pickle spearheads an' mammoth teeth to keep 'em."

"That's so," Bettles agreed. "I'll study on it. Maybe I can think up somethin' to collect that needs picklin'."

"Make it sound reasonable, Gordon," McQuesten said. "Remember the hull damn celebration is dependin' on you. I'm gittin' off at Anvik. Want to see Steve Boardman about buyin' the biler out of that steamboat of his that burnt last fall. I'm goin' to try thawin' out the gravel with steam this winter. I'll go back up with you when the *Arctic* comes along—an' for cripes' sake, fetch that alcohol!"

III

Captain Baggs Finds His Deserter

Til Carter followed Kootlak into the house, a single-room structure some fourteen feet square. A woman, slightly taller than the man, lifted a teapot from the stove and set it on the table placed before the single window overlooking the slough. Kootlak spoke a few words to her in the native tongue. He turned to Til. "Dis my 'oman nem Nowak."

Til bowed and smiled. "I'm glad to know you. I'm Til Carter." As the woman returned the smile Til noted that although her face was swarthy as the man's, it was more oval, the features regular, actually handsome in outline. He noted, too, that she smiled with her eyes as well as her lips —a friendly smile.

"Kootlak say you wet an' col'. Tak' you clo's off. Get dry."

Til glanced about the room, the entire furnishing of which consisted of the stove and table, four wooden chairs, a wide bunk built along one wall, and a low bench upon which stood a water pail and a washdish, also against the wall. He noted with surprise that everything—floor, bunk, table, and the dishes on the rude shelf—was scrupulously clean. A round-faced baby, apparently about two years old, sat on the floor, stared up at him through bright beady eyes, smiled, and extended a hand in which was a curiously carved wooden canoe.

Nowak's smile widened. "Baby like you," she said. "He want give you kayak."

Stooping, Til prodded the youngster in the ribs and was rewarded by a gurgle of laughter. Straightening up, he hesitated a moment. "I can just stand there by the stove and dry off," he said.

Noting his evident embarrassment, the woman giggled. "No. Git clothes off. Dry on rack." Stepping to the bunk, she picked up a blanket and handed it to him. "Git in warm blanket. You no git seek. Clo's dry queek on rack."

Kootlak seconded the opinion and handed Til a bit of sealskin line. "Tie blanket roun' you belly. Den we eat."

As the woman busied herself about the stove Til succeeded in removing his wet clothing and wrapping the blanket about him, fastening it at the waist with the bit of thong. When he had finished, the woman set a dish heaped high with smoked-salmon strips on the table and placed a bowl of oatmeal before each of the three places she had set, while Kootlak hung the wet clothing on the rack above the stove.

Bare to the waist, Til seated himself beside Kootlak, while at the end of the table the woman sat with the baby on her lap, after filling the three thick porcelain cups with steaming hot chocolate. Not until then had he realized that he was ravenously hungry. His bowl of oatmeal, condensed milk, and sugar disappeared, and he thought the salmon strips, washed down by draughts of hot chocolate, by far the most satisfying meal he had ever eaten.

When it was finished he turned to Nowak. "That's the best breakfast I ever had," he said. "Gosh, that greasy mess they shove to you on the *Cormorant* isn't fit for a dog to eat!"

Kootlak grinned. "W'en dey git cuttin' up whale, den she git worse. De cabin stink. De fo'c'sle stink. De grub stink. De men stink. Everyt'ing stink. But git so dam' hongry got to eat."

Til nodded. "I can well believe it," he said. "We ran onto a big herd of seals swimming in the ocean a short time before we sighted St. Paul's Island, and the boats were lowered and all hands except the captain and the mate and the watch attacked the seals with harpoons and rifles. It was a shame. They were all females, heavy with young, and in the two days we kept up with the herd we killed over two hundred of them. They were hoisted on deck, skinned, and the bodies thrown overboard. The skins were salted and stowed in the hold. And if a couple of hundred seals can stink up a ship like those did, I can well imagine what it will be like when they begin to work on whales."

As the woman continued to feed the baby gruel from a spoon Kootlak stepped outside and returned shortly with an armful of firewood. "Com' boat from *Cormorant*. Four, fi' mans. Com' mebbe-so hont for you. Cap Baggs git mad you knock hell out heem an' jomp ship. *Arctic* com' in too. Com' down Yukon, jus' drop anchor in front tradin' pos'. Way off iss smoke. Mebbe-so de *Bear* com' in too. Lot of ship com'. De *Bear*, she gov'mint ship."

"Government ship!" Til exclaimed. "Gosh, if Captain Baggs and his crew succeed in finding me and I refuse to go back with 'em, he could report me to a government official, and he'd either make me go back or arrest me for assaulting an officer on the high seas, and for desertion!"

Kootlak shook his head. "Me, I'm ain' t'ink Cap Baggs fin' you. I ain' t'ink he tell Cap Heally 'bout you knock hell out heem an' jomp ship. Cap Heally good man. All good mans on *Bear*."

Again the Eskimo started out, and turned in the doorway. "Me, I'm go to tradin' pos' fin' out w'at Cap Baggs say." A huge black-and-white cat slipped into the room carrying a

22

lemming in his mouth. The man stepped from the room and a moment later was back. "Com's man from tradin' pos'! Mebbe-so Cap Baggs! Qweek git onder bunk!" Jerking the drying clothing from the rack, the man spread it on the bunk under which Til was wriggling and drew a caribou-skin robe over the garments, allowing its edge to touch the floor, concealing the aperture beneath. Rising, Nowak placed the baby on the floor, where he promptly seized hold of the limp lemming and tried to pull it away from the cat. Crossing to the bunk, the woman seated herself upon it and began industriously stitching at a shirt. Loud howls came from the baby as the cat succeeded in pulling the lemming from his grasp and darting under the bunk, where it squatted within a few inches of Til's face and with low growls proceeded to tear the little animal to pieces.

A few moments later Kootlak opened the door in answer to a lusty knocking, and a voice greeted him heartily. "Hi, Kootlak, you ornery son-of-a-gun! An' there's Nowak too! Doggone if you don't get better-lookin' as time goes on! An' look at the kid! Last time I saw him he wasn't no bigger'n my fist. How you folks ben, anyhow?"

The man grinned. "We a'ri'. Long time no see. W'at you com' St. Michael? Goin' ship on whaler?"

The newcomer laughed. "No whaler for me. Even if I wanted to ship on one, I shore as hell wouldn't ship with that damn Cap Baggs. If you're hell-bent on whalin' this summer, you can prob'ly ship with him. He's over to the tradin' post madder'n a hornet. Claims one of his crew knocked him out last night with a belayin' pin an' then let himself over the rail with a rope. Nelson says no one showed up at the post durin' the night, an' the chances are that the fellow never made shore. That's a hell of a long swim in this cold water. I shore wouldn't want to try it."

"Man com' shore a'ri'. Him here."

"Here! Where?" the newcomer asked, glancing about the room. "An' why did he come here?"

"W'en he swim from ship he kin see light in tradin' pos'. Before he git to lan', Nelson put out de light an' gon' to bed. He 'fraid he wake Nelson up Nelson git mad on heem an' give heem back to Cap Baggs w'en he com' hont for heem. Iss git daylight an' he walk 'way from pos' so Cap Baggs no kin fin' heem, an' com' 'long here w'en I'm go out to git wood, an' he say he lak to git dry, so I breeng heem in de house."

"But—where is he now?"

Kootlak grinned as Nowak arose from the bunk, threw back the robe, and replaced Til's clothing on the drying rack. "Heem onder de bunk. Me, I'm goin' out for git mor' wood, an' I'm see man com' from tradin' pos', I'm t'ink mebbe-so Cap Baggs com' hont for man, so I'm tell heem git onder bunk, an' I'm tak' de clo's off de dry rack an' put de robe on dem, an' Nowak sit on de robe." Pausing, he called to Til, who wriggled out from under the bunk, adjusted his blanket, and smiled.

"Carter's my name," he said. "Til Carter. I overheard what you said. I deserted from the *Cormorant* last night and swam ashore. But Captain Baggs is a damned liar if he says I knocked him out with a belaying pin. I used my fists—and he knows it."

The man returned the smile. "I'm Gordon Bettles, from here an' there along the river. So you don't like Cap Baggs, eh?"

"No, I don't like him, nor his drunken mate, nor his crew, nor anything else about his stinking ship. I signed on for a whaling voyage hoping for some excitement and adventure. It didn't take me long to find out what kind of an outfit it was, so when we stopped at a salmon cannery dock somewhere along the coast I told the captain I wanted to quit. The only satisfaction I got out of that was the information that I'd signed on for the voyage and there was no backing out. The statement was emphasized by a punch on the jaw that knocked me flat on the deck while the mate and crew looked on and laughed. I could have killed the damn cuss then and there—but the way things stood, the odds weren't right for me to start anything. So I shut up, but I made up my mind to desert at the first opportunity.

"It came, last night. I had hidden a coil of rope in a boat, and shortly after I went on watch I got the rope and made one end fast to the rail and tossed the coil overboard. As I was about to lower myself into the water and try to swim ashore, the captain flashed a dark lantern on me and asked me if I was going somewhere. He said that one of the crew had reported seeing me sewing my money into a waterproof covering, so he figured I was going to try to desert ship, and he promised me that in the morning the mate would go to work on my bare back with a cat-o'-nine-tails.

"The odds were different this time, with only the two of us there on deck, and I laced into him with my fists—got in three or four good stiff swings to his jaw, and he went down and stayed down. I tossed his lantern overboard and went over the side. It sure was a cold swim and a long one. But I made it. And I'm not going back."

Bettles grinned. "I'll say it was a cold swim," he agreed. "An' I can't say as I blame you for not wantin' to go back. But"—and his grin widened—"from your angle the trip didn't turn out so bad, at that. You signed on for some excitement an' adventure. You got it, didn't you? By God, I'd claim it was an adventure—knockin' a captain cold on his own deck an' swimmin' damn near half a mile in ice water! Took guts to start it, an' more guts to see it through."

Til shrugged. "It would have taken more guts than that to have stuck out a whole summer on that damned ship," he said. "The way I figure it, I took the easy way out."

"Guess you're right, at that," Bettles agreed, and turned to the native. "There's a new strike ben made way up the Koyukuk," he said. "Al Mayo was tellin' me about it. It's somewheres up around your old stampin' ground—the Jim River country. I'm goin' up an' take a look-see. Thought maybe you'd like to go along. That's what I came to see you about."

Kootlak's brow wrinkled and he glanced at his wife. Nowak shook her head emphatically. "No," she said. "No like Koyukuk. Too mooch col'. Too mooch no peoples. Too far to pos'. Too mooch no grub. Got baby now. Got to git good grub."

"But cripes, Nowak," Bettles argued, "Kootlak might strike it lucky up there. Might make a big strike—lots of gold. Then in a year or so you could come back down an' live wherever you wanted to!"

The woman smiled. "See lot of mans try for mak' de beeg strike. Work hard all time. No mak' strike. Mebbe-so wan man, two man mak' strike. Rest of mans work hard, got nuttin'. We git 'long good here. Kootlak work, som'tam Mission, som'tam tradin' pos', som'tam hont an' feesh. Git 'nough to eat. Lots of peoples here. No go to Koyukuk. W'at you call too lonesome."

"Well, how about Kootlak goin' up there with me an' you stayin' here?"

"No. Kootlak my mans. He stay wit' me."

"Well, I guess that settles it," Bettles grinned. "Don't know's I blame you. That is a kind of a tough country up there."

A loud knock sounded on the door, and Kootlak opened it, then quickly stepped outside, closing the door behind him—but not before the sound of a harsh voice caused Til Carter to stiffen. Bettles also heard the voice and, with a wink at Til, joined Kootlak outside. The minute the door closed behind him Til reached for his half-dry clothes and, as Nowak turned her back, wriggled into them.

Outside Captain Baggs greeted the native heartily. "Hello, Kootlak! Lookin' fit as ever, I see. Allus claimed you was a good man. Best damn native I ever had. How about signin' on fer the summer? I kin pay you five dollars more on the month than last year, on account you ain't no green hand.

Lost a man last night, an' I'm shorthanded. Green hand. He was on watch, an' I took a turn around the deck to see how he was gittin' along, when he whammed me over the head with a belayin' pin an' slipped overboard. The damn fool never made shore, though. Nelson ain't seen nothin' of him at the post, an' Mr. Jackson, here, patrolled the beach for half a mile each way an' didn't find nothin'—not even his body. No one could swim that fer with heavy clothes on an' the water cold as it is. Prob'ly drownded an' the sharks got him."

"Damn good reddence, I says," the mate added. "He wasn't no good. Didn't fit in with the crew. Fetched some books aboard, an' when he'd git the chanct he'd read in 'em. What I claim, a guy that would read a book would rape his gran'mother!"

"I wish't he'd of made shore, at that," the captain said. "I'd like to got even with him fer whammin' me over the head with that belayin' pin."

The door opened and closed swiftly and Til Carter stood facing the captain. "I did make shore," he said in a flinty tone. "And you've got your chance to get even right now. And when you say I whammed you over the head with a belayin' pin you're a God-damned liar—and you know it!"

As Til spoke Kootlak unobtrusively lifted a sixteen-inch snow knife from its peg in the wall beside the door.

The captain's eyes widened at sight of Til and his lips drew into a snarl. "How the hell did you git here?" he cried.

"Swam part way and walked the rest."

The mate, who had been standing behind the captain, leaped forward with clenched fists. "Come on, Cap—grab the son-of-a-bitch! We'll learn him——" The flow of words ceased abruptly and the mate drew back, his eyes on the sharp point of the harpoon that a moment before had been leaning against the wall.

"One at a time, Jackson," Bettles said, advancing the point of the weapon slightly, "unless you want to find out how the

27

mate of a whaler would feel wigglin' around on the end of a spear."

The captain's eyes shifted from Til to the long-bladed snow knife and then to the harpoon. He appealed to Bettles. "This man assaulted a superior officer on shipboard an' then jumped ship. He's a deserter. He signed on fer the voyage all fair an' reg'lar, an' we got a right to take him back to the ship. The law's on our side. We don't aim to harm him—jest take him back. If he knows what's good fer him he'll come peaceable. If he don't, we got a right to take him back forcible. That's the law."

Til's fists clenched as he stepped toward the captain, who backed away. "I assaulted you, all right," he said, "and I deserted your stinking ship. The law may be on your side—but you're going to have a hell of a time enforcing it. In the meantime pull off your coat and get even with me for knocking you down. You said you wanted to—come on and do it! And when I get through with you, I'll take *Mister* Jackson on—if he's sober enough, and has guts enough to fight. I'd like to find out how good he is when he hasn't got a cat-o'-nine-tails in his fist and the captain and most of the crew backing him up—like he had that day on the ship when that poor devil let the winch slip."

Captain Baggs backed a couple of more discreet steps away from Til's clenched fists and narrowed eyes. He jerked his thumb over his shoulder in the direction of the *Bear*, which had dropped anchor not far from the *Cormorant*. "You claim we'll have a hell of a time enforcin' the law," he said. "There's the *Bear*. She's a gov'mint ship, an' they's officers aboard her that'll tend to enforcin' maritime law. We're lucky."

Kootlak scowled at the two officers. "You cheat me las' year 'bout twenty dolla. I no go on you ship no mor'." He paused and pointed to Til. "Dis mans no go on you ship no mor', neider. Him good mans. No good mans go on you damn ship. You say officer on *Bear* mak' heem go back.

Mebbe-so w'en you tell 'em 'bout dis man jomp ship you tell 'em 'bout dem two hondre sealskin you got in de hold, eh? Mebbe-so you ain' so damn lucky you t'ink."

"What the hell do you mean—two hundred sealskins!" cried the captain.

"He means the skins we salted down and stowed in the hold. The skins of those female seals, every one heavy with young, that we butchered when we ran onto that herd near St. Paul's Island. It's a damned shame, and I wondered if it wasn't illegal when I noticed you kept a lookout at the mast-head all the time the boats were out, and again when you made the crew clean up every last trace of blood and blubber from the deck where we skinned the seals. I knew it wasn't from any sense of cleanliness you might have. Below deck, from galley to fo'c'sle, your ship stinks like a latrine. Come to think of it, I guess I'll have a talk with the officers of the *Bear* myself."

The belligerent, outthrust jaw of Captain Baggs drooped, his shoulders seemed to sag as he nervously wet his lips with his tongue and cast an appealing glance at his mate.

Jackson shrugged. "Don't look at me. You're the captain. Anythin' I done I done under orders."

Bettles grinned as he eyed the captain. "Looks like you've shrunk about three sizes in three minutes, Cap. Better reef yer belt in a couple of holes or yer pants'll drop off."

Captain Baggs cleared his throat nervously. "Listen, Carter," he said, "you didn't fit in with my crew. I seen that. An' I felt kinda sorry fer you. I'd of let you go when you wanted to, down there at the cannin' factory, but I needed every man I had—an' you'd signed on fer the voyage."

"Is that why you knocked me down when you told me I couldn't quit the ship—because you were sorry for me?"

"Well, hell—I hadn't ort to done that, mebbe. I got a lot on my mind, an' I'm kinda short-tempered, like, when things don't go to suit me. I don't want you to have no hard feelin's. I'll make a deal with you—if you don't say nothin' to Captain Heally of the *Bear* about them seals, I won't say nothin' about assaultin' me on my own deck an' then desertin'. If we go shootin' off our mouth, it would make it mean fer both of us."

"And I'm free to go where I please?"

"That's right. I kin ship a native in yer place, either here er somewheres along the coast."

"How about my duffel? Will you have that set ashore at the trading post?"

"Yes, I'll do that."

"And my pay?"

"Well—you got a month's pay comin'. That's thirty dollars. I ain't got my wallet along, er I'd pay you right here. But I'll send it ashore with yer bag."

"You told me when I signed on that the pay, figuring in my board an' bonus and all, would figure right around a hundred dollars a month."

"Yeah—I said it could come to about that. Tell you what I'll do—jest to show there ain't no hard feelin's. I'll make it the hundred, instead of thirty."

"You told me the voyage would last five months. I signed on for five months—I'm entitled to five months' pay. I'm a long way from home. I need the money."

"Five months' pay!" the captain cried. "You mean—five hundred dollars!"

"That's what I mean!"

"By God, I won't pay it! It's robbery! That's what it is!"

Til grinned. "Okay. It's all right with me. Just forget the whole thing—and we'll both go and talk things over with Captain Heally."

The captain hesitated. "You got me," he said finally. "I'll pay. Yer five hundred will be in yer bag along with yer duffel."

"Just see that it is," Til replied. "And don't make any mistake about the amount. And don't try to haul anchor and sneak out of your bargain, either. It wouldn't take the *Bear* very long to overhaul you."

As the two discomfited officers turned and strode off in the direction of the trading post, Bettles roared with laughter and thumped the younger man on the back. "By God, you handed it to him, boy—all done up in as neat a package as I ever seen! An' say, bein' as Kootlak won't go up the Koyukuk, how about you takin' a shot at it? There's gold along the rivers. Lots of it bein' taken out. But I'm tellin' you the big strike ain't come yet! But it's comin'! An' you an' me might be in on it. If we don't hit it on the Koyukuk, we'll hit it somewheres else. You claim you're huntin' excitement an' adventure. I'm tellin' you there's more excitement an' adventure along the rivers in a month than there is on a whaler in a year! We don't go much on chechakos in this country. But you're different. I kinda like the way you work. I'm bettin' you'll make good."

Til grinned. "Okay," he said. "You can count me in. I always did think I'd like to try my hand at prospecting. I'll be ready to pull out as soon as my dear old captain sets my duffel and my money ashore."

IV

Bettles Dabbles in Science

As Captain Baggs and the mate disappeared in the direction of the trading post, the three re-entered the house. Til glanced down at his bare feet. "I sure hope Baggs makes good on his promise to send my duffel ashore—and that five hundred too. I've got some money with me, but I expect there'll be quite a few items of outfit I'll be needing."

Bettles grinned. "You don't need to be afraid that Baggs'll renig on sendin' that stuff to the post. You shore called his bluff when you told him you'd both go to Cap Heally with your troubles. He knew damn well there was no one on the *Bear* with authority to force you back on his ship. The *Bear's* a Coast Guard cutter. An' he knew that one word to Heally about those sealskins in his hold an' he'd do plenty of time in jail an' lose the *Cormorant* to boot. When it comes to seal poachin', those Coast Guard boys don't fool!"

"The credit belongs to Kootlak," Til said. "It was he who mentioned the sealskins. I had a sort of inkling that the killing was somehow illegal, but I hadn't thought of pulling it on Baggs till Kootlak mentioned it and I saw how it hit Baggs where it hurt." Reaching into his pocket, he withdrew a small packet and, picking up a knife from the table, cut the stitches of its oiled-silk wrapping and disclosed a roll of bills. "I'd never have got a nickel out of Baggs, and I'd have lost my duffel too—so the way I figure it, Kootlak is entitled to half that five hundred. I've got four hundred here." Pausing, he counted out two hundred and fifty dollars and offered it to the Eskimo, who drew back, his hands behind him. "No," the man said emphatically. "Dat you money. Me, I'm no tak'." Despite Til's urging, the man stubbornly refused the money, and he turned to Nowak. "You take it, then. It's yours. Kootlak sure earned it."

The woman shook her head. "No. Kootlak no earn heem. No kin earn so mooch money so queek."

Frowning, Til glanced down, and on the floor the baby smiled up at him and extended the little wooden kayak. Til's lips widened in a broad grin. "Okay, kid," he said. "It's a deal!" Stooping, he took the toy, pocketed it, and thrust the roll of bills into the chubby hand. Then, still smiling broadly, he turned to the two Eskimos. "I bought the kayak from the baby—and there's nothing you can do about it. The money is his. Keep it for him. Sometime it may come handy. We'll be hitting for the trading post now. So long—and thanks for everything. I owe you people a lot more than I'll ever be able to repay. I don't know what would have happened to me if I hadn't run onto you."

On the way to the post Bettles slanted the younger man a glance. "You're a square shooter, Til," he said. "That was a damn fine thing to do. Time'll come when that kid can use that money—you bet."

"It was no more than fair. Anyway, they've got it. If the kid can't use it, his parents can."

Bettles shook his head. "Kootlak an' Nowak are honest. Most Eskimos are. They're a damn sight different from the Siwashes. No matter how bad they might need that money, neither one of 'em will ever touch a damn cent of it. When the time comes they'll turn every nickel of it over to the kid—you can bet on that. An' here's another thing—you made an investment there that might pay damn big dividends."

"What do you mean?"

"I mean that maybe a month from now, or six months—maybe a year, or ten years—maybe here in the delta country, maybe a thousan' miles from here—sometime—somewhere—you might need help, an' need it bad. An' if you do, an' there's an Eskimo around, by God, you'll get it! Moccasin telegraph. An Eskimo never forgets." As they neared the trading post Bettles pointed seaward with a grin. "Here comes your duffel, an' your five hundred dollars," he said. "That boat just put off from the *Cormorant*. Cap Baggs ain't wastin' any time. He'll be haulin' up his hook an' headin' north as quick as that boat gets back. He's too damn close to the *Bear* for comfort. The wind might shift, an' Cap Healy might get a whiff of them sealskins. An' that reminds me, we'll be payin' the *Bear* a call before we head upriver."

Til glanced at the older man and shook his head. "Not me," he said. "A bargain's a bargain. Much as that damned Cap Baggs deserves all he'd get for butchering those seals, I won't squeal on him—not if my duffel and that five hundred reach the post, I won't."

"Who the hell said you would? I've got some important business to transact with Doc McCall, an' you might as well come along an' get acquainted. Damn fine bunch of men on the *Bear*, an' in this country a man never can tell when he's goin' to need a friend."

Arriving at the post, Bettles introduced Til to Nelson, the trader, who smiled when Til told him he hadn't dared to wake him up. "You needn't have ben afraid of wakin' me up," he said. "I wouldn't return a deserter to Baggs if I'd go to jail for hidin' him out. He's a God-damn bully an' a crooked son-of-a-bitch. Him an' Jackson hit here this mornin', madder'n hell an' threatenin' what they'd do to you when they got you back on the ship. They started out to hunt you, an' when they come back they wasn't sayin' a damn word—jest ordered the crew back into the boat an' shoved off."

A native stepped into the room, and as the trader turned to wait on him a sailor appeared, swung a duffel bag from his shoulder to the floor, and departed. Opening the bag, Til withdrew an envelope, opened it, and counted the money. As he slipped it into his pocket he grinned and winked at Bettles. "All there," he said in an undertone. "The deal is closed."

The native departed with his purchase, and Nelson eyed the bag at Til's feet. "What the hell!" he exclaimed. "Did Baggs have your duffel put ashore? You must of bought him off."

Til nodded. "Yeah—that's right. I bought him off. He said he'd ship a native to take my place."

"Yer lucky," the trader opined. "I wouldn't ship under that damn Baggs fer no money. An' he ain't goin' to find a man to take yer place, neither. There ain't a native between here an' Hershel Island that would ship with him—not after the way he done Kootlak last summer—beat him out of a month's pay. Take them Eskimos—what one knows they all know. Beats hell how the word gits around. Charlie Brower stopped in last fall an' he told me the natives had heard about it already at Barrow."

The door opened, a man stepped into the room, and Til was introduced to Lieutenant Jarvis, of the *Bear*. "Compliments of Captain and Mrs. Heally," he said when the introduction was over, "and you're all invited aboard for refreshments. I swung in by the *Arctic* and told Captain Brown I'd pick him up as we came by."

"You got to give us time to shave an' change our shirt," Bettles said.

"And I've got to get a whole new outfit," Til added, and turned to Bettles, "and you'll have to help me pick it out. You know what I'll need, and I don't."

When the items were purchased, Nelson turned to the officer. "Wait here till we git cleaned up," he said. "If anyone comes in, tell 'em I'll be back. It won't take but a few minutes." And motioning for the others to follow, he led the way to his living quarters adjoining the post in the rear.

Fifteen minutes later the three reappeared, spruced up for the occasion. Nelson locked the trading room, and they followed Jarvis to the beach, where the *Cub* was waiting to take them out to the ship.

As they approached the *Arctic*, where Captain Brown was waiting at the rail, Bettles turned to the lieutenant. "You've got to give me time to slip aboard for a minute," he said. "I've got a little present for Doc McCall—an old skull I picked up, an' a mammoth tooth, an' some slate spearheads."

The officer nodded. "Sure—go ahead. The doctor's keen for that stuff. Anything that has to do with archaeology, anthropology, ethnology, or any other branch of science is right down his alley."

"How about frogology?" Bettles asked.

The lieutenant looked puzzled. "What?" he asked.

"Oh, jest somethin' Al Mayo an' I run onto a while back. I'll bet I can fetch him down some specimens he'll be interested in—if I had some way of savin' 'em."

The *Cub* drew alongside the *Arctic*. Captain Brown stepped aboard as Bettles boarded the larger vessel and returned a few moments later carrying a package wrapped in a bit of old sailcloth. A few minutes later they were being welcomed on the deck of the *Bear* by Captain and Mrs. Heally and the good Dr. McCall.

The breeze had died down, and the afternoon sun shone warmly—one of those rare spring days when one could find comfort and enjoyment loafing on deck in Norton Sound. Refreshments, both solid and liquid, were passed; the company seated themselves. The people of the ship related news from the "outside," and in turn listened to news of the coast and the river—the latest gold strikes, the ravages of floods on rivers, epidemics among various tribes of natives, unusual adventures of prospectors, trappers, and traders.

When, finally, interest lagged, Bettles opened his package and turned to Dr. McCall. "Here's a skull, Doc, that I dug out of that old Eskimo buryin' ground I was tellin' you about last year. The one in back of Paimute. I remember you said you wanted some old skulls—from natives that died before the Russians came—so you could compare 'em with later ones. I'll bet this one is old, all right. There were good-sized trees growin' right out of the old graves. I had a hell of a time gettin' this skull out from amongst the roots. An' here's two or three old slate spearheads I found there too."

The doctor viewed the skull with interest and examined the spearheads. "You are undoubtedly right, Gordon," he said, "about this being a pre-Russian burial. The old-time Eskimos ground or polished their slate implements into shape. The chipping technique seems to have been developed later. I wonder if you could do some further excavating at this old burial place?"

"Oh, shore! Next time I come down-river I'll stop off an' do some more diggin'. Can't go very deep, though. Couple of feet down you strike the frost—ground froze hard as iron the year around—never does thaw out." Pausing, he drew the last piece from the canvas wrapping. "An' here's somethin' I'll bet you'll like—a mammoth's tooth. Found it a little ways back from the river where high water had gouged out a cutbank. Looks like it's kind of petrified or somethin'."

The good doctor carefully examined the object, turning it over and over in his hands. "Yes, it is partially fossilized. I certainly appreciate your collecting these things for me. I wish there was something I could do for you in return."

Bettles laughed. "Nothin' you can do, Doc. Not a damn thing—unless I should happen to get sick sometime. But speakin' of collectin' things—this old prehistoric stuff is all right. But take the things that are livin' here in the country right now—I remember you had a native paddlin' you around amongst the channels an' sloughs here in the delta a couple of years ago, so you could collect specimens of bugs, an' little lizards, an' birds an' things. Are you still interested in stuff like that?"

"Certainly I am."

"Okay. Then listen to this—Al Mayo and I were lookin' over a new buildin' site two, three weeks ago. We figure on callin' it Mayo's Landin'. While Al was lookin' over the flat along the river I struck off up a deep ravine that slanted up into the hills. There's a little crick comes down the ravine, an' I took my pan an' shovel along to see if I could strike any colors. I didn't. But I kept on goin', an' finally I come out on the lake that the crick starts in. It ain't a very big lake, but the first thing I noticed was that it was shallow an' the shore was flat an' muddy, with lots of rushes growin' along the edge. Most of these mountain lakes are steep-sided an' deep. I started to walk along the shore an' found them mudbanks an' rushes was alive with frogs. They'd jump off the mud when I come along an' swim out amongst the rushes. I noticed they looked sort of different from other frogs I'd seen, an' I caught one of 'em. Its back was a sort of a dull greenish color, with hardly any spots on it, an' its belly, instead of bein' dead white, like other frogs, was a sort of pale pinkish color. But what got me was the fact that the damn thing was transparent."

"Transparent!" the doctor exclaimed. "Surely you don't mean transparent!"

"The hell I don't! That's jest exactly what I mean. An' not only that one was—so was every one of 'em I caught—an' I'll bet I caught fifty before I got tired of it. I've ben around this country quite a bit, an' I've seen lots of frogs—but never none like them."

"Let's get this thing straightened out," the doctor said, his brow furrowing. "You certainly don't mean that these frogs are transparent—like glass."

"Well," Bettles grinned, "they ain't exactly like glass.

38

They won't crack or fly to pieces if you drop 'em. An' I don't claim a man could read fine print through 'em. But if you hold one of 'em up by the hind flipper, you can see his heart beat. You can see every damn bone in the skeleton. An' you can see the bugs they've et in their stummicks. An' you can see the eggs in the she ones."

"Remarkable!" the doctor exclaimed. "Never heard anything like it. And there's certainly nothing in the books about any such frogs!"

"I don't know about the books," Bettles said. "But I've ben around this country since the Yukon wasn't nothin' but a crick, an' I never saw anythin' like 'em."

"Could you get me some of them?" the doctor asked.

"Shore thing. But—how'm I goin' to keep 'em?"

"Pickle them."

"In what?"

"In alcohol, of course."

"Where can I get the alcohol?"

"Why," the doctor said, "I can let you have some."

"How much can you spare?" Bettles asked.

"How many frogs can you get?"

"No limit to the frogs. It's how much alcohol can I get."

"I can let you have five gallons, if you can use that much."

"I can use ten gallons, if you want that many frogs," Bettles replied.

"Fine!" the doctor exclaimed. "I want all of those frogs I can get. I'll share them with other scientists, dissect them, and write a paper. It isn't often in these days that a man is able to discover a new species, or even a subspecies. I'll name this new species after you—*Rani bettlesi*. I tell you, Gordon, it is a signal honor for a man to have his name go down in history as the discoverer of a new species!"

"Oh, shore," Bettles grinned. "I'll bet the boys will jest more than whoop 'er up when they hear about what I accomplished."

"No—really, Gordon—I'm serious about this. You don't

appreciate your outstanding contribution to science—and neither will your cronies along the river."

"Oh, I think they'll appreciate it, Doc," Bettles replied. "Once they realize what it means, they're goin' to be real pleased."

Captain Brown glanced toward the southwest and sniffed the air. He turned to Captain Heally. "I don't like to hurry away, Captain," he said, "but I feel a blow comin' on. I'm headin' back as quick as I pick up the mail, an' I'd like to get into the river before she hits."

Just before the *Cub* reached shore Lieutenant Jarvis shifted his glance from the two five-gallon cans of alcohol to the face of Bettles. "I'll sure be interested in seeing those transparent frogs when you bring them down," he remarked gravely.

Bettles nodded. "Yeah. They're goin' to be quite a sight —ain't they?"

V

The Arctic *Arrives at Nulato*

As the *Arctic* neared Nulato on the evening of July third, Captain Brown turned to Bettles, who stood beside him in the wheelhouse. "Fred Martin aims to pull out day after tomorrow on his first run up the Koyukuk in his new boat. Figgers he can make regular trips in her clean up to Bettles. That's a good five hundred miles, ain't it? You ort to know. That's your old camp."

"Yeah, it's a good five hundred miles, all right. I know it's a hell of a long trip in a canoe."

"Well, there's four, five camps up above Bettles now, besides those below—Moses Village an' the Mission. Fred's built him a good shallow-draft boat. He might do all right on that run, if he don't rip her bottom out in some rapids or get trapped up there on low water. Anyhow, the boys are aimin' to pull off a celebration tomorrow to give Fred a good send-off. Guess I'll lay over an' take in the fun. I won't lose no time. I can wood up here as well as anywhere. An' besides, I've got all them supplies that Fred ordered from Nelson to take up the Koyukuk. If he gits up there with 'em he'll shore make him a good profit on his first run."

As the *Arctic* made fast to the bank just astern of Fred Martin's new *North Star*, Jack McQuesten stepped aboard, accompanied by Moosehide Charlie, who together with Camillo Bill and Burr MacShane had just returned to the big river from a prospecting trip on the Kuskokwim. His glance shifted from Til to Bettles, who stood beside him on the deck. "This the Eskimo you figgered on takin' up the Koyukuk with you?" he asked with a grin.

"No, this is another fella. Til Carter, his name is. He's a chechako." He turned to the younger man. "Til, meet Jack McQuesten an' Moosehide Charlie, a couple of dubious characters that have ben in the country about as long as I have."

Moosehide Charlie swept Til with an appraising glance. "Glad to know you," he said. "You goin' up the Koyukuk with Bettles?"

Til nodded. "That's right."

Moosehide grinned. "Well, take it from me, brother—when you git back you'll shore as hell know you've ben somewhere. Yer headin' into the toughest country there is in Alaska with the toughest old sourdough outside of hell. Time you hit the big river agin you won't be a chechako no more. You'll be a sourdough, right."

"Til's a chechako, all right," Bettles said. "But he's a sort of special brand of chechako. He knocked hell out of a whalin' skipper on his own ship, then jumped over the side in the middle of the night an' swum damn near half a mile to shore in water so cold his cap froze to his hair. An' when the skipper an' the mate come to hunt him in the mornin', he offered to scrap both of 'em. An' not only that, he bluffed the skipper into settin' his duffel ashore an' his season's pay along with it. I found him in Kootlak's shack dryin' out his clothes. So when Kootlak wouldn't go up the Koyukuk with me, I asked Til how he'd like to go, an' he took me up. Any man with the guts he's got is good enough for me—chechako or no chechako."

Jack McQuesten nodded. "That's right. By God, we was all chechakos oncet! Trouble with chechakos is so damn few of 'em pans out. But say, Gordon, how'd you make out with Doc McCall?"

"Oh, not too bad. He let me have ten gallon. It's in the captain's cabin. Stuck it in there so the crew couldn't get at it."

"Ten gallons!"

"Yeah, five for me an' five for you to take up to Fortymile."

"We don't need it at Fortymile," McQuesten said. "Like I told you, we've got a saloon there. But I'll take it along. There'll be four of us goin' up on the *Arctic*, an' what with stoppin' at Rampart, an' Fort Yukon, an' Circle, an' Eagle, we kin prob'ly find use fer it."

"Ten gallon of what?" Moosehide asked.

"Alcohol, of course," Bettles replied. "What the hell would Jack be askin' about? It's for picklin' specimens."

Moosehide chuckled. "With ten gallon of alcohol the chances is a lot of us old specimens'll git pickled, all right. But what good is that goin' to do Doc McCall? If it makes us sick, he shore ain't comin' clean up here to fix us up."

"No, I mean this stuff is for picklin' real specimens—scientific ones—frogs, to be exact."

"Frogs! Where the hell you goin' to git any frogs?"

"That's up to you boys," Bettles replied. "I got the alcohol. An' you fellas have got to furnish the frogs."

"You mean—jest any kind of frogs?" Moosehide asked. "What the hell would Doc want with a lot of pickled frogs?"

Jack McQuesten eyed Moosehide gravely. "It's fer his wife," he explained. "She wants ten gallon of pickled frogs to serve at parties, along with the cocktails. Ain't you never moved around in high society none?"

"Cripes—no! An' what's more, I ain't never goin' to, if I would have to eat a pickled frog!"

"Jack's kiddin' you, Moosehide," Bettles said. "Don't pay no attention to him. Doc don't want jest any kind of frogs. These have got to be transparent ones."

"Transparent!" Moosehide exclaimed. "You mean you kin see through 'em? Who the hell ever heard of a transparent frog?"

"Doc McCall."

"Who told him about 'em?"

"Me."

"You! Where the hell is these frogs s'posed to be?"

"Well, accordin' to the way Doc heard it, me an' Al Mayo was locatin' a buildin' site somewheres upriver, an' I follered a ravine up into the hills till I come to a shallow lake an' found the shore of it jest workin' alive with these transparent frogs."

"If they're transparent, how the hell could you see 'em?"

Bettles hesitated a moment and ran his fingers over his chin. "They was kind of hard to see at first. You rec'lect a couple of years back when the measles hit that Siwash village over on the Kuskokwim, an' Carmack an' Swiftwater Bill come along an' found every last Siwash dead. Well, sir—when I hit that lake I saw thousan's of frog skeletons settin' around on the mud, an' I figured the measles or some such epidemic had hit the frogs. I reached down to pick up a skeleton to examine it, an' before I could grab it the damn thing jumped in the lake an' swum off. I reached for another, an' it done likewise, an' then they all begun jumpin' in the water when I'd get near 'em. Finally I caught one, an' then I saw right away what the answer was—they was transparent —all but their bones. I held some of 'em up to the light by the hind legs, an' damned if I couldn't see their heart beat an' see the blood squirtin' around through their veins. It was quite a sight."

"Yeah," said Moosehide, "it must of ben. So now you figger on gittin' Doc some of these frogs fer his collection, eh?"

"Like I said—I got the alcohol—it's up to you boys to get the frogs."

"Where's this lake at?"

"If me an' Til, here, wasn't headin' up the Koyukuk, I'd go along an' show you. But you boys won't have no trouble locatin' it. Jest keep your eyes open when you're goin' up-river, an' if you see some place that looks like a good buildin' site, an' a ravine runnin' up into the hills, an' foller up the ravine, an' find a shallow lake at the end of it, an' find a lot of transparent frogs settin' around on the mud, you catch a tubful an' pickle 'em, an' save 'em till you run onto me again, an' I'll deliver 'em to Doc when I get the chance."

Moosehide Charlie's brow furrowed. "It don't sound reasonable. Hell—they ain't no transparent frogs!"

"Cripes, Moosehide!" McQuesten exclaimed. "You don't think Gordon would lie to us, do you? Even if he might—he shore as hell wouldn't lie to Doc McCall!" He turned to Bettles. "We'll keep our eyes open fer that buildin' site, an' if we find it, we'll git the frogs, all right. But jest in case we don't happen to find that lake, it'll be all right if we'd sort of drink up the alcohol to keep it from spilin', won't it, Gordon?"

Bettles nodded. "Oh, shore. That's jest common sense. I wouldn't see the good in lettin' a five-gallon tin of alcohol lay around an' rot. I'll explain how it was to Doc next time I see him, if you boys should happen to miss out on them frogs. I know where there's a cutbank with a piece of mammoth ivory stickin' out of it. In a year or so it ort to be caved off enough so I can dig out the whole tusk. I'll give that to Doc for his collection. It stands to reason he'd ruther have an ivory mammoth tusk than a tub of pickled frogs. Hell—most anyone would!"

Til Carter and Bettles moved their duffel, together with one of the five-gallon tins of alcohol, from the *Arctic* to the *North Star*, where at the invitation of her owner the entire white population of Nulato forgathered, augmented by the visiting sourdoughs, to celebrate the new vessel's christening.

After all hands had pitched in and transferred the cargo of merchandise from the *Arctic* to the *North Star*, the alcohol, cut to half its strength with river water, was dispensed free. Several stud games got under way, and all during the night and most of the next day the celebration continued. A good time was had by all, with the exception of Hooch Albert and Dog Face Nolan, who found no sale for their vile concoctions of homemade hooch. The story of Til's knocking out the whaling captain and his cold swim ashore passed from lip to lip, and when during the festivities he proved to be a good man at the stud table, and one who could drink glass for glass with the best of them and hold his liquor well, the sourdoughs accepted him as one of themselves.

VI

On the Koyukuk

Early on the morning of the fifth of July the two steamboats cast loose from their moorings and headed upriver. At the mouth of the Koyukuk, from the deck of the *North Star*, Bettles waved his cap to the sourdoughs who lined the rail of the *Arctic*. "So long, boys! It won't be long before all you gravel hogs'll be hittin' up to the Jim River country too. An' when Fortymile heads for the Koyukuk country, fer cripes' sake tell Bergman to fetch his saloon along! In the meantime don't forget to keep your eyes open for those frogs!"

The run up the Koyukuk was accomplished in twenty days. No difficulties were encountered other than a few inconsequential groundings in various rapids. Fred Martin, the captain, was an experienced riverman, and he was taking no rash chances in his first exploratory run of the river. The scattering of white prospectors along the banks greeted the steamboat with cap waving and shouts of good luck as she passed, and the natives at Moses Village and the Mission, many of whom had never seen any craft larger than a poling boat, stared in wide-eyed awe.

As they approached the camp of Bettles, at the foot of a long, shallow rapid that precluded any thought of steam navigation, Martin smiled as he eyed the crowd that lined both banks of the river. "Well, by cripes, we made her! The folks up here'll be damn glad of the chance to get their freight hauled in without waitin' all summer for polin' boats to fetch it. It's took twenty days for the first run. I'll make the next upriver one in sixteen, an' I'd ort to run back down in twelve. I'll bet I can pay for this boat the first two trips. To hell with prospectin'! This river business is a shore thing."

Bettles grinned. "The only difference is if we make a strike we're all set. But if you make one—in some of them rapids—yer busted. I'll take a chanct in the gravel."

When the boat was made fast the entire population of the camp turned in to transfer the cargo of goods to the warehouse of Kemper, the trader. Among the hundred or more men were half a dozen old sourdoughs who greeted Bettles vociferously. Old Tim Condon thumped him on the back. "By God, I figgered you'd be comin' back!" he roared. "That there upriver Yukon country ain't worth a damn, an' never will be! I told you you was a damn fool when you pulled out of here! Didn't do no good along the big river, eh?"

"Well, I ain't made no hell of a strike. Hit a few locations that paid better'n wages—but nothin' to brag of. Was workin' a location at Old Station when Al Mayo came along an' told me there'd ben some strikes made up on the Jim River, an' I figured I'd come up ahead of a stampede. None of the camps along the river—not even Fortymile—are doin' so good that news of a rich strike wouldn't send 'em all kihootin' off on a stampede. What do you think of this Jim River proposition?"

Condon glanced at the men of the camp, who were busy packing goods from the boat to the warehouse. "Hell," he said, "there's enough of 'em workin' on that freight without us. We'll slip over to the Swede's, where we can hist a few drinks, an' I'll tell you about it. Accordin' to law, we ain't civilized enough here in Alaska to have saloons, but the Swede, he was smart enough to fix it up with the marshal. Some says the marshal is in pardners with him. Anyhow, he's runnin' a damn good imitation of a saloon an' gettin' away with it." He led the way to a sizable log building at the edge of the camp, and Bettles followed.

Til Carter joined the others in packing the goods from the boat. Half a dozen women were also doing their share, and among them Til noticed a young girl with fiery red hair whose deep blue eyes regarded him quizzically as she passed and repassed him going to and from the warehouse. As he was returning empty-handed from one of the trips, he smiled as she stumbled just at the top of the bank and allowed a fifty-pound sack of flour to slip from her shoulder. "Sort of bit off more than you can chew, didn't you, sis?" he said as he stooped to retrieve the sack.

The blue eyes flashed angrily as she snatched up the sack and shouldered it. "No, I didn't!" she snapped. "And even if I had, I don't need any help from a chechako!"

Til's grin widened. "Kind of spunky, eh? Well, guess you've got a right to be. Redheads generally are."

She strode off without replying, and Til noticed that during the remainder of the unloading her eyes were averted as she passed him in the line.

Reaching the Swede's, Condon led the way to the rude bar built along one end of the room. Six or eight tables were distributed about the floor, the center of which was occupied by a huge cannon stove. The proprietor served them, and when the drinks were downed Condon picked up the bottle and glasses from the bar and led the way to a table where the two seated themselves. "Fill up," he invited, shoving the bottle toward Bettles. "It's ben a hell of a while since you an' I've drank together. Remember that time down to Rampart when Jack Bedoe married Sid Carney's gal? Cripes, we whooped her up for a week! At that, I guess me an' you was the only ones on our feet when the jamboree was over."

Bettles grinned. "Yeah—an' what we kept it up for God only knows. Jack an' his bride pulled out on their honeymoon right after the weddin'—an' us damn fools kept right on celebratin'. Never even missed 'em for three days!"

"Well, hell, Gordon—after all, there ain't so many white wimmin in the country. A man don't run onto a weddin' every day!"

As he filled his glass Bettles eyed a powerfully built man with a scraggly yellow beard who was sprawled in a chair, apparently asleep, at the next table, an empty whisky glass before him. Noting the glance, Condon frowned. "That's Ear Bitin' Finley. He's a no-account bastard. Workin' a location up on South Crick. Wasn't fer his pardner, young fella name of Harmon, they wouldn't be takin' out wages. Finley, he comes in about oncet in so often an' gets soused an' picks a fight an' gits the other fella down an' chaws his ears. Someday someone's goin' to knock hell out of him, an' I hope I'll be there to see it."

"What about this Jim River country?" Bettles asked.

Condon glanced about the room, the only other occupants of which were the Swede and two men playing cribbage at a table near the bar. "She's spotted," he said. "But she's good. An' she might turn out big. Pavlo, the Finn, put me wise to it. He'd ben up there all last summer snipin' the bars along the Jim River, an' along toward fall he hit some coarse gold in a rapids. He filed a location there, an' when he come in he tipped me off. I done him a good turn a couple of years back, an' he hadn't fergot it. Me an' Davey went up an' staked a couple of claims."

"Davey!" Bettles exclaimed. "You mean that little kid of yours?"

"That's right. Wasn't nothin' but a little shaver when you pulled outa here. He's nineteen now, an' Julie's sixteen. My wife died four years ago up to Coldfoot. After that I fetched the kids down here where there's a school. You rec'lect Julie. She's a couple of years younger'n Davey."

Bettles grinned. "Hell, yes! I used to call her the Pest. It was 'Uncle Gordon' this an' 'Uncle Gordon' that—everything from makin' a harness for a litter of pups to givin' her a ride in a canoe."

"She's grow'd up now. The schoolmarm they had here got married this spring. An' they hired Julie to teach school next winter."

The two old-timers emptied their glasses and refilled them from the bottle that stood between them on the table. "How'd you make out on yer claims?" Bettles asked.

"We didn't do so bad fer the time we put in. We didn't get up there till late in the fall, an' the timber's kind of scatterin' along the Jim, so it was damn near Chris'mas before we'd got wood enough cut an' hauled to burn in with. We sluiced out twelve hundred ounces between the two of us. I fetched two hundred down with me an' we've got a thousan' ounces cached." Condon paused, and again the two emptied and refilled the glasses. "Yes sir," he continued, his voice rising a little as the potent liquor took hold. "A thousan' ounces cached right there on the claim." Bettles, whose glance had strayed to the face of Ear Bitin' Finley, thought he caught just the faintest flicker of an eyelid at the words, and he winked at Condon as he kicked his shin under the table. Condon glanced at the sprawling figure. "Oh, hell," he said. "I ain't worryin' about him. You see, I know'd when I left the claim I was liable to do more er less drinkin' with the boys. An' you know how it is—when a man's drinkin' he's liable to run off at the head an' let go of somethin' he might better of kep' to himself. So I told Davey to change the cache after I pulled out—jest in case I might do too much talkin' in the wrong place. The way it is, I couldn't let on where that cache is at, 'cause I don't know myself."

"Davey stayed up on the location, eh?"

"Yeah. Wasn't no use in the two of us comin' down.

Hadn't been fer Julie bein' down here to the school, I could of got the supplies at Coldfoot an' saved a couple hundred miles. But I wanted to see how she's gettin' along, an' arrange fer her board an' keep this winter. We're in my cabin down by the river now. But when I pull out she'll move over to the tradin' post an' winter with Kemper an' his wife. It's better that way than her bachin' it all winter there in the cabin. But I'll bet she could do it, at that."

"Guess I'll slip up an' have a look at the Jim River country," Bettles said. "When you goin' back?"

"Oh, mebbe a week—ten days. There ain't no hell of a hurry. Davey's up there gettin' out wood. Can't do nothin' in a shaft in the summertime. It's coarse gravel up there, an' the seepage fills a shaft up as fast as a man can dig it. That ain't no one-man job up there. You got a pardner?"

"Well, not exactly what you'd call a pardner. I fetched a young fella along with me, an' if we hit somethin' up there we could damn well go pardners."

"Chechako?"

"Yeah, he's a chechako. But he won't be one very long. He's got what it takes. When I heard about this strike up here I hit down to St. Michael. There's an Eskimo down there name of Kootlak that used to live somewheres up on the Jim River, an' I figured on gettin' him to come up here with me. But both him an' his wife turned it down. They don't neither one of 'em want no part of it. So I hooked up with this young fella that deserted from a whaler."

Condon shook his head doubtfully. "He might be all right. But you know damn well, Gordon, this ain't no chechako country. By God, she's tough."

"Cripes, Tim, we was all chechakos oncet!"

"Shore we was, but we got broke in, what you might say, by degrees—down along the Yukon. This is a damn pore country fer brass monkeys."

Voices sounded outside, and a moment later the door opened and a dozen or more men entered the room and advanced to the bar, led by Kemper, proprietor of the trading post, who ordered a round of drinks, then turned and eyed the two at the table with a grin. "Hey, you two, what the hell do you mean by settin' over here lappin' up likker whilst the rest of the camp was unloadin' the boat?"

Condon solemnly thumbed his nose at the speaker. "We don't belong to the workin' class," he said. "We're 'ristocrats."

"That's right," Bettles agreed. "We don't mingle with the rabble."

Kemper bowed low in mock respect. "Well, step up, me lords, an' jine us in a drink."

"Have patience," Condon replied, indicating the bottle on the table with a jerk of the head. "We'll be with you when we finish this."

"We shore will," Bettles agreed, downing his drink and refilling his glass. "An' you won't need no hell of a lot of patience, at that. This ain't goin' to take long."

"Yer a couple of damn lazy old hooch-guzzlin' loafers," grinned Kemper.

"You can't get no argument there," Bettles replied. "Ain't that jest what we got through tellin' you?" Noticing Til among the newcomers, Bettles beckoned to him. "Til," he said, "I want you should meet Tim Condon, one of the best damn men on the Koyukuk, or any other river." He turned to the other. "An', Tim, this is Til Carter. He's a chechako now. But he won't be one in a year from now."

"I'll say he won't," Condon grinned, "if he sticks with you!" Rising from his chair, Condon poured the last drink from the bottle and downed it. "Come on now an' we'll get over to the bar an' help these boys collect their pay before Kemper quits buyin'."

An hour later Condon looked at his watch. "Cripes, I got to get outa here!" He turned to Bettles. "Where you an' Til stoppin'?" he asked.

"Why, on the boat, I guess," Bettles replied. "I hadn't give it a thought."

"Not by a damn sight, you ain't stoppin' on no boat. Yer comin' home with me—you an' Til both. An' we better be gittin' over to the cabin, er we'll ketch hell. Julie she don't like fer me to be late fer supper—special when I ben mebbe drinkin' jest a mite."

Kemper grinned. "Hell, Tim, how's she goin' to find out you ben drinkin'?"

"Well—she might sort of smell my breath."

Bettles chuckled. "We can fix that, Tim. You an' me an' Tim will all breathe together, an' she can't tell whose breath she's smellin'. We can practice it while we're goin' to the cabin."

"If you get it down pat," Kemper said, "by God, you better warn her not to light a match in the cabin—er you'll all git blow'd to hell!"

VII

Supper at the Condons'

Julie Condon looked up from the stove as her father stepped into the room followed by Bettles and Til Carter. The next instant she leaped forward, both hands extended. "Why, Uncle Gordon!" she cried. "Where in the world did you come from?"

"Well, doggone if it ain't the Pest herself! Lordy, how you've grow'd! I come up on the boat. How'd you think I got here?"

"But I didn't see you while we were packing the freight to the warehouse. Come to think of it, I didn't see Daddy there either."

Bettles grinned. "Certainly not. You couldn't expect such notorious characters as Tim an' me to be associatin' with the rabble, could you? Fact is, we had some important business to transact over to the Swede's."

The girl sniffed. "You must have transacted quite a lot of it," she said.

Tim Condon chuckled. "We done all right fer the time we had. You see, darter, the camp's grow'd quite a bit sence Gordon pulled out, an' I had to kinda show him around."

"Shore he did," Bettles seconded. "I'm a man that likes to keep posted on the growth of these camps."

"So you got as far as the Swede's, and never got any farther?"

"That's right. Somethin' come up to detain us."

"You mean something went down that detained you, don't you?"

"Well, of course—there's that angle too. I tell you, Julie, a man shore appreciates a dram of good likker after puttin' in a couple of years on the damn stuff they make you drink down along the Yukon."

The corners of the girl's lips twitched. "Who makes you drink it?" she asked.

"Why—er—a man's conscience does. There ain't no two ways about it. He's got to drink that, er nothin'."

The girl giggled. "Did you ever try drinking water?"

Bettles nodded gravely. "Yeah, I tried it oncet. Three, four years ago, it was—over on the Kuskokwim. I didn't like it. It tasted kinda fishy."

Tim Condon's glance rested for a moment on Til, who stood just inside the doorway, and shifted to the girl. "Julie," he said, "I'll make you acquainted with Til Carter. He come upriver with Gordon."

Til stepped forward, smiling. "Miss Julie and I have met before," he said. "Not formally. It was quite by accident."

"Why didn't you tell me you came up with Uncle Gordon?" the girl asked.

"Why didn't you ask me?"

"You called me a redhead."

"You called me a chechako."

"It was horrid of you to make fun of me when I tripped and dropped that sack of flour."

"I wasn't making fun of you," Til smiled. "I was trying to help you. But you wouldn't let me. Little girls shouldn't carry big sacks of flour."

The blue eyes flashed. "I'm not a little girl! I'm sixteen.

I was born and raised in this country. I can carry a pack all day on the trail. I wouldn't ask odds of any chechako. I'd die first!"

Bettles grinned. "Pour it into him, Pest, while you've got the chanct. Til's a chechako now—but he won't be very long. We're goin' up on the Jim River with Tim, when he goes back. Time a man puts in a winter in that country he'll be a sourdough or a dead man, one of the two."

"Anyway," the girl said, "he pitched in and helped unload the boat. And that's more than you two old scamps did. Get busy now, all of you, if you want any supper. I'll open a couple more cans of corn. Daddy, you cut two more good thick steaks and——"

"Thick steaks!" Tim exclaimed. "What'll I cut 'em off'n?"

"Joe Illivik brought in a caribou about an hour ago, and I bought a hindquarter. It's outside in the tub. And don't forget to put that netting back over it when you get through, or the flies will blow it. And you two throw your packs in the other room and then move the table out from the wall so we can all sit down, and set a couple of more places. The dishes are there on the shelf."

Til picked up his pack from the floor and followed Bettles. As he passed the girl he grinned. "Ever been in the Army?" he asked.

"What?"

"Oh, nothing. I was just thinking what a swell top sergeant you'd make."

"You were, eh? Well, just for that, when you and Uncle Gordon get the table set you can go out and split me a couple of armfuls of wood. That is, if a chechako can split wood."

"Chechakos can do lots of things," Til laughed. "You'd be surprised."

"I sure would. The only thing I've ever seen 'em do is get in other people's way."

As Til deposited the second armful of wood in the box

behind the stove, the girl set a platter of sizzling steaks on the table where Tim and Bettles were already seated. As she seated herself she glanced at her father and pointed to the woodbox. "I'm learning things," she said. "I've learned that chechakos can pitch in and help unload steamboats, and they can split wood the way it ought to be split—not just left in big chunks you can hardly get in the stove."

Tim eyed the wood. "Takes longer splittin' it thin," he said. "Lasts longer if you leave it big. But he's young yet. He'll learn."

"I suppose so," the girl replied, tossing her head. "I guess if they live long enough to be sourdoughs they've got to learn all the bad tricks as well as the good ones. Wood split fine, like that, is a lot easier to cook with, though."

As the meal progressed Bettles recounted the news from the "outside," as reported to him by Dr. McCall and the officers of the *Bear*, and listened to various happenings of interest along the Koyukuk. When it was over, Tim and Bettles put on their caps. "We might be a little late gettin' in tonight, Julie," he said. "The boys was sort of talkin' up a stud game fer this evenin' down to the Swede's."

As the two old-timers stepped out, the girl glanced across the table at Til. "Don't chechakos play stud?" she asked. "I know they drink whisky, because I got a whiff of your breath."

"Oh, sure, chechakos drink whisky and play stud too. But before they do, they like to stick around and help pretty girls do the dishes."

The girl laughed. "Really? You know, even with the bad start you got, I'm beginning to think I might learn to tolerate a chechako—after a long time I might even learn to like one."

"Yeah? And I'm beginning to think that I can go for this land of the midnight sun in a big way."

"It's the only land I know," the girl said. "It's the land of the midnight sun in summer—but in winter it's the land of the noontime dark. That doesn't sound quite so romantic, does it?"

"Oh, I don't know. I imagine that romance is like what the sourdoughs say about gold—it's where you find it."

The girl rose from the table, piled the dishes into the pan, and poured boiling water over them. She handed Til a towel, and as he wiped them he laid them away on the shelf. "I wonder when we'll be hitting out for the Jim River country," he said. "I overheard Bettles and your father talking about it there at the Swede's."

"I expect Daddy will stick around here for about a week yet. These old sourdoughs are all alike. They hit camp and for a couple of weeks they hang around and guzzle whisky and gamble. Then they pull out for the creeks. It's all right, I suppose. They sure work hard, and don't get much fun out of life while they're out. Daddy won't hit camp again until spring."

"You say your daddy won't be back till spring—aren't you going up there too?"

The girl shook her head. "No, I'm staying here. I haven't lived out in the creeks for ever so long. I've lived with the Kempers and gone to school. This coming winter I'm going to teach. Miss Bancroft, the teacher who was here, was married this spring and moved down to Fort Yukon."

Til grinned. "Guess I'll pass up the Jim River and go to school this winter. Come to think about it, there's quite a lot of things I haven't learned."

The girl tossed her head, sending a cascade of bright red curls flashing in the sunlight that streamed in through the window. "You might better learn 'em from Uncle Gordon, then. I can't waste my time teaching chechakos."

"You've taught me one thing already," Til said, his grin widening. "And that is—why Bettles called you 'the Pest'!" He hung the towel on the line stretched above the stove, picked up the dishpan, carried it out and emptied it, returned it to the table, and picked up his hat. "Guess I'll loaf over to the Swede's and horn in on that stud game. Good night. See you in the morning."

The girl stood in the doorway, her eyes on his broad back, until he disappeared among the cabins. She stamped her foot and frowned as she realized that he had not once glanced back. Then she took a book from the shelf and settled herself in a chair. It was Darwin's *Origin of Species*.

VIII

The Caribou Hunt

During the week that followed, Bettles and Tim Condon devoted themselves assiduously to stud poker. Together with several old sourdoughs who were marking time until the freeze-up would allow them to sink shafts that wouldn't fill up with seepage water, they would forgather shortly after noon each day at the Swede's and play until suppertime. After supper the game would start again and run until far into the night. Til Carter sat in these night sessions, then the three would sleep until noon and awake to devour the hearty breakfast of caribou steak, pancakes, and coffee that Julie always had ready for them. Then, when the oldsters would head for the Swede's, Til would help with the dishes, split the wood, and carry water from the river.

"Did you ever hunt caribou?" the girl asked as he returned with the water on the first day.

"No. Never even saw one."

"This quarter we've got isn't going to last long the way we're tearing into it. Joe Illivik told me there's a band of them hanging out' in the hills about five miles up the river."

"What are we waiting for? Let's go," Til said. "I bought a rifle at St. Michael and I'd like to try it out."

"I'll put up a lunch and leave a note telling Daddy where we've gone. If we don't get back in time, they can get their own supper. It won't hurt 'em any—even if they should miss a few hands of their beloved stud. Why do men gamble, anyway?"

"Well—it's a good way to pass the time."

"It's a good way to waste time, you mean," the girl replied. "I'm not talking about professional gamblers that make a business of cards. But take those old sourdoughs that play together whenever they hit camp. They all play about equally well. Once in a while some newcomer sits in that don't play well, but he loses continually for a while and then quits playing. But the regulars—one of 'em wins one night, and another one the next, and so on. It's just a question of who carries the dust around until the next game. I'll bet there isn't one of those men that are playing right now that is fifty ounces ahead, or behind either—and they've been playing for years."

Til smiled. "Sure. But look at the fun they've had."

"And look at the time they've wasted! Why, if they'd spent all that time reading good books—books that are really worth while—they would have improved their minds and gained a world of valuable information. Instead of that they sit around, night after night, and watch three of a kind beat two pairs, and flushes beat straights! I should think it would bore them to death!"

"Yeah—but look at the kick a fellow gets when he makes a little pair of deuces beat three big aces! And besides, what valuable information would a sourdough get by reading Gibbon's *Rome* or trying to follow Schopenhauer's philosophy?"

The girl shrugged, slipped the lunch she had prepared into a packsack, and picked up her rifle. "I guess men are all alike," she said. "I thought maybe you'd be different."

Til stepped into the other room and returned with his rifle. Julie was waiting outside. She shot him a glance. "What are you going to help pack the meat back in—your pocket?"

He re-entered the cabin and returned with his packsack. "That's the way a man gets valuable information," he grinned. "By experience. Not by reading it out of a book."

The two struck off upriver, following the portage trail that paralleled the long rapid. At the head of the rapid the girl slanted off to the west toward a range of low, sparsely wooded hills some three miles distant. Til followed, his gaze sweeping the vast expanse of level tundra in search of some living, moving thing, to return to the trim figure of the girl. Clad in faded-blue denim trousers, checked flannel shirt, and light pacs, sheath knife and light ax at her belt, gun slung over her shoulder, from which dangled a pair of field glasses in their leather case and the limp packsack, she held a fast and apparently effortless pace toward the ever-nearing hills.

Ascending the first ridge, she led the way to a bald dome of rock that commanded a view of a wide valley. Laying her rifle aside, she removed the glass from its case and handed it to Til. "See if you can find any caribou while I get the lunch out," she said.

Til took the glass, raised it to his eyes, focused it, and, standing erect, slowly swept the sparsely timbered valley or basin and the slope of the next ridge, a mile or more away. He handed the glass back. "Nothing doing," he said. "Guess we'll have to hit the next valley."

The girl smiled. "Maybe," she admitted. "But sit down and we'll eat half our lunch. We'll save the rest till later. You never know how long you're going to be out. We might need the other half for supper."

"Even if there were caribou down there in the valley, they couldn't help seeing us up on this bare knob," Til said.

The girl shook her head. "They'd never see us if we don't

move around. Their eyes don't seem able to distinguish stationary objects. If a person remains perfectly still, they can't tell him from a rock or a tree stub. I've had 'em walk up to within fifty feet of me. They depend more on scent than sight. Wolves do too. As long as we keep down-wind from 'em we're all right."

When the allotted portion of cold caribou sandwiches had been consumed, she reached for the glass, drew a clean piece of flannel from her pocket, and carefully wiped the lenses. Remaining seated, she drew up her knees, rested her elbows on them, and sighted on the upper reach of the basin. For long minutes she sat motionless, then shifted the glass slightly to the right and again concentrated her gaze on the terrain. Again and again she repeated the performance until she had scrutinized every foot of the wide basin and the slope of the ridge beyond. When she finally lowered the glass, Til smiled.

"You sure must have enjoyed that scenery. You've been looking at it for more than half an hour."

The girl nodded. "Yes," she replied. "I did. Especially the twenty-three caribou and the four wolves."

"Caribou and wolves!" Til exclaimed. "I sure didn't see any caribou and wolves! And I covered the whole valley."

"I didn't expect you to—the way you 'covered the whole valley' in about two minutes. There could have been a herd of elephants there and you'd never have seen them. I never saw a chechako yet that knew how to use a glass. A caribou, either standing up or lying down, blends perfectly into a background of rock or heather, even if there are no trees. So does a wolf or a fox. If they had been moving, you'd have probably seen them. But caribou are seldom moving at this time of day. They feed until they fill up, then they camp for several hours. It takes long and careful scrutiny to tell them from the rocks. There are three bunches of 'em. Five are about halfway up the ridge. Eleven are just to the right of that little bunch of spruce. And seven are about a quarter of a mile to the right—almost in line with that rock pinnacle there on top of the ridge. Those seven are the closest—but we better try for those by the spruce thicket, on account of the wolves."

"I guess we don't have to worry much about the wolves," Til said. "With the two rifles, we could stop 'em if they should attack us."

"Attack us!" cried the girl, a note of ill-concealed contempt in her voice. "Did you ever hear of wolves attacking anyone outside of a storybook? No wolf or pack of wolves ever yet attacked anyone, whether he had a rifle or not! These stories you hear about wolves attacking people are all the bunk. They'll follow you—sure. Sometimes for days. And they'll hang around your camp at night just outside the circle of firelight. They're waiting to devour what you throw away—not to attack you. You never saw a sourdough who was afraid of wolves.

"Those four wolves are slipping up on that lower bunch of caribou. They're about a quarter of a mile down-wind from 'em, and they're working slowly up. They lie still for a few minutes, then snake along on their bellies, and then lie still again. I'm afraid they would stampede the caribou before we could get a shot at 'em. Come on—we'll slip back over the ridge and get that clump of spruce lined up with that other bunch, and maybe we can slip up on 'em. But we've got to hurry, because if that lower bunch stampedes they'll come charging up the valley and the whole band will hit out, and we'd never see 'em again this day."

Walking swiftly, the girl led the way along the side of the ridge for some five hundred yards, then, turning abruptly, she climbed to the crest and peered over. "We're all right," she said to Til, who was close behind her. "We can slip down behind that spruce grove and get within fifty or sixty yards of 'em. But we haven't got much time. Those wolves must be pretty close to that lower bunch by now." The next instant she uttered a cry of dismay and pointed down

65

the valley, where the seven caribou broke from the sparse timber in headlong flight, pursued by two of the four wolves that had stalked them. The terrified animals headed across the open basin straight for the spruce clump. Swiftly Til adjusted the sight of his rifle. The girl shook her head. "No use," she said. "When they pass us they'll be a good five hundred yards away." Even as she spoke the eleven caribou that had been concealed by the grove broke into sight, ran a short distance, and stopped to look at the on-coming seven. Til raised his rifle and fired. Again he fired, and again. At the third shot the band broke into a run. One of the animals suddenly staggered, went down on its knees, struggled to rise, and rolled over on its side, and a few moments later the whole band disappeared over the ridge.

The girl's eyes dwelt for a moment on Til's gun, then raised to his face. "What kind of a rifle is that?" she asked.

"It's a Ross. The trader at St. Michael recommended it for this open country."

"It's a good gun," she said. "I couldn't have begun to reach 'em with this carbine. And even if you are a chechako, you made a mighty good shot."

Til laughed. "Oh, I can do lots of things. Really—as I told you once before, you'd be surprised."

The girl smiled. "I'm surprised already. You're the first chechako I've ever seen that could do anything right."

"We better slip down there before those wolves beat us to our meat," he said.

"There's no hurry. We won't see the wolves again. They'll stick around and clean up what we leave. But we'll never see 'em."

They made their way into the valley, and as they stood for a moment looking down at the dead animal Til smiled ruefully. "I *would* pick out an old bull to shoot at," he exclaimed, "when there must have been plenty of younger animals in that bunch!"

The girl nodded. "Yes, there must have been. But it's a

good thing you didn't get one of 'em. This time of year the cows and young bulls are hardly fit to eat. They are lean and scrawny, and the meat is stringy and tasteless. But the old bulls are fat—and the fat is what counts. From now on the cows and young bulls begin to put on fat and the old bulls will soon begin to lose it. So in the fall the cows and young bulls are the best to eat." As she spoke the girl drew her knife from its sheath and, stooping, slit the animal's throat close against the breast. As the blood gushed in a torrent onto the ground, she began slitting the skin around one of the legs just above the knee. Til drew his own knife and went to work on the other leg.

"By gosh, if this bull's meat is tough as his hide," he said, "we'll never be able to chew it!"

The girl paused and held out her hand. "Let's see your knife."

He handed her the knife. "It's brand new. It ought to be sharp."

"It's brand new—so it oughtn't to be sharp, you mean. New knives are never sharp." Drawing a small stone from her pocket, she handed it and the knife to Til. "Better sit down and work on that edge for ten or fifteen minutes," she advised, "while I get on with the skinning. I'll bet we'll get two hundred pounds of meat off this fellow—and thirty or forty pounds of fat."

"And that hide ought to make a good warm winter coat," Til said.

"That hide isn't worth a cent for anything," the girl replied. "It'll be as full of holes as a salt shaker."

"What do you mean—full of holes?" Til exclaimed. "I only fired three shots—probably only one of 'em hit him."

"I don't mean bullet holes," the girl said, slanting him a pitying glance. "I mean grub holes. The botflies lay their eggs under the hide in the fall, and the grub grows all winter and burrows out in the spring, leaving a half-inch hole in the hide. I've seen almost a hundred of 'em in one summer-killed hide. The holes begin closing up soon after the grub comes out, but the hide is no good till well into August."

Two hours later the two stood and regarded with approval the pile of meat from which all bone had been removed, and the slabs of luscious fat that was piled on the hide. "We better start packing now," the girl said. "I can handle fifty pounds. We'll have to double back, but it won't take long. We ought to make the round trip in half an hour."

"Half an hour!" Til exclaimed. "It must be a good seven miles from here to the cabin. What are you going to do—fly?"

For answer the girl pointed to a thin line of timber a half mile away. "The river swings in and cuts through the hills there. We'll cut some poles and raft the meat down to the head of the rapid. Then we'll make Daddy and Uncle Gordon pack it from there home. We've done our share. It won't hurt 'em to miss a few hands of stud. They ought to be glad that Mr. Kemper has an icehouse to keep it in, so they won't have to put in a couple of days sun-drying it or smoking it."

The packing completed, the two cut a dozen poles which were laid side by side on a flat sand bar at the edge of the water. "How are you going to fasten 'em together?" Til asked. "We didn't bring any rope."

From the bottom of her packsack the girl produced a couple of dozen spikes. "These are easier to carry than rope," she said, and proceeded to spike a couple of cross-pieces that held the poles firmly in place. The raft was launched, loaded, and shoved out into the current.

"I hope it holds together when it hits that whitewater there in the rapid," Til said as the two followed along the bank. "We ought to have a rope to hold it back."

"We don't need one," the girl replied. "There are plenty of rocks sticking out of the water for the raft to catch on above the head of the canyon. It'll never hit the white-water."

Til grinned. "How much does a chechako have to learn before he becomes a sourdough?"

The girl regarded him with a puzzled frown. "What do you mean?"

"I mean I wouldn't have missed this trip for the world. I've learned how not to use field glasses, that caribou and wolves can't see very well, what kind of caribou to kill when, that caribou hides are no good till August, that wolves never attack people, that the fat is more important to save than the lean meat, that new knives are never sharp, and that you can get rid of a lot of useless packing by eliminating all the bones. And not only that, but it wouldn't have occurred to me to let the river do the bulk of the packing. I'd have packed the meat all the way to the cabin on my back."

The girl laughed. "The saying is that a man isn't a sourdough until he's seen the ice go out on the Yukon. That means he must have wintered in the country, as no one comes in from the outside in winter. But let me tell you this —if you winter on the Jim River with Uncle Gordon, you'll be a sourdough by spring, if you never see the ice go out on the Yukon. He's got the reputation of being the toughest sourdough of 'em all—except, maybe, Father Judge."

"Anyway," Til said, "it proves that I was right—a man could never learn to be a sourdough out of a book."

The two arrived at the cabin to find that Tim Condon and Bettles had finished their supper and were on the point of returning to the Swede's. Old Tim scowled ferociously. "Doggone you two young whiffets! Kihootin' all over the country, an' leavin' me an' Gordon to cook our own supper. We've missed a good hour of stud a'ready—an' I don't see no meat, neither!"

The girl smiled sweetly. "You're going to miss some more stud too. And you're going to see plenty of meat—and heft it besides. So get your packsacks and get busy. You'll find the meat—a couple of hundred pounds of it on a raft—stuck on some rocks at the head of the rapids. When you get it stored away in Mr. Kemper's icehouse, you can go back to your stud. Til and I are hungry. We're going to eat supper as soon as I get it cooked." Reaching into her packsack, she drew out a morsel and held it up. "And we're going to have nice fresh tongue."

"Why an' the hell couldn't you have fetched the meat down when you come?" Tim asked as he took a packsack from a peg driven into the log wall.

"Because we were tired, and besides, the raft is hung up on some rocks in the middle of the river, and we didn't want to get wet to our waists—and the longer you stand around and argue, the more stud you're going to miss—so there."

Bettles grinned and winked at Tim. "Kinda looks like we're elected. An' at our age, too."

"Cripes, age ain't got nothin' to do with it when it comes to augerin' with a woman—not our age, nor theirn neither. A man can't win no oftener'n he kin fill an inside royal flush. He might better save his breath. Come on—let's git that damn meat packed down to Kemper's an' git back to the Swede's. The boys'll be wonderin' what's keepin' us."

One morning a week later Til Carter stood with Julie, Bettles, and Tim Condon at the head of the rapid beside a nineteen-foot freight canoe loaded with supplies for the hundred-mile upriver trip to Coldfoot, where they would outfit for the winter on Jim River.

Old Tim turned to the girl. "Good-by, darter. Take care yerself. You'll have it a lot easier there teachin' them kids than what you would winterin' up on the Jim."

"I don't mind wintering on a creek," the girl replied. "I've done it most of my life."

Til stepped closer to the girl. "I sure wish you were going with us," he said in a low voice. "Or that I was staying here. I'll bet you could teach me everything Bettles can—and a lot more."

The girl tossed her head as she felt the pressure of the

hand that closed over hers. "I'll be too busy teaching the children to bother with chechakos," she said.

Til grinned. "Okay. Well—good-by—Pest. But remember —I'm coming back in the spring."

Bettles, who had inadvertently heard the conversation, grinned broadly. "That's right, Julie—Til will be comin' back in the spring. An' I'm warnin' you, you won't have no chechako to deal with then. He'll be a sourdough—an' don't you fergit it!"

IX

Ear Bitin' Finley Returns to His Claim

Shortly after Tim Condon and Bettles finished their bottle at the table in the Swede's saloon and joined the men who had crowded into the room, Ear Bitin' Finley roused from his apparent drunken stupor at the next table, slipped unobtrusively from the saloon, and struck out for his claim on South Creek, where his partner, young Bob Harmon, greeted him with surprise.

"What—back already! I didn't look for you to show up for three or four days. What's the matter—did the boys clean you out in a stud game?"

"No, I didn't set in no game," the man replied as he seated himself on the edge of the sluice box and eyed the shallow shaft half filled with seepage water. "I jest got to thinkin' how we're workin' like hell here an' ain't takin' out no better'n wages. How'd you like to hit out fer the Jim River country?"

"The Jim River! Cripes, that's way up somewheres beyond Coldfoot! What makes you so anxious to hit for there all of a sudden?"

"It's like this—I has me a few drinks down to the Swede's

place an' I gits sleepy, an' so I goes over to a chair by a table an' goes to sleep there. By and by I hears someone talkin', an' it's old Tim Condon an' some other old sourdough. They goes to the bar an' has 'em a drink er two, then Tim he picks up the bottle an' a couple of glasses, an' him an' this other guy comes over an' sets down at the next table to where I'm layin' kinda slunched over.

"They begin talkin', an' I let on like I was dead to the world. A man can't never tell when he might hear somethin' he kin cash in on, 'cause when guys is drinkin' they might spill somethin' they wouldn't if they wasn't. Well, I heerd somethin', all right—an' you an' me's goin' to cash in on it. I'll learn old Tim Condon to go 'round tellin' folks I'm a no-'count bastard—like he told this here other guy! He claimed I hang 'round an' pick fights an' how if it warn't fer you we wouldn't even be takin' out wages here on the claim. He says sometime someone's goin' to knock hell outa me, an' he hopes he'll be there to see it. By God, I'd ort to knocked him cold an' chawed his ears off!" The man paused, drew a bottle from his pocket, and took a drink.

"How are we goin' to cash in on that?" Harmon asked.

"We ain't—on that. I hung onto myself an' played dead to the world, 'cause I figgered that when Tim an' this other guy goes to work on that bottle they'd spill somethin'. An' I was right—the more Tim drunk, the more he talked. An' I laid there an' tuk it all in. He claims him an' his kid, Davey, has got 'em a good proposition up on the Jim River. Says they've got a thousan' ounces of dust cached there on the claim. He says how they git their supplies at Coldfoot, but he come down here this trip fer to see how his darter's comin' along an' fix it up fer her board an' lodgin' this win-ter. She's that there redhead that stays to Kemper's. He left Davey on the location, an' bein' as how he know'd that if he got to drinkin' he might spill his guts about that cache, before he came away he told the kid to shift the cache to some other place after he'd gone, so if he got to runnin' off at the head, he couldn't let on where it's at, 'cause he wouldn't know.

"This other guy, he says how he figgers he'll go up an' have a look at the Jim River country. An' he asks Tim when he was headin' back, an' Tim says in a week er ten days. Now what I mean—what's the sense in you an' me stickin' around this here proposition an' workin' like hell when we can't take out no better'n wages?"

"You mean you want to hit out for the Jim River? It's quite a trip up there. An' how do you know we'd hit it any better up there than we did here?"

Finley's eyes narrowed. "I ain't figgerin' to file no location up there. I'm thinkin' about that thousan' ounces in Condon's cache."

"You mean—rob the cache?"

"Shore. It's a cinch. If we pull out tomorrow, we kin beat Condon to his location by a week er ten days. The kid's alone there on the claim. When he tells us where the cache is we'll——"

"Hell, he won't tell where the cache is!" Harmon interrupted. "He'd be a damn fool to."

Finley's eyes held an evil gleam. "He'll tell. After I've worked on him awhile he'll tell anythin' I want to know. An' after we git the dust, we rap the kid on the head an' plant him in the muskeg. Oncet a guy's shoved down in the muck in under that moss they can't no one in God's world ever find him. Then me an' you'll hit fer the Yukon. I'm damn well fed up with this Koyukuk country. Hell, I'd ruther snipe the bars on any of them cricks that runs into the Yukon than work the best location the Koyukuk kin show."

"You mean—murder the kid after we got the dust?"

Finley shrugged. "Well—some calls it murder. But no one could ever prove nothin'—'specially that damn pot-gutted marshal."

74

Harmon shook his head. "You can count me out. I don't want no part of it."

"A thousan' ounces is sixteen thousan' dollars—eight thousan' apiece," Finley said. "We never could lay by that much dust workin' this location. Hell, it takes all we kin git out to buy our clothes an' grub an' mebbe a little likker now an' then."

Harmon shrugged. "We could take out a lot more if you'd spend more time here on the claim an' less at the Swede's," he said.

Finley scowled. "Is that so! Well, I ain't spendin' no more time on this location! I'm through here—an' so be you!"

"What do you mean?"

"Meanin' that I'm goin' after that thousan' ounces—an' you're in on it, whether you want to er not!" He paused and leered at the younger man. "If you try to back out—how about me goin' to the marshal about the Bert Townley case?"

The younger man paled. "I didn't kill Bert Townley—an' you know it!"

"Oh, shore. I know it." The man's lips twisted into an evil grin. "Townley wasn't killed only oncet—an' I killed him. You see, I ain't afraid to tell you I did. You couldn't never prove it. An' if you was to say I told you I did, I'd say yer a damn liar. But a word from me would hang you fer that job damn quick. I shot him with your revolver—the revolver that's got yer name engraved on it. The marshal saved the bullet he dug outa Townley's skull. Two different men kin swear that they seen you on Rat Crick near Townley's claim the day he was shot. After shootin' Townley, I cached yer revolver. All I'd have to do is tip off the marshal to that cache—an' you'd swing. There ain't another revolver in the hull damn country that bullet would fit—an' you know that." The man paused and took another drink from his bottle. "You goin' to throw in with me on this Jim River job an' git yerself a nice easy eight thousan'? Er be you goin' to stay here on the Koyukuk an' git hung?"

The younger man's shoulders drooped as for several moments he stood digging at the gravel with the toe of his pac. "Okay," he said. "When do we start?"

X

The Man on the Cabin Floor

The trip up the Koyukuk in the freight canoe was uneventful, and toward evening of the fifth day after bidding Julie Condon good-by Old Tim, Bettles, and Til Carter beached the canoe at Coldfoot and made their way to the trading post. As they approached the low log building a man stepped from the door and with a glance in their direction disappeared swiftly around a corner of the building.

Bettles slanted Tim a glance. "Ain't that the same cuss that was layin' spraddled out over that table down to the Swede's the other day soused to the gills? What's he doin' up here?"

Tim nodded. "Yeah—Ear Bitin' Finley. Like I told you, him an' a young punk name of Harmon ben workin' a location on South Crick. But they ain't ben takin' out no better'n wages. Chances is they pulled out an' figger on tryin' their luck up here."

As they stepped into the trading room Crim, the proprietor, nodded to Tim, and at sight of Bettles his eyes lighted. "Well, dog my cats, if it ain't Gordon Bettles himself! Welcome back to God's country! I know'd you wouldn't never be satisfied down there on the Yukon. When you pulled out, couple year ago, I says to the boys how you'd be back. It's too damn civilized down along the big river fer old sour-doughs like me an' you. But we're gittin' civilized up here too. We got a doctor now, an' a damn good one, too. Young feller name of Sutherland. An' on top of that I hear how Fred Martin is buildin' a steamboat to run the Koyukuk as fer up as Bettles. I kinda hate to see the country goin' to hell that way. But, even at that, it would save a lot of time gittin' freight in here. Damn sight cheaper, too."

Bettles laughed. "The steamboat's built. The *North Star*, Fred named her. I come up on her first trip—me an' my friend here. Crim—meet Til Carter."

The two shook hands as the trader eyed the younger man. "Chechako?" he asked.

Til smiled. "Yes, I'm afraid I'm pretty much of a chechako."

"What's Ear Bitin' Finley doin' up here?" Tim asked. "We seen him come out the door as we come up from the river."

"Oh—him. Yeah, he said his name's Finley. Ben hangin' 'round here three, four days. Claims he's huntin' his pardner —young feller name of Harmon. Finley, he claims this here Harmon robbed their cache down on South Crick an' skipped out on him whilst he was havin' hisself a couple days' drunk down to the Swede's. Says he figgers Harmon hit upriver. But they ain't no sech party showed up here. Leastwise I ain't never saw him—an' no one else in Coldfoot has neither."

"Couldn't of ben no hell of a job of robbin' Harmon pulled," Condon opined. "They wasn't takin' out no better'n wages. You got that there list of supplies ready that I left when I went down to Bettles? I'll be hittin' out fer the claim in the mornin'."

Crim nodded. "All broke out an' laid to one side, there in the storeroom." He turned to Bettles. "How about you,

Gordon? You'll be needin' a bill of goods. Yer figgerin' on winterin' here, ain't you?"

"Me an' Til might winter on some crick. It's accordin' to what we find. Al Mayo told me there'd ben some pretty good strikes made up here, so I thought I'd have a look-see. Me an' Til will be wantin' a light canoe an' a stampedin' outfit of grub. If we strike somethin' that looks good, we'll knock us up a shack an' come back for our winter's supplies."

Crim smiled and glanced at Til. "You heard what he said. When you git that shack built, don't let him fergit to come back fer supplies. Be jest like him to fergit all about it. That old devil could winter through in a country that would starve a wolf. You might be a chechako now, but by God, you won't be come spring. You'll be a sourdough—er you'll be dead."

The three pulled out the following morning. The first day's travel on the Koyukuk was easy, with Til paddling the front end of Condon's freight canoe, loaded with his winter's supplies, while Bettles handled the light canoe with the stampeding outfit.

When they headed up the smaller river, progress was slowed by innumerable shallow rapids that necessitated much heaving and hauling and track-lining and by a mile-long canyon through which the river roared in a welter of seething whitewater, around which the canoes and their contents had to be portaged.

Late in the afternoon of the fourth day out of Coldfoot they rounded a bend and Condon pointed to a small log cabin at the head of a quarter-mile stretch of slack water. "There she is," he said. "That's our location. We struck the first colors in a rapids jest above the shack."

As the two canoes approached the cabin, Condon's brow drew into a frown. "Somethin's wrong," he said. "We've ben in sight fer a good ten minutes. Davey'd ort to be out there on the bank waitin' fer us."

"Maybe he's workin' somewheres above an' ain't seen us," Bettles suggested from his canoe, which was gliding along close beside the larger craft.

Condon shook his head. "He'd be knocked off by now. An' besides, look at them dogs runnin' along the bank to meet us. They're hungry—that's what they be! Look at 'em! By God, they ain't ben fed fer three, four days—mebbe longer —to be ganted up like they be! There's somethin' damn good an' wrong!"

Under the redoubled effort of the paddlers the two canoes shot forward and a few minutes later were beached in front of the cabin. Leaping from the canoe, Condon hurried up the bank, closely followed by the others, and threw the door open. For a long moment he stood there staring at the man who lay sprawled on the floor.

Bettles peered over his shoulder. "Is—is it Davey?" he asked.

Condon shook his head. "No," he replied in a bewildered voice. "It's—Harmon."

"Harmon? You mean Ear Bitin' Finley's pardner—that robbed their cache an' skipped out?"

"Mebbe he robbed the cache—an' mebbe he didn't," Condon replied. "I'd have to have more than Finley's word fer it. But what the hell's he doin' here? An' where's Davey?"

Pushing past Condon, Bettles stepped into the room and, dropping to his knees beside the prone man, grasped him by the shoulder and turned him over. "My God, he ain't dead!" he cried. "Come on—give me a hand an' we'll lift him onto the bunk." With the man on the bunk and a pillow under his head, Bettles examined him further. "He's got a pulse, but it's damn feeble," he announced, and turned to Til. "Go fetch that bottle of liquor out of my pack," he said. "A good stiff shot might fetch him to." When Til disappeared, Bettles scrutinized the unconscious man's face. Gently his fingers explored a slight depression just above the left temple. His brow drew into a frown as he glanced up at Condon. "He's ben hit a hell of a crack with somethin' heavy. The skull's smashed. Not jest cracked—it's smashed. Maybe he'll never come to."

"Mebbe he come along here an' tried to rob Davey, an' Davey slugged him with somethin'," Condon said. "But if that's the way of it—where the hell's Davey?" Til stepped into the room with the liquor, and Condon continued. "You go ahead an' try to fetch him to whilst I feed the dogs. Then we'll hunt fer Davey."

As Til handed the bottle to Bettles his brow drew into a frown. "If Harmon came here with the intention of robbing the cache, Davey may have clouted him over the head and then, when he thought he'd killed him, he may have got panicky and pulled out."

Bettles shook his head. "That ain't the way of it, Til. If Davey'd hit him, it would have ben with the first thing he got holt of when he found Harmon aimed to rob him—like a stick of stovewood, or an ax, or a rock. Harmon was knocked out with some padded weapon—like a blackjack or a rock in a sock. The man that hit Harmon never done it on the spur of the moment. It was planned."

Drawing the cork, Bettles slopped out half a tin cup of liquor, which he held to the man's lips, allowing a few drops to trickle down his throat. Failing to produce any result, he tilted the cup farther.

Til, who was watching the performance, cried a warning. "Hell, go easy there! You'll drown him!"

Bettles replied without looking up. "This man's bad off. It'll take quite a bit of liquor to fetch him around. Anyways, a man would ruther drown in whisky than die of a rap on the head any day."

The man's eyelids flickered feebly, and he coughed slightly as his throat muscles moved. Then his lips moved slightly, and both bent down to catch the words. "Finley . . . burnin' his feet an' hands . . . candle . . . tried . . . to stop

. . . him . . ." Then the whisper died into silence, and Bettles glanced up swiftly into Til's face. "For Christ's sake, don't tell Tim what he said. Back there in the Swede's place Tim got to shootin' off about havin' a thousan' ounces cached up here an' Davey know'd where it is. This Finley was playin' drunk an' listenin'. The way it looks, Finley an' Harmon came up here to rob that cache, an' Finley was tryin' to torture its location out of Davey, an' Harmon couldn't stand for it, so Finley jerked out a blackjack an' let him have it. After that maybe Finley tortured Davey into talkin'—an' maybe he didn't. But don't never let Tim know that Davey was tortured. He'd figure it was his own fault for talkin' about the cache. He'd never forgive himself—an' feelin' like he would about it, God knows what he might do."

Til nodded. "That's right," he agreed. "No matter whether we ever find Davey or not. Old Tim must never know."

"Did the likker fetch him to?" Condon asked as he re-entered the room.

Bettles shook his head. "Nope. Looks like he's a goner."

Old Tim frowned. "We're in a hell of a jam, any ways you look at it. We can't jest let this feller lay there an' die, even if he did try to rob Davey. Looks like we got to git him down to Coldfoot. Crim says there's a good doctor there now. Then there's Davey. I ben studyin' about him whilst I was out there feedin' the dogs. Soon's I stepped into the room here I seen that his packsack an' blankets was gone, an' how there's more grub missin' off'n the shelves than what he'd of et whilst I was down to Bettles. But he ain't off on no prospectin' trip, 'cause his pan an' shovel is here. So he must of pulled out.

"Then there's the cache. It's empty. I told Davey to move it after I pulled out. Mebbe he did, an' then agin, mebbe he took them thousan' ounces with him when he pulled out. Looks to me like when he seen this damn cuss aimed to rob him, he whammed him over the head, an' then, figgerin' he'd killed him, he got scairt an' hit out. Me or you would know that we had a right to kill anyone that was tryin' to rob us. But Davey's only a kid."

"If he pulled out," Bettles ventured, "it looks like we'd ort to met him on the river. It can't be so damn long ago that this man was hit."

"It could be quite a while," Condon said. "I rec'lect the time a fella name of Simmons got his skull caved in when a tree fell on him over on Myrtle Crick. There wasn't no doctor in the country then, an' his pardner drug him into the cabin an' he laid there ten days 'fore he died, an' he never did come to.

"But we wouldn't of met Davey on the river, nohow. I had the canoe. If he pulled out, he pulled out afoot, an' he'd of held back from the river, where the ground's higher. There's a hell of a lot of muskeg along the river, with deep, mucky sloughs windin' through 'em. It might be that he hit off into the hills an' will camp there waitin' fer me to git back. If that's the way of it, he'll be slippin' down here pretty quick. He know'd I wouldn't be gone more'n a month at the most. Then agin, he might of hit upriver instead of down. Amos Krump an' Ed Hanson is located up above the big canyon, an' so is Pete Jones an' Frank Este. He might have hit out fer there, figgerin' to hole up with them fellers till I got back."

Bettles eyed the unconscious man. "There's a doctor in the country now, so we can't set here an' let this man die like you say this Simmons did. We'll lay him in the big canoe, an' Til an' I'll run him down to Coldfoot. It might be we could get him there in time for the doctor to save him. I doubt—but we've got to try. If he dies on the way down, that's his hard luck. You stick around here on the chanct that Davey might show up."

Condon nodded. "Looks like that's the way to work it. I can sort of slip up the river a ways an' mebbe hit back in the hills lookin' fer Davey—like if somethin' might of happened. Anything could happen to a man out alone. You're

83

the ones that's got the tough job, though. It's goin' to be a hell of a chore gittin' him down to the doctor, what with all them portages."

"It won't be so bad," Bettles said. "We'll make a stretcher out of a blanket an' a couple of poles, an' the two of us can handle him all right."

XI

"This Man Is Dead"

The run down to Coldfoot was made in three days. As the two loaded the unconscious Harmon into the canoe at the foot of the last portage, Bettles heaved a sigh of relief. "Three, four hours now an' we can turn him over to the doctor. He shore must be a tough cuss, stayin' alive without nothin' to eat er drink except that swaller er two of whisky I poured down him."

"Sort of suspended animation, I guess," Til said. "Like a hibernating animal. I don't believe he's got much chance of pulling through, though. I tried to take his pulse there at the head of the portage, and it was so feeble I could just barely feel it. When we hit Coldfoot, I'll skip over to the trading post and ask Crim where the doctor lives, and we'll rush him there as quick as we can."

Young Dr. Sutherland opened the door of his cabin in answer to a knock and glanced down at the form on the stretcher that the two had lowered to the ground.

"This fella got a hell of a rap on the head, Doc," Bettles explained. "You better get to work on him pronto. He's in bad shape."

Dropping to one knee, the doctor felt for a pulse. With his thumb he drew back an eyelid and glanced at the exposed eye. He nodded. "Yes," he agreed. "He's in bad shape. This man is dead."

Bettles shrugged. "Well, we done our damnedest. Found him layin' on the floor of Tim Condon's shack up on Jim River. His head's stove in there jest above the left temple. I wish you'd kind of look him over an' see if you can tell what he was hit with—an' how long ago. We'll step over to the tradin' post an' be back directly."

"I'm goin' to have some words with this Ear Bitin' Finley," Bettles said as he and Til walked toward the trading post. "An' he's goin' to have to talk pretty fast. Like I told you back there in the cabin, I know damn well he laid there spraddled acrost that table pretendin' to be dead to the world an' listened to Tim tellin' me about that cache up there on the claim—an' how Davey was s'posed to move it after Tim had gone. If him an' Harmon wasn't takin' out no better'n wages on their claim, you can bet Harmon never robbed their cache an' lit out. What happened—Finley went back to the claim an' got Harmon, an' the two of 'em hit out fer Tim's claim an' done away with Davey, after torturin' him till he told where the cache was. Then, either because Harmon objected to the torturin' or because Finley didn't want to split that thousan' ounces with Harmon, he knocked him off, too, an' hit back here to Coldfoot an' told Crim that yarn about huntin' fer his thievin' pardner."

"Sounds reasonable, all right," Til agreed. "But how are you going to prove it if Finley sticks to his story?"

"Maybe we can't prove it," Bettles admitted. "But anyway, I'm goin' to hear what he's got to say—an' watch him damn clost while he's sayin' it. He might slip up somehow in what he says. Or Doc might find out by the shape of that smashed place in Harmon's skull what he was hit with. Or someone might have seen Finley somewheres along the river between here an' Tim's claim. Or some other bit of evidence er information might pop up so we could call a miners' meetin'."

"What's a miners' meeting?" Til asked.

"A miners' meetin' is a device we've worked out up here where there ain't no courts, an' damn few marshals, to try such damn scoundrels as are suspected of committin' such crimes as robbery, murder, arson, an' other form of skull-duggery. The evidence is laid before a gatherin' of miners, an' then the prisoner is given the chanct of presentin' his side of it, an' then a vote is taken. If he's convicted, he's hung. If he's acquitted, he's turned loose. It's crude, maybe —but it comes a damn sight closer to metin' out justice than a court does—like when some damn cuss that everyone knows is guilty as hell gets off scot free because some clerk spelt his name wrong or some lawyer left some word out of an indictment."

Stepping into the trading post, Bettles faced Crim across the rude counter. "Where's Ear Bitin' Finley? You rec'lect he's the one Tim asked you about when we come through here."

"Oh, him. Damn if I know where he's at. He hung around here a few days jest before you fellas come along, claimin' he was huntin' his pardner which had robbed their cache an' skipped out. He had a little A tent down by the river. He broke camp jest after you pulled out, an' I ain't saw him sence. Prob'ly he tuk out huntin' his pardner agin when he didn't find him here."

"If he was still anywheres around Coldfoot, you'd know it, wouldn't you?"

"Shore I would. He ain't around here. Some of the boys was inquirin' about him the other day. They figger like me, that he shoved on huntin' his pardner."

"He'd ort to stayed here an' he'd have found him," Bettles said dryly.

"You mean his pardner's here in Coldfoot?"

"Yeah—he's here. He's up to the doctor's. We found him

layin' on old Tim's floor with his head stove in. We fetched him down to the doctor's—but we was too late. He was dead when we got here. An' on top of that, Davey Condon's missin'. Old Tim's up there huntin' him. Me an' Til are hittin' back there. If Finley shows up, you send word up to Tim's, an' we'll come down. Looks like a case fer a miners' meetin'."

"I shore will," Crim agreed. "It would be a damn shame if anything has happened to Davey. He's a good lad, an' him an' old Tim's got 'em a good location up there."

Returning to the doctor's cabin, Bettles inquired, "What did you find, Doc?"

"I found," replied the doctor gravely, "that the man had been struck a terrific blow with some padded weapon. The crushed area is three inches in diameter and could have been made by a padded stone, or a padded head of an iron maul, or by a blackjack."

"But not by anything a man might happen to pick up—like a stick of stovewood or a rock?"

"No. There is no surface laceration whatever, such as would result from a blow by an unpadded weapon. Frankly, this looks like a deliberately planned assault—like a murder."

Bettles nodded. "That's the way I figure it. An' can you tell how long ago he was hit?"

The doctor shook his head. "No. A man might conceivably live for several days—maybe even for a week or more —with an injury of that kind. There is no way of determining that point."

XII

Old Tim Meets a Bear

The two reached the Condon cabin on the evening of the third day after leaving Coldfoot. Tim was nowhere in sight, and the light canoe was missing.

"Prob'ly paddled upriver a ways huntin' Davey," Bettles opined as they ate their supper. "But I'm bettin' he never will find him. My guess is that Finley knocked him off an' sunk him in the muskeg somewheres. Chances are Tim will show up before mornin'."

Til nodded. "It looks that way," he agreed. "I sure hope not. It would be mighty hard on Julie. She thinks a heap of her brother."

Bettles grinned. "You seen quite a lot of the Pest whilst we was there, didn't you? Come to think of it, you never did show up in them stud games at the Swede's till late in the evenin'."

"Yeah, I sort of helped around with the chores. And she and I went on that caribou hunt. Cripes, we were staying there. It was the least I could do."

The grin widened. "Oh, shore. But it wasn't the most you could do. Tellin' you about me—I'd think twice before I'd fall for one of them redheads. They're hell on wheels when they get their dander up. It would take a damn good man to handle one."

Til returned the grin. "I guess I'm safe enough. She hasn't got much time for chechakos."

Bettles nodded solemnly. "There's one pint yer overlookin', Til. If a man's an Irishman, or a Siwash, or an' Eskimo, he's got to be one till he dies. But a chechako—one that's got guts enough to stick in this country—don't stay a chechako. He grows into a sourdough. Next time you see the Pest you won't be a chechako. I'm just mentionin' this fer yer own good."

Til laughed. "Thanks for the warning. I'll sure have to watch my step. But, at that, she's by all odds the most efficient and capable girl I have ever seen. There don't seem to be a damn thing she can't do. Come on, let's clean up these dishes. I'm getting sleepy."

The two awoke in the morning to find that Tim Condon had not returned. Bettles frowned as he mixed up a batch of pancakes. "What the hell are we up against? First Davey disappears, an' now it's Tim. I shore expected to find him here this mornin'."

"So did I," Til agreed. "I sure hope nothing's happened to him."

"Chances are he's all right. Tim ain't no kid, like Davey. He's used to hittin' out alone. Ben up in this country since God knows when. The canoe's gone, so he's somewheres along the river. An' he's upstream, or we'd have run across him. We'll throw a pick an' shovel an' pan in the canoe after breakfast an' shove up the river. We'll keep an eye out for Tim an' do a little prospect pannin' here an' there. Tim told me the river is spotted. We might pan for a month an' not hit anything. An' again, we might run onto a damn good location in a day. That's what makes prospectin' fun—a man can be a bum one minute an' a millionaire the next."

It was well along in the afternoon when they rounded a

bend several miles up from the cabin and saw Tim Condon's canoe pulled up on a sand bar at the foot of a series of falls and turbulent rapids flanked by high rock walls. Beaching their canoe beside the other, Bettles stepped out and stood for several moments staring down into the sand. Frowning deeply, he raised his eyes to Til's. "That rainstorm we run into comin' up from Coldfoot—when was it?"

"Why, it was day before yesterday. Don't you remember, it hit about noon and rained like the devil for a good three hours."

Bettles nodded. "That's right. I just wanted to be shore." He paused and pointed down at the sand. "An' Tim left the canoe here before that. His foot tracks are rained out. Not only that—his grub an' blankets are in the canoe, wet as hell an' layin' in a good three inches of water. So he ain't ben back here for two nights, an' better'n two days. Get to work now an' we'll spread this stuff out to dry. We're hittin' out to hunt for Tim—an' by God, we ain't goin' back till we find him! We might be campin' here tonight."

"Tim said there were a couple of locations staked above the big canyon and that Davey may have gone up there," Til replied, eying the foaming whitewater that cascaded between the high rock walls. "This may be the big canyon, and Tim may have gone on up to inquire whether they had seen Davey. If so, he may have stayed over a couple of days with those men."

Bettles shook his head doubtfully. "That ain't the way it looks to me. Admittin' this is the big canyon, Tim didn't say how far above it these fellers are located. If he aimed to visit 'em, he'd figure on stoppin' over anyways one night with 'em. If their locations are quite a ways above the canyon, he'd have portaged his canoe to the head of the canyon an' gone on upriver. If they're only a little ways, he'd have packed his blankets up there. Either way, he'd never have left his canoe pulled up on the sand right side up with his stuff in it. He'd have tossed his grub pack out on the sand an' turned his canoe upside down over it. No sir—Tim figured on comin' back here before night, no matter where he went. It's my bet that Tim ain't no hell of a ways from here right now—an' I'm shore dreadin' what we're goin' to find. We'll hit up to the head of the canyon, an' if those locations are anywhere close, we'll get those boys to help us hunt."

The little-used portage trail slanted steeply upward for a quarter of a mile, then swung wide of the canyon to avoid a high-piled jumble of rock fragments. Bettles was in the lead, and as he rounded a sharp angle of rock he leaped backward, nearly knocking Til off his feet, as a deep, snarling roar filled the air. "A bear, an' a damn big one," he cried, "an' us without a gun! Climb up the rocks quick!"

The two climbed frantically and, taking advantage of whatever offered in the way of hand and toe holds, were soon high enough above the trail to peer over the projecting angle of rock. There, directly in the trail, glaring up with hate-blazing eyes and emitting deep-throated, snarling growls, was an enormous grizzly. His belly was flat on the ground with hind legs stretched backward, the fore part of his body raised on his forelegs, the long claws of which scratched frantically in a futile attempt to pull himself up the steep rock pile.

"His back's broke!" Bettles exclaimed. "Look at the blood there on his hide! By God, he's been shot! We're safe enough—but where the hell is Tim?"

For answer, Til, whose glance swept that steeply slanted face of the rock pile, pointed to an object that showed at about their own level and a dozen or more yards farther on. "I'm afraid we'll find him there," he said. "That looks to me like the body of a man wedged in among the rocks."

As quickly as possible the two worked their way along the rock face and a few minutes later reached old Tim, who lay face downward among the rock fragments, held there by a block of stone that had shifted, crushing his left leg and holding it firmly pinned against the edge of a deep rock crevice.

"By God, he's alive!" Bettles cried. "We've got to get him out of here! That rock don't weigh more'n three, four hundred pounds. We'll cut a pole, an' one of us can pry it up while the other one frees his leg. You wait here an' I'll cut the pry."

Retrieving Condon's rifle, which lay among the rocks a few inches below his outstretched hands, Bettles made his way swiftly down onto the trail. Stepping close to the infuriated but helpless bear, he dispatched him with a bullet between the eyes, then with his belt ax he cut a ten-foot length of three-inch spruce and returned to the injured man, where it was but the work of a few minutes to raise the rock with the lever sufficiently for Til to free the imprisoned leg.

The unconscious man was carefully lowered to the trail and laid on his back. Dropping to his knees, Bettles cut away the man's trousers, and the two gazed at the leg, crushed and mangled horribly at the knee.

Bettles shook his head sadly. "Pore old Tim. He got three, four bullets in that bear before he stopped him. He was a damn good man, anywheres you put him. But he'll never walk on that leg again. Cripes, it's swollen an' black from his toes damn near to his hip, an' I could feel the smashed bones grittin' together when we was easin' him down. It's another trip down-river fer us, Til. We've got to get him to the doctor."

Til nodded. "I only hope we have better luck getting him there than we had with Harmon," he said. "Wait here, and I'll go and get one of his blankets to make a stretcher."

"We won't need no stretcher to get him down to the canoe with. He don't weigh over a hundred an' fifty, an' it ain't more'n half a mile, an' we can back-pack him. Hold on—I'll rig us a tumpline that'll take the bulk of the weight off our arms." Stepping to the carcass of the bear, he drew his belt knife and cut a strip of hide some four inches wide and seven feet long. Tying the two ends about Condon's body, he turned to Til. "Go easy, now, an' hist him onto my back an' I'll show you how it works." When the man was in place, Bettles slipped the line over his forehead and, reaching backward, grasped the thighs with his hands.

"I get it," Til said. "Put him down and let me pack him. I'm younger than you are."

"You might be younger, but, by God, you ain't no tougher," Bettles replied. "I'll pack him halfways, an' you can take him on from there. I shore hope he don't come to till we git him to the canoe. It won't be so bad from there."

Til took over at the top of the slope and had almost reached the level when the wounded man opened his eyes. "What—what the hell?" he muttered feebly.

"Take it easy," Til said. "We'll be at the canoe in a few minutes."

As they eased the man onto the sand he again opened his eyes. "What happened? That damn bear—did he git me?"

"No," Bettles replied. "You got the bear. Then a rock got you."

"Water. Give me some water. I'm all dried up." Til filled a tin cup and held it to the man's lips. He swallowed the water in great gulps, and Til refilled the cup. When the second cupful had been swallowed, Condon eyed his injured leg. "That Godam bear! I run onto him at the turn of the trail. He rared up an' I let him have it right plumb in the chest. He went down an' started to git up, an' I let him have it agin. He was rollin' around, snarlin' an' bitin' at himself, an' I was goin' to give him another, but my rifle jammed, an' whilst I was workin' at it, he got to his feet an' come at me. I clumb the rocks an' stuck my leg in a crack to hang on whilst I fooled with the gun. Then I got it, an' the bear was halfways up to me an' I let him have it agin. He rolled back onto the trail, an' I was goin' to give him another when that rock hit me. Jesus! I never had nothin' hurt like that! I dropped the rifle an' tried to git my leg loose. But I couldn't—an' that damn bear snarlin' an' growlin', an' clawin' at the rocks to come back up. I tried to grab my rifle, but I couldn't reach it. The bear kep' on raisin' hell, but he didn't git no closter. Then I seen how his back was broke, an' I know'd he couldn't git to me. I worked at the rock, tryin' to lift it off'n my leg. But I couldn't. After a while it quit hurtin'—turned kind of numb. I laid there a hell of a while. Then mebbe I fainted—mebbe went to sleep. I woke up—an' went to sleep, mebbe half a dozen times. One time it was rainin'. It was hell layin' there in the rain. Then the next time I woke up, Til, here, was packin' me down the trail."

Bettles nodded. "That rain was two days ago. You must be hungrier'n hell. I'll build a fire an' fry up some bacon an' them bannocks you had in yer pack—they're kind of soggy, but they're a damn sight better'n nothin'."

"Yeah, I'm hungry, all right. I'd shore ben in a hell of a fix if you boys hadn't of found me. Chances is no one would of used that trail till spring—onlest Davey had come along. Them boys upriver has already took their winter supplies up. You ain't seen nothin' of Davey, have you?"

Bettles shook his head. "No, he ain't showed up. An' they hadn't heard nothin' of him down to Coldfoot."

When the man had consumed a huge ration of bacon and half a dozen soggy bannocks, his eyes again rested on his injured leg. "Guess I'm through," he said. "Smashed up like it is, that leg's prob'ly got to come off."

"The leg might have to come off," Bettles agreed. "But you ain't through—by a damn sight. Cripes, a one-legged man can get along, all right. A hell of a lot of 'em has."

"Oh, I'll get along—but not prospectin'. Snow, or sand, or muskeg has got a peg-legged man stopped cold. I dunno. Davey—he'll either show up somewheres er he won't. If he does, he kin keep on workin' the location. If he don't, I'll sell it. Crim knows it's a good claim. He'll be glad to buy it. I used to run a restaurant years ago, back in St. Cloud, Minnesoty. Might be I could start one in some goin' camp down along the Yukon. This country's good enough fer me. I ain't never goin' outside."

"Me neither," Bettles agreed. "Oncet a man's lived in this country every place else seems plumb puny."

"Like I told you, this Jim River country's spotted," Tim said. "You might strike it lucky—an' you might never make wages. You an' Til better winter in my shack an' prospect along the river an' cricks. If Davey shows up, he kin work the claim. There's room enough, an' grub enough, fer the three of you to winter through. If you don't hit nothin' agin the freeze-up, you better run a shaft down along them riffles jest above our location. I've got a hunch it might be as good as ours. If Davey don't show up, you can use our wood to burn in. Then in the spring, if you ain't done no good, you could hunt a new location."

"Okay," Bettles said. "We'll leave it that way. If we use your wood an' grub we'll pay you for it. First off, though, we've got to git you down to the doctor."

XIII

Farewell to the Koyukuk

"By God, if we've got to make many more trips up an' down this river we'll wear the damn thing out," Bettles grinned as he and Til beached the canoe at the cabin after taking Condon to Coldfoot.

Til grinned. "I've sure learned a lot about getting around the country."

"Yeah, an' by the time the freeze-up comes you'll know a hell of a lot about prospectin'," Bettles added, "an' by spring you'll know all about winter minin'—burnin' in—diggin' out—test pannin'—shootin' meat an' cachin' it away from the wolves—sluicin' out the dump. Then you can go back down to Kemper's an' tell the Pest you're a sourdough."

"She'll have to find that out for herself," Til laughed. "I'll never tell her. What about this winter darkness? I've read about men becoming depressed and killing themselves because of it."

"Huh," Bettles snorted. "Anyone that would kill himself on account of the darkness can be damn well got along without. What's depressin' about darkness? It never gets too dark outdoors to work—damn seldom too dark to hunt. Inside we light up a coal-oil lamp or a candle. Let me tell you this—the more a man reads about the North, the less he knows about it. You've got to live in this country to know it—an' when you know it you'll like it."

Day after day the two worked—taking test pans from bars, panning the gravel scooped from among the rocks of rapids, exploring tributary creeks. "She's spotted, all right, jest like Tim said," Bettles grinned one day as they ate their lunch near the head of a small tributary. "But the hell of it is the spots are a long ways apart. We've covered quite a bit of territory, an' we haven't found nothin' yet that's worth stakin'. We'll keep at it till the freeze-up, an' then we'll hole up in Tim's shack for the winter an' sink a shaft beside them riffles above his location. We found more colors amongst the rocks of that rapids than anywheres else. We can prob'ly take out better'n wages, so we might as well winter here as anywhere."

"I'd sure like to know what's become of Davey," Til said. "If he hit out and is lying low, he's had plenty of time to show up before this. And if he hit out down-river, he'd have showed up at Coldfoot. He couldn't pack enough grub to see him clear through to Bettles."

"Davey's dead," Bettles replied with conviction. "Like I told you down there in Coldfoot, Ear Bitin' Finley knocked him off, then he knocked off Harmon too. Maybe he got them thousan' ounces Davey recached an' maybe he didn't."

A few days later a canoe beached at the cabin and a man stepped out and eyed the two questioningly. "Who be you?" he asked. "An' wher's Tim Condon?"

"I'm Gordon Bettles. An' this is my pardner, Til Carter."

"Gordon Bettles!" the man exclaimed. "You mean him that the camp of Bettles is named for, down wher' Kemper's post's at?"

"That's right. I've ben down along the Yukon the last couple of years. You come from upriver. You must be one of the boys old Tim told us was located above the big canyon."

"Yeah. Amos Krump, my name is. I'm headin' for the doctor's down to Coldfoot. Got an infected hand, an' I want to git it doctored 'fore blood pizen sets in. You fellas buy Condon out?"

"No. An' speakin' of Condon—you ain't seen Davey, have you?"

The man shook his head. "Not sence early in the summer, when we come by here with our supplies. I seen a funny thing, though, there on the portage trail around the big canyon. There's a hell of a big bear layin' dead right on the trail. He'd ben shot, looks like about three, four weeks ago, an' a strip of hide four, five inches wide was cut out of his back from his ears clean back to his tail."

Bettles nodded. "Yeah, I cut the strip of hide. Made a tump strap out of it to pack Tim Condon over the portage. Tim had shot the bear a couple of days before, whilst he was up there huntin' fer Davey. He knocked the bear over with a couple of shots, but the bear got up an' come at him an' then Tim's gun jammed an' he climbed up the rocks. He got his gun workin' again an' broke the bear's back. Then he got his leg wedged in a crack, an' a big rock slid down an' crushed it. We found him then an' took him down to Coldfoot an' the doctor amputated the leg. Tim's the second one we took down there. When we came up here with him from Bettles we found a fella layin' here on the floor with his head stove in. He died before we got him to the doctor. Looks like Davey was robbed an' done away with whilst old Tim was down to Bettles. Me an' Til are holin' up here for the winter. We aim to work Number One above Tim's Discovery claim."

Krump frowned. "I'm shore sorry to hear about Tim an' Davey. They had a good thing here, an' they was damn good neighbors. Well, it jest goes to show. Don't make no difference how good a man's doin', he might run into bad luck. Take me, now. Me an' Hanson's doin' all right up on our claim. But if this here swole-up hand of mine runs into blood pizen, that would be bad luck too. The way I look at it, a man's got jest so much luck comin' to him—an' part of it's bound to be bad."

During the days that remained before the freeze-up Bettles and Til covered a wide area, even prospected several dry gulches back in the hills.

Then as the days shortened, the lakes froze, then the rivers, and the two settled down to the long grind of "burning in"—to the endless repetition of building fires of dry spruce in the shaft and, when they burned out, of removing the ashes and shoveling the few inches of thawed gravel onto a dump to be sluiced out in the spring. Frequent test pannings showed that they were taking out from three to five ounces a day.

Late in May the ice went out of the river, and using the Condon sluice, the two cleaned up their dump, which totaled eight hundred and forty ounces.

"That figures thirteen thousan', four hundred an' forty dollars," Bettles announced. "It ain't nothin' to write home about. But it ain't too bad, at that. We'll find out from Crim what Tim's grub bill come to, an' pay Tim, an' on top of that we ort to give him five hundred fer the wood we used. We won't bother to record this location. It ain't ben gettin' no better as we went down, an' it ain't worth while winterin' up here agin for what we'd get out of it. I'd ruther take a chance somewheres down along the big river. I s'pose, though, you'll stick around Bettles, seein' the Pest is teachin' school there. Or you might even throw in pardners with old Tim an' work his claim in Davey's place. Might not be sech a bad proposition, at that—if the Pest would quit her job.

She's a sourdough—you bet. You an' her might do all right winterin' here."

Til shrugged. "Tim spoke of selling out to Crim. And——Hell, you talk as if I was already married to her."

"A man might go further an' do a damn sight worse," Bettles replied. "I tell you, Til, I've got faith in this country. I don't mean here on Koyukuk, maybe. But somewheres, on some river—maybe down along the Yukon—the big strike's comin'. An' when she comes, an' the news of it hits the outside, there's goin' to be the damnedest gold rush the world ever seen. An' us fellows that's here are goin' to get the cream of it. Mind what I'm tellin' you—chechakos will come pilin' in by the thousan'—good men an' bad. They'll freeze, an' they'll drown, an' they'll starve to death. Some of 'em'll get rich. A lot of 'em'll make expenses. But most of 'em'll go broke an' take their pay out in experience. The camps will fill up with whores an' gamblers an' dance-hall floozies till hell won't have it. There'll be hell a-poppin' when that time comes—an' the man that's located on a good claim, an' married to a good woman—one that knows the country an' loves it—will be settin' on top of the world."

Til caught something of the older man's enthusiasm. "I'll do my damnedest to get in on a good claim," he said. "But the woman part—that's something that time will have to tell."

At Coldfoot the two called at the trading post. "How did Tim make out?" Bettles asked.

"Well, sir—he done all right. Doc cut off his leg just above the knee, an' we kep' him here with us till the break-up, an' he went on down to Bettles. Tom Armstrong, he's handy with tools, an' he made Tim a peg leg, an' Tim got so he kin git around pretty good. Course he won't never be able to do no prospectin'. He waited till jest before the breakup, hopin' that Davey might show up. When he didn't, Tim sold the claim to me. Says he figgers on goin' on down to the Yukon on the *North Star* an' sort of look them camps over along the big river—Nulato, Rampart, Fort Yukon, Eagle, Circle, Fortymile, an', if he sees a good openin', he aims to start a restaurant. Claims he used to run one back in the States somewheres. By God, he might do all right, too. Anyways, it'll beat layin' around doin' nothin'. An' if Julie'll quit her job teachin' an' throw in with him runnin' this here restaurant, they might have a damn good thing."

"He might, at that," Bettles agreed. "An' speakin' of the *North Star*, me an' Til will be hittin' out for Bettles. We aim to hit fer the Yukon on her first trip down."

Crim grinned. "Yer outa luck, then. The *North Star* has already pulled out. Fred Martin figgered on winterin' her at Nulato, but the freeze-up ketched him 'fore he could git back down-river, an' he wintered at Bettles an' run down last week on the high water."

"Okay," Bettles said. "We ain't in no hurry, then. We'll drop on down to Bettles an' wait there. We can get a hell of a lot of stud played at the Swede's before he can make the round trip back. We red up Tim's shack before we left, an' stuck the light canoe inside. How much was that last bill of grub Tim got? We used the most of it, an' we'll pay him when we see him. We used up damn near all his wood. So we'll pay him fer that too."

Crim consulted his book. "It come to seven hundred an' eighty dollars," he said. "It won't come so high from now on. Havin' a steamboat on the river cuts the freight bill jest about in half."

Arriving at Bettles, the two moved into the Condon cabin to await the return of the *North Star*. At the trading post Kemper shook his head sadly. "I was shore sorry to see the Condons pull out of the Koyukuk. With Davey gone, old Tim ain't fit to do no more prospectin', nor to work his claim alone—the shape he's in. Damn funny about Davey. Tim was tellin' me about him disappearin' an' findin' Harmon layin' on the floor with his head stove in. Julie shore tuk it hard. She thought a heap of Davey. She swears she'll find out what become of him if it takes her all her life. Old Tim was tellin' about you fellas winterin' up there on his claim. You didn't find out nothin' about Davey, did you?"

"Not a damn thing."

Kemper wagged his head slowly. "That's hell, ain't it? Old Tim, he figgers on startin' a restaurant somewheres along the Yukon. But, even more than Tim, I hated to see Julie go. By God, there's a woman fer you! She's the smartest kid that ever went to the school here, an' then when the teacher got married an' quit, Julie stepped right in an' took her place. An' she done a better job than the reg'lar teacher. She didn't try to *make* 'em learn—she made 'em *want* to learn. An' when that big lout of a kid of Bob Kling's told her to go to hell one day when she told him to quit pesterin' the little kids there in front of the schoolhouse, by God, she tore into him with her two fists an' knocked the livin' b'jesus outa him—an' him half agin as big as her. An' he went home an' told Bob, an' Bob went back to the school with him an' marched him right up to the desk in front of all the other kids an' told Julie she done a damn good job—an' go ahead an' do it agin. An' Julie, she jest laughed an' she says, 'Why, Mr. Kling, I'll never have to do it agin. You see, Bobby an' I jest had to find out who's boss around here. We understand each other now—an' we'll get along fine, won't we, Bobby?' An' young Bob, he sort of grins an' he says, 'That's right, Miss Julie. I guess I had it comin'.'

"An' ever sence then young Bob's worked like hell at his learnin', an' on top of that, he won't let Julie carry in no wood, an' he's over there every mornin' an' got the fire built an' the room warm 'fore Julie shows up. An' if any of the other kids starts raisin' hell he boots their hind end fer 'em. By God, them redheads is hell on wheels when they git their dander up! There's a fine young woman fer some man. She was the first white child born on the Koyukuk, an' every year when her birthday comes we pull off a celebration. Take them old fellas like George Worshintin an' Abe Lincoln—their birthdays is legal hollerdays down in the States, but they wasn't neither one of 'em born on the Koyukuk, an' by God, Julie Condon's birthday is a damn sight legaler than what either one of theirn are up in this neck of the woods. You bet—she's the pick of the hull damn country when it comes to wimmin. But it's goin' to take a damn good man to handle her."

XIV

Those Frogs!

It was well toward the end of June when Bettles and Til boarded the *North Star* for the run to Nulato. The captain told them that Tim Condon and Julie had taken passage upriver on the *Hannah*. "Old Tim, he talks to some of the boys an' they told him how Fortymile has grow'd in the last year. Accordin' to their tell, she's quite a camp now. There's a lot of prospectin' goin' on, an' some damn good locations has ben staked, not only on Fortymile River but on a lot of cricks an' gulches. So Tim, he figgers on goin' up an' lookin' things over, an' mebbe startin' a restaurant. The boys says they's one restaurant there now, but it's run kinda sloppy, like, an' the grub ain't none too good. I'm bettin' that if Tim does start a restaurant up there, an' Miss Julie throws in with him, it won't be no time at all till they'll run that other guy outa business. By God, she won't stand fer no sloppy work! An' I'll bet she'll dish out good grub, too."

"She shore would," Bettles agreed. "I've known her ever sence she was knee high to a grasshopper."

"A lot of the old-timers has," Martin said. "An' that's why

her an' Tim would git the trade." He paused and chuckled. "They've got a new name fer her now. The other evenin' a bunch of the boys was here on deck whilst I was tied up at Nulato. They'd got holt of a few bottles an' was sort of celebratin' Jack McQuesten's birthday an'——"

"Jack McQuesten's birthday!" Bettles exclaimed. "Cripes, here last year, up to Rampart, Jack got holt of some liquor, an' we celebrated his birthday late in the fall!"

The captain grinned. "Yeah—an' at Fort Yukon, three, four years ago, we celebrated it along about Chris'mas time. Trouble with Jack, he has a birthday any time the boys kin git holt of some likker. Anyways, like I says, we was settin' around here on deck chawin' the fat an' drinkin', an' Miss Julie, she'd went up the hill a ways to pick some flowers, an' Al Mayo happened to look up an' see her standin' there with the sunlight ketchin' that red head of hern jest right so it looked it was fair blazin'. 'My God, boys,' Al says, 'look at the fireweed!' An' seein' it there agin that green hillside, it shore did look like a bunch of fireweed shore enough. So after that the boys got to callin' her the Fireweed—an' she liked it."

Arriving at Nulato, they learned that the *Arctic* was due from St. Michael shortly. Bettles slanted Til a glance. "Guess we might's well head upriver on her. We might do a little prospectin' around Rampart, er maybe Eagle."

Til cleared his throat. "I kind of figured I'd like to have a look at the Fortymile country," he said. "Captain Martin said there have been some good strikes made up there."

Bettles grinned. "That's so. I'd plumb forgot about Fortymile. Wouldn't mind sort of lookin' it over myself. Yer on yer own now, Til. You ain't a chechako no more. You're a shore enough sourdough—an' I'm bettin' you'll make good."

Al Mayo stepped into the trading post and greeted Bettles with a hearty thump on the back. "How are you—you damned old gravel hound? What you doin' down here? Thought you'd gone back to the Koyukuk fer good."

"No. When you told me there was somethin' doin' up above Coldfoot, me an' Til, here, went up an' looked her over. By the way, Al, meet Til Carter. Til an' I wintered together up on Jim River."

Mayo wrung the younger man's hand. "Heard about you from old Tim Condon—how you an' Bettles found him jest in time with his leg smashed in some rocks an' run him down to the doctor." He grinned and winked. "Heard about you from the Fireweed too. She claims yer nothin' but a chechako—but she did allow you was the pick of all the chechakos she ever seen. It couldn't be, I s'pose, that you'd be headin' fer Fortymile?"

Til returned the grin. "Yes, we thought we'd slip up there and sort of look things over."

"Well—good luck to you, boy. If you see somethin' up there that looks good to you, grab it off." He turned to Bettles. "Jack McQuesten an' me are headin' fer Fortymile on the *Arctic*. She'll be along any day now. You two go on back to the *North Star*, an' I'll hunt up Dog Face Nolan an' git holt of three, four quarts of hooch an' fetch Jack down to the boat, an' we'll celebrate my birthday."

"Your birthday!" Bettles grinned. "What's the matter with celebratin' Jack's?"

"Hell—we jest celebrated his the other day—fer the third time this year!"

Two days later, when the *Arctic* nosed into the bank and tied up, Bettles and Til, together with McQuesten and Al Mayo, boarded her.

As the four stepped on deck they were greeted by Dr. McCall.

"Hello, Gordon!" the good doctor exclaimed. "Where are my frogs?"

"Why, hello, Doc! What you doin' 'way up here? You quit the *Bear*?"

"No. I heard about an old Indian burial place up near

Rampart, and I want to do some anthropological explora-
tion, so I got a thirty-day leave while the *Bear* makes a run
up north. But how about my frogs—those transparent frogs
you were going to get me?"

"Frogs? Oh—yeah—transparent frogs. Doc—meet Al
Mayo an' Jack McQuesten. You ort to know these boys.
They ben in the country ever sence the mountains wasn't
nothin' but little hills." He turned to the two grinning
sourdoughs. "Boys, meet Doc McCall, one of the best damn
men that ever dug around in the dirt fer old skulls an' spearheads an' stone lamps. An' that reminds me, Doc—I know
where there's a whole mammoth tusk stickin' out of a cutbank up near Old Station. I'll see the captain an' have him
wood up at Old Station when we get there, an' me an' Til
an' Jack an' Al will slip out an' dig that tusk out an' fetch
it to you. Damn seldom a man ever sees a whole ivory tusk.
It'll go fine in your collection."

"That will be great, Gordon. I'll certainly be glad to get
it. But about those transparent frogs——"

"Oh, shore—them frogs! Well, sir, Doc, we shore run
into tough luck with them frogs—didn't we, boys?" he
appealed to Mayo and McQuesten, who nodded emphatically.

"We shore did," McQuesten said. "You see, Doc, we
ketched damn near a worshtub full of them transparent
frogs an' was picklin' 'em in that there alcohol Gordon
fetched up, an' we had 'em settin' there in the cabin, an' we
went back to git more frogs, an' whilst we was gone along
come fifteen, twenty fellas that had got ashore off'n a steamboat that run aground a couple of mile above, an' they
went in the cabin, an' bein' damn near starved, they figgered
them frogs was some we was picklin' fer winter—an' they et
the whole damn tubful, alcohol an' all!"

"That's right, Doc," Mayo agreed. "We was shore sore
at them guys. You see, we'd went back to the lake where

we found these frogs, aimin' to git enough more of 'em to fill the tub clean full, an' damned if we didn't find the lake had practically dried up. Yes sir—there wasn't hardly no water left in it at all. So we hustled around an' finally managed to ketch about a quart of frogs—an' when we got back to the cabin, here we finds these damn cusses, sittin' around that tub, with a tin cup in one hand an' a frog in the other. They'd reach in the tub, grab up the frog by the hind leg, pop him into their mouth, an' worsh him down with a swig of alcohol. They was clean down to the bottom of the tub when we ketched 'em at it."

The doctor nodded gravely. "That was tough luck. But I presume you won't have any trouble collecting me some more of these frogs?"

McQuesten shook his head. "No chanct, Doc. That's where the hard luck comes in. Like Al says—when we went back we found the lake had dried up, an' after we ketched that there last quart of frogs there wasn't a damn one left. No sir—I doubt if there's another transparent frog left in the hull of Alaska."

"But," persisted the doctor, "how about that last quart of frogs you caught? Surely you saved those for me, didn't you?"

"That's more hard luck, Doc," Bettles said. "Shore, we saved 'em all right—er tried to. We hunted up Hooch Albert an' got a couple of quarts of hooch from him, an' then we poured out about half the hooch from each bottle——"

"You poured it out?"

"Yeah—part of it down each of us. An' then we poked them frogs into the bottles, one to a time, an' put back the corks, an' set 'em away on the shelf. In about a week we took 'em down to look if they was picklin' all right—an' by God, there wasn't a frog in either one of them bottles! No sir—every damn frog had dissolved! You want to remember that, Doc. If you ever want to save some frogs. Alcohol dissolves frogs—it don't pickle 'em. You better use formaldehyde."

"I'll remember. Thanks for the tip. And by the way, Gordon, the next time you visit the *Bear* remind me to slip you ten gallons of formaldehyde, so you can save me some of those transparent frogs if you should happen to run onto any."

"You bet I will, Doc! If I can locate another lake that's got transparent frogs in it. But I'm doubtin' if I ever will. I'm like Jack—I'm doubtin' there's another transparent frog left in Alaska."

"Okay," the doctor grinned. "I guess I'll have to settle for the mammoth tusk, then. I think I'll go along to that cutbank and help you dig it out. And by the way, what became of those two quarts of hooch with the frogs dissolved in them?"

"Oh, we drunk 'em. Yes sir, we didn't see no use in throwin' away good hooch jest because there was frogs dissolved in it. Them frogs sort of flavored it up. It was the best-tastin' of any hooch we ever got off'n Albert. An' on top of that, we found out we could jump about four times as far as we ever could before—ain't that so, boys?"

"That's right," McQuesten agreed. "But that wore off in a week er so. Too bad it didn't last. An' it's too bad there ain't no more of them transparent frogs. I figger if a man drunk enough of that frogged-up likker he could jump clean acrost the Yukon."

"At least he could try it," the doctor smiled. "You fellows are all right," he added, turning to Bettles. "And if you got as much enjoyment out of that alcohol as I have, I'm glad of it. And I must tell you this, Gordon—I realized, right from the first, that the transparency was in your story of those frogs, rather than in the frogs themselves. Now—do I get my mammoth tusk?"

"I'll say you do!"

"Yer damn right you will!"

"You shore will," Bettles added. "An' bein' as Al an' Jack an' me ain't in no hell of a hurry to get to Fortymile, we'll lay over at Rampart an' help you dig up them old Siwash skulls. Til, here, he wasn't in on the frog deal, so he won't need to stop. Besides that, he's got some personal prospectin' to do up Fortymile way."

XV

Julie Condon Speaks Her Mind

While the *Arctic* took on wood at Old Station, the four sourdoughs, armed with picks and shovels and accompanied by Dr. McCall, struck out for the cutbank which Bettles assured them bordered a small creek only a few hundred yards back from the river. Two hours later they returned to the boat carrying an enormous ivory tusk which the good doctor proclaimed was worth more to him than all the frogs in Christendom, transparent or otherwise. As they deposited it on the deck, the doctor slapped Bettles on the back. "I knew when I turned over that alcohol to you down there on the *Bear* that I'd get value received for it, somehow. I didn't expect any transparent frogs, but I knew you old devils wouldn't let me down."

At Rampart, Til stood at the rail and waved good-by to the doctor and the three sourdoughs who had accompanied him to help excavate the old Indian burial ground. As the boat pulled out into the river, Bettles called from the bank.

"Good luck, Til! Be seein' you in Fortymile! If you should happen to run acrost the Pest up there, tell her Uncle Gordon wishes her luck!"

Arriving at Fortymile, Til stepped into Bergman's saloon to inquire as to the whereabouts of the Condons. No sooner had he entered the room than Old Tim, peg leg thumping the floor, detached himself from a group at the bar and advanced to meet him shouting a greeting. "Damn me, if I ain't glad to see you!" He turned toward the bar. "Boys, meet Til Carter, the best damn chechako that ever stood in shoe leather!" One by one Til was introduced to Swiftwater Bill, Mooseshide Charlie, Burr MacShane, and Camillo Bill. Old Tim continued. "It was Til, along of Gordon Bettles, I was tellin' you about findin' me with my leg smashed in them rocks up on the big canyon an' takin' me clean down to Coldfoot so the doc could cut off my leg. Hadn't ben fer them two, by God, I'd be hangin' there in them rocks yet—what would be left of me. Him an' Bettles aimed to winter up there in my shack."

Burr MacShane grinned. "If he wintered up in that damn country with Bettles, he ain't a chechako—by a damn sight."

"An' accordin' to old Mathew, he ain't, neither," Camillo Bill added.

Til looked puzzled. "Who is Mathew?" he asked. "I don't seem to remember any Mathew."

"That ain't surprisin' bein' as you never seen him," Camillo grinned. "But he's a friend of yourn jest the same. If you ever git in a spot when you need help, jest holler for Mathew an' he'll come a-runnin'. Mathew, he's a Siwash. Lives in the first log shack you come to, down by the Mission. His wife's an Eskimo, an' her brother lives down to St. Michael. Accordin' to Mathew, this brother passed the word that you give his little kid two hundred and fifty dollars last spring when him an' his wife wouldn't take no money off you fer some favor they done you. Them Eskimo is queer folks—do one of 'em a good turn, an' the word gits passed on—an' every Eskimo is yer friend fer life."

Til smiled. "Bettles told me the same thing. It's good for a man to know he's got friends, even if he never has seen 'em!" He turned to MacShane. "We wintered up there, all right."

"Do any good?" Swiftwater Bill asked.

"No. We prospected up and down along the Jim River, and lots of side cricks and gulches, but we didn't run onto anything. When the freeze-up came we sunk a shaft beside the rapids just above Tim's claim. We sluiced out eight hundred and forty ounces. It looked like a lot of gold to me, but Bettles didn't seem to be impressed. We abandoned the location without even recording it."

"Four hundred an' twenty ounces apiece ain't no hell of a pay-off fer a winter's work," Moosehide Charlie opined. "But it's a damn sight better'n wages, at that."

Camillo Bill grinned. "I've seen winters when I'd ben damn glad to cash in four hundred an' twenty ounces come spring."

Til drew a moosehide pouch from his pocket and tossed it onto the bar. "I'm buying a drink," he said, "and while you're about it, weigh out six hundred and forty dollars' worth of dust and give it to Tim."

"What's that fer?" Condon asked.

"We used nearly all the grub you laid in for the winter. Crim said the bill came to seven hundred and eighty dollars. And we used pretty near all the wood you'd got out, and Bettles figured that at five hundred. So I figure my half of the expense comes to six hundred and forty—and there it is."

"Hell, you fellas is welcome to that grub—an' the wood too. I'd never of used the stuff. I sold out to Crim this spring, when Davey didn't show up."

"We used the stuff and we're paying for it. We'd pay you rent for the cabin too—but Bettles said you'd probably bust us one on the jaw if we tried to."

Tim grinned. "Bettles is right. But where the hell is he?"

"He'll probably be along on the next boat. He and Al Mayo and Jack McQuesten stopped off at Rampart to help Dr. McCall dig up some Indian relics. It seems that they felt they owed him something for gypping him out of some frogs."

"Frogs!" Camillo Bill exclaimed. "Did you say *frogs?*"

"Yes—transparent frogs. Bettles will tell you about it when he comes."

The sourdoughs roared with laughter. "Transparent frogs!" Swiftwater Bill howled. "By God, that ort to be good!"

More drinks were had, and the talk ran, as always when sourdoughs forgathered, to gold.

"Clem Whitefield was tellin' me how Jake Breen hit it lucky on Anvil this spring," Camillo Bill said.

"That's right," Moosehide Charlie concurred. "Joe Ashton was tellin' me about it. Accordin' to Joe, Clem made his strike in a dry gulch way back off'n the crick."

"Trouble with them dry gulches," Swiftwater Bill opined, "you have a hell of a time sluicin' out yer dump. The water comes down hell a-tearin' when the snow melts in the spring —an' in a few days she's dry agin."

"Larue's prospectin' upriver," Bergman said. "An Bob Henderson's off up there somewheres too. They might do all right up there."

"To hell with the upriver country," Swiftwater Bill said. "I took a shot at it last year an' never found nothin' to speak of. An' Jack McQuesten put in two year up on a river they named after him—up there in the Stewart River country. I'm tellin' you, this here Fortymile country has got 'em all beat. Ain't that so, Burr?"

MacShane toyed with his glass. "Well, there's a lot of good locations bein' worked here. An' there's a lot more room to locate others. But that ain't sayin' the upper country ain't jest as good. Personally, I'd just as soon take a chance there as I would here. There's a hell of a lot of territory upriver—an' it ain't hardly ben scratched yet. Take all the country between here an' the Mackenzie—what does anyone know about it? Not a damn thing. It stands to reason there's just as much gold upriver an' out there in the back country as there is here—an' no competition prospectin' it, neither."

"Why ain't you up there, then?" Moosehide asked.

"I ain't up there because I've got a damn good thing right here on Fortymile. But that ain't sayin' I wouldn't get a hunch to sell my claim an' hit out on a prospectin' trip. An' if I do, it'll be upriver—an' back amongst them mountains to the east."

Til listened with interest as the sourdoughs discussed the pros and cons of the upriver country. After a while he drew old Tim aside. "Where's Julie?" he asked.

"Julie? She's down to the restaurant. We seen a good openin' here, so we started up a restaurant, an' we're doin' all right with it. There's another one here, but we're gettin' the bulk of the trade. We got a Chink cook an' a breed gal waitin' table, an' Julie, she sticks around an' keeps 'em humpin'. It's down the street a ways. Julie painted a sign. Aurora Borealis, she calls it—but the boys cut it down to Rory Bory an' let it go at that."

Til slipped unobtrusively from the saloon and a few minutes later stepped into the restaurant to find Julie Condon seated on a stool behind the long counter with an open ledger before her, while the half-breed girl was busily scrubbing the top of one of the dozen or more tables scattered about the room.

Julie greeted him as he approached the counter. "Hello, Til! What brings you up here?"

"I came up here to find someone."

"Have any luck?"

Til smiled. "Not until just this minute."

"You mean—you came to Fortymile to find me?"

"That's right."

"How did you get here?"

"Canoe from your dad's location to Coldfoot. Canoe from Coldfoot to Bettles. The *North Star* from Bettles to Nulato. And from Nulato I came up on the *Arctic*."

"The *Arctic* docked two hours ago. It took you quite a while to find out I wasn't hanging out at Bergman's."

"Tim was there, and I paid him my share for the grub and wood Bettles and I used last winter, and he introduced me to several sourdoughs and they wanted to know what we found up there in the Jim River country. And then they got to talking about the upriver country and I listened."

"You didn't find out anything about Davey, did you?"

"No. Not a thing. He seems to have vanished completely."

"Somebody knows what happened to him," the girl said, "and I'm going to find out if it takes me all my life. And if it hadn't been for you and Uncle Gordon, Daddy would have vanished too. He couldn't have lasted much longer, hanging there with his leg crushed between those rocks, and the chances are the wolves wouldn't have left enough of him for anyone to find."

"I'm sure glad we came along when we did," Til said. "I'm sorry the doctor couldn't save his leg."

"It isn't as bad as it might have been. At least I don't have to worry about his hitting out alone on some prospecting trip 'way back to God knows where. And with Davey gone that's just what he'd have done if he had two good legs under him. A man's a fool to hit out alone into country that nobody knows and nobody is apt to explore. If anything happens he's sure out of luck—just as Daddy would have been out of luck if you two hadn't happened along."

"Bergman mentioned that a fellow named Larue and another by the name of Henderson are prospecting somewhere in the upriver country. They're not together. They're each prospecting alone."

The girl shrugged. "Huh—the upriver country! It's no good and never will be! Larue and Bob Henderson might better have stayed around Fortymile. We know Fortymile is good."

"Gold's where you find it," Til reminded her.

"Sure it is. But a man's a fool that will leave a district

that everyone knows is good to go wandering around a country that never has amounted to anything. Swiftwater Bill prospected that upriver country, and so did Jack McQuesten, and neither one of 'em did any good. And both of 'em are sourdoughs that would have found gold if there had been any to find."

"This man Burr MacShane is a sourdough too," Til argued. "And he said that if he didn't have a good thing here, he'd take a shot at the upriver country."

The girl nodded. "Yes, Burr MacShane is a sourdough—one of the best. But Burr's a gambler. I don't mean with cards and faro and roulette—though he gambles with those too. But he gambles his life against gold. He's made some of the longest, toughest trips anyone ever heard of—and made them alone. Once he was gone for nearly two years 'way out in the back country. No one ever expected to see him again. But he got back—went clear through to the Arctic Ocean, living off the country. He's made several big strikes. But he gets fed up with living in a camp, and he always sells out and hits out on another lone trip. As he said, he has a good thing here on Fortymile—but I'll bet you he'll get tired of it inside a year and sell out and hit out again for some Godforsaken part of the country. How did you and Uncle Gordon do up on the Jim River?"

"We did a lot of prospecting without finding anything worth while. So when the freeze-up came we holed up in your dad's camp and worked the next location above his Discovery claim. We sluiced out eight hundred and forty ounces in the spring. Bettles didn't seem to think it was a worth-while proposition, so we abandoned it."

"About six thousand clear apiece for a winter's work," the girl said. "No, that's nothing to brag of. You'll do better than that here, I'm sure. You said you were hunting for me. Why?"

Til flushed and glanced toward the half-breed girl, who was busily scrubbing a table top across the room, and leaned over the counter. "Well—because—because—damn it, I might as well come right out with it! Because I've been thinking about you all winter—every day and every night—and I love you—that's why! I want to marry you. I never saw another woman I wanted to marry. I never will marry anyone but you. We two could go a long way together."

The girl smiled slightly as her eyes met his. "I've been thinking about you too, Til. But—here's the restaurant. Daddy would have a hard time running it without me. The truth is, Til, he—he spends rather too much time over at Bergman's. Six thousand isn't very much to start with, with prices what they are. But, even at that, you might buy into a paying proposition. Jerry Manton was telling me the other day that he might have a pretty good proposition up on a creek that runs into Fortymile if he could get money enough to pipe some water from a little lake near the rim down to his claim. He said that for five thousand he could buy enough pipe from a man who went broke down at Circle and that he'd sell a partnership in his claim to anyone who would put up the five thousand." The girl paused, and her smile widened slightly. "I like you, Til—maybe I love you— I'm not sure. But really, I don't know a whole lot about you. If you settle down and maybe buy a half interest in Jerry Manton's claim, we could see a lot of each other—I might marry you. But I won't marry you till I'm sure I love you."

Til returned the smile, then his face took on a serious expression. "I wouldn't want you to marry me, Julie, unless you love me. But it won't work out like you said. In the first place, I haven't got five thousand dollars to put into that proposition. When I hit Fortymile, I had just about a thousand dollars in gold in my pocket. I paid your dad five hundred and forty dollars. You see, we had to lie around Bettles for quite a while waiting for the *North Star* to get there, and the stud sessions at the Swede's didn't do my pile any good. But even if I had the money, I wouldn't invest it in any proposition that, as Manton told you, 'might be pretty good.'

"I'm on my own now, and I'm going to hit out alone and keep on going till I find gold—and plenty of gold. Later, if you marry me, you won't be marrying a pauper. And you won't be marrying a man who's willing to be a partner in a proposition that 'might be pretty good.' You'll be marrying a man who has made good—and made good by his own effort."

The girl's face clouded and she frowned. "You mean you're going to hit out on a lone prospecting trip—after I just got through telling you that a man that does that is a fool?"

"That's right, Julie. You may think I'm a fool, but I'll bet there were plenty of people that thought Burr Mac-Shane was a fool when he started on those trips that you told me about. But—he found gold. Those people aren't calling him a fool now."

"Where are you going on this prospecting trip?"

"I'm going to try the upriver country. Burr MacShane says that's where he'd hit for."

The girl scowled. "I just got through telling you that the upriver country is no good, and never will be any good, and that a man was a fool for prospecting it. And you say that's where you're going! All right—go, then! And for all I care, you can keep on going! I'll never marry a fool! You'll probably never come back anyway. You may think you're a sourdough—but you're no Burr MacShane!"

Til straightened up. "Good-by, Julie," he said. "When I come back I'll hunt you up again. And I'll ask you again to marry me. And you'll do it—because by that time you'll know you're not marrying a fool." And without waiting for a reply, he turned on his heel and stepped out onto the street.

Back in Bergman's, Til bought a drink and sat in a stud game. He knew that the money he had left was insufficient to outfit him for a long prospecting trip into a country where supplies were unobtainable, and he hoped that the run of bad luck that had dogged him at the Swede's would change. But after an hour's play he cashed in what few remaining chips he had left and, stepping to the bar, ordered a drink.

Old Tim Condon cashed out and joined him a few minutes later. "D'ye see Julie?" he asked.

Til nodded. "Yes, I saw her. The fact is, I asked her to marry me. She told me of a proposition I could buy into for five thousand—fellow named Manton wanted the money for pipe to get water to his claim. But I haven't got the five thousand, and I told her I wouldn't buy into that kind of a proposition if I had it. I told her I was going to hit out alone into the upriver country and keep going till I made a strike. She called me a fool—and told me she'd never marry a fool."

Old Tim grinned. "Don't pay no heed to what Julie says. Take a tip from me an' keep right on pesterin' her to marry you—if you want her. She thinks a heap of you, Til. I know that—an' not only fer what you an' Bettles done fer me, neither. So yer hittin' out upriver, eh?"

Til ordered another drink. "I am—when I can get enough money to buy an outfit. I didn't have enough after paying you. So I sat in the stud game, hoping to win enough for a grubstake. But now I'll have to hunt a job and work till I can save wages enough to finance my trip."

Old Tim smote the bar with his fist. "No you don't! Not by a damn sight, you don't! Not whilst I've got the dust to grubstake you! Not after what you an' Bettles done fer me, you don't!"

"You mean you'll grubstake me for a trip upriver?"

"Yer damn right I will!"

"But—Julie and some of the sourdoughs here say the upriver country's no good."

"Let 'em say it. You heard what Burr MacShane said about it, didn't you? Well, by God, if it's good enough fer

Burr to take a shot at—like he said he would—it's good enough fer me to take a chanct on grubstakin' you fer a trip up there. Come on over to the recorder's an' we'll file the grubstake papers an' then go over to the A.C. store an' get yer outfit. Then you hit out—an' to hell with what Julie an' them damn sourdoughs says!"

XVI

Gold—in a Moose Pasture!

Til Carter topped a ridge and stood looking down into a little valley through the center of which wound a slow-flowing creek. Swinging the pack from his shoulders, he seated himself with his back against a rock, drew his pipe from his pocket, and proceeded to take a "cold smoke." He had been out of tobacco for a month.

During the twelve months he had been prospecting the mountains to the eastward for gold he had seen no white man. Nor had he found much gold. The sixty ounces in his pack was a poor return for twelve months of grueling toil. He could have done much better sniping the bars on Birch Creek or the Fortymile, or even by buying a half interest in Jerry Manton's claim, as Julie Condon had suggested. Bettles would have loaned him the five thousand if he'd asked for it. The sourdoughs at Fortymile had said that the upriver country was no good—Swiftwater Bill, and Moosehide Charlie, and Camillo Bill. Julie Condon was a sourdough too, and she had told him the same thing. She had called him a fool for hitting out alone, and especially into the little-known upriver country. Of all the sourdoughs, only Burr

MacShane had expressed faith in the unexplored upper country—Burr MacShane and old Tim Condon, who had grub-staked him for the venture.

But there is not much excitement in sniping the bars—only hard work. And there was only hard work and little profit in sinking shafts in lean gravel. His winter on the Jim River had convinced him of that. So, disregarding the doubts of the sourdoughs and the advice of Julie Condon, Til had hit out upriver and struck eastward into the high hills.

He had prospected creeks that no other white man had seen, had wintered in a tiny pole shack he built on a nameless feeder to the upper McQuesten, had escaped death by drowning, by freezing, and by starvation. And now he was returning to Fortymile to tell Julie and the old-timers that they were right—and to go back to sniping the bars for little better than wages.

He flushed at thought of Julie Condon. He visualized the scorn that would flash in her blue eyes when he admitted his failure. He frowned and shrugged. She had called him a fool—said she would never marry a fool—so what the hell!

Glumly he sat there sucking at his cold pipe. As the girl's parting words recurred to him he flushed angrily. "All right —go, then! And for all I care, you can keep on going! I'll never marry a fool!"

"No, by God," he blurted aloud, "I'll never tell her she was right! And I won't stick around Fortymile and be satisfied with sniping the bars or working lean gravel!" His lips clamped tightly about the pipestem as he laid his plans. He'd show Julie Condon he wasn't the fool she thought him. He had proved that he was a sourdough—had stuck it out alone in the back country for a year—and he could do it again! And he'd make a strike, too! The sixty ounces in his pack would finance another trip. The big jamboree he had planned as he sat beside his lonely campfires would have to wait. Those sixty ounces would last for only a few days of drinking and swinging the dance-hall girls, anyway. Yes, the jamboree would have to wait. The sixty ounces would finance another trip into the hills—another six months or a year—what did it matter? He'd make his strike sometime—then he'd pull off the damnedest jamboree Fortymile ever saw! He'd make Julie Condon wish she had married him. But he'd never let old Tim down on that grubstake. He'd keep the grubstake agreement alive until he did make a strike —no matter where or when he made it!

The upper country was no good for gold. Only Burr MacShane and Bob Henderson and Larue had faith in it. But none of them had showed gold to justify their faith. And his own sixty ounces was nothing to brag about.

Til wondered how far it was to the Yukon. He was out of tobacco, out of tea, out of meat. His packsack contained a scant five pounds of flour and a handful of salt. He had just six cartridges left for his rifle. For a week he had sighted no game except ptarmigan, and he hated to waste his scant ammunition on the little birds. He had eaten the last of his smoked moose meat the day before. For breakfast he had eaten a ground squirrel that he had killed with a stick and boiled up with flour.

A movement caught his eye in the birches at the foot of the ridge below him, and as he looked a big bull moose stepped out into the open and sniffed the air not a hundred yards away. Reaching for his rifle, Til took careful aim and fired. The huge animal started down the creek at a trot. Again he shot, and again, and again—four of his six precious cartridges—and the moose broke into a lumbering gallop. He cursed roundly and wholeheartedly, then he grinned. "That's shooting! I ought to get a job tending bar, where I wouldn't have to kill anything bigger than flies! And me with two shells left to take me, God knows how far, to the river."

Half a mile down the creek the galloping moose lunged heavily forward, struck on his horns, turned a complete somersault, and lay very still. Til's eyes lighted at the sight, and his grin widened. "I knew I never missed a moose as big as a steamboat at that range," he muttered, slipping into his pack straps and picking up his rifle. "Bet I hit him every time! And now for the first regular feed I've had since I can remember. I'm fed up on smoked meat. Ground squirrels are all right—but a man ought to have about three of 'em to the mile."

Making his way down the steep slope, he fell to work on the moose and soon had the tongue and some choice chunks of red loin meat cut out and laid on the hide. The animal lay close to the stream, and hungry as a wolf, Til cast about for wood to make a fire. A short distance downstream a birch tree grew on the edge of the bank. Beyond it were several more.

Picking up his ax, he started toward the trees. A few yards from the first birch tree he halted and stared at the ground with a puckering frown. Claim stakes had been set into the sod. Two creek claims had been staked—and not very long ago. The ashes of a recent fire showed near the lone birch tree. And the chips from the claim stakes were freshly cut. Til threw back his head and laughed. "Well—of all the damn fools! Staking claims in a flat moose pasture! And the whole country full of good, steep-sided cricks! I didn't know anyone except Bob Henderson and Larue was in the upper country. They're both sourdoughs, and neither one of 'em would stake a claim on a mud flat."

Walking to the stakes, he read the notice, which, as the law allowed, described two Discovery claims, of five hundred feet each, along the base line of the creek. The notice, only ten days old, was jointly signed by Carmack and Skookum Jim. Til remembered that Bettles had mentioned Carmack, a squaw man, and Skookum Jim, his Indian brother-in-law, who worked for wages, at times, but preferred to hunt meat for the camps.

He noted that the surface of the sod had been disturbed

near the birch tree, and kicked idly at the muck and gravel that had been dumped back into the shallow hole.

"Sure is a Siwash trick," he laughed, and procuring an armful of wood, returned to his moose, where he cut up the tongue and enough loin meat to fill his kettle and set it to boil.

It was late in August. The nights were cool, but the days were still too warm to risk the packing of raw meat, so Til decided to camp where he was and boil up all he could conveniently pack. Drying or smoking the meat would be a slower process, and after all, it couldn't be so very far to the Yukon—and Fortymile.

Alone in the far hills, Til Carter had longed for the lights and delights of Fortymile—the saloons, the dance-hall girls, the commingling with his kind over glasses of raw red liquor. But most of all he knew that deep down in his heart he longed for Julie Condon—the Pest, as Bettles had called her before Al Mayo renamed her the Fireweed. He knew she would despise him for a fool and a failure—but even so . . . Well, he had lost Julie. And the drinking and dancing must wait.

In the twelve months since he had left Fortymile he had made no strike, but he had satisfied himself at first hand that Julie and the old-timers were right in deriding the upper country. On no river or creek had he taken out as much gold as he could have taken from the bars and creeks of the Fortymile valley in one fifth of the time, and with one tenth of the effort.

Idly he noted that one huge, palmated horn had plowed through the sod and broken off close to the skull when the animal fell. The horn lay nearly buried in the loose gravel and muck of its shallow furrow. As he looked his eye caught a tiny glint of yellow, and the next moment he was kneeling beside the broken horn, intently staring at the gravel on its palmated surface. The fire was forgotten, and grabbing up his pan, he slipped the gravel from the horn into it, gouged up some more loose stuff from the furrow, and hurried to the river, where he dipped his pan and started washing for the glints of yellow he had seen on the broken horn.

Impatiently he flirted the mucky water from the pan and clawed the coarser gravel out with eager fingers. Then, for long moments, he sat staring down into the bottom of the pan, liberally sprinkled with raw gold! Returning to the carcass, he added fuel to his fire, cut a square from the green hide, and returned to the creek bank, where he emptied the gold from the pan onto the piece of hide.

From that moment until sunset he panned gold. His kettle boiled dry and his meat and tongue burned to a cinder. His fire burned out—but still he panned gold, not noticing. He had forgotten he was hungry. With pick and shovel he attacked the tough sod, leaving twenty shallow scars within what would roughly be the confines of the claim that would be numbered One Above Discovery. And in every panful was gold! Right in the grass roots—and more gold than he had ever seen, or hoped to see, in any pan!

When the sun finally sank behind the high western hills, he paused and sat staring down at the little yellow pile on the strip of green moosehide. In less than half a day he had panned out more gold than even the richest bars of Fortymile had ever yielded in half a month! He shouted! He sang snatches of song! He danced about like a crazy man!

"She's come!" he yelled to the high hills. "The big strike that old Bettles predicted was bound to come sometime! And the sourdoughs were wrong! She came upriver—*in a moose pasture!* 'Gold's where you find it!' and—ain't that the truth!"

Til suddenly remembered that he was hungry. Walking to his fire, he stood staring down at the wreck of his supper. Canted among the dead ashes, the interior of his kettle showed only a blackened gob of charcoal. He laughed and, scraping out the mess, refilled the kettle with meat and water and kindled a new fire.

As the water boiled, and the savory odor reached his nostrils, he cut other strips of meat, skewered them on the end of a birch switch, and held them over the coals. These he chewed slowly and contentedly while the water bubbled in the pot.

"A man never knows when he's lucky," he mused. "Here I was cussing my shooting—and if that moose had dropped where I first shot, it would have cost me a million! This claim, now—I'll call her the Moosehorn."

In the morning he shaped and planted his stakes, carefully stepping off the two hundred and fifty feet along the creek that locations, other than Discovery, are allowed. Then, with the handle of an iron spoon, he burned his inscription into the flatted sides of his stakes.

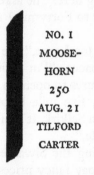

NO. I
MOOSE-
HORN
250
AUG. 21
TILFORD
CARTER

All that day and the next he boiled meat and panned gold, until the gold in the pouch he had fashioned of green moose-hide outweighed the gold in the smoke-tanned pouch in his packsack. He had panned more gold in less than three days than he had taken out in the preceding twelve months! And he hadn't scratched the surface!

That evening he sat long over his little fire and sucked at his cold pipe. Julie couldn't call him a fool now. He grinned broadly and watched the little flames lick at the dry wood. He'd kid her about it, but he wouldn't rub it in. They'd be married there in Fortymile and come here and put up a cabin on the claim. And then—then they could go outside and—— No, by God, they'd never go outside! This is her country—and from now on it's mine!

The following morning he struck out with a full pack and a light heart. When he reached the Klondike River he built a raft, lashing its spruce poles together with strips cut from the hide of a cow moose he shot as she emerged from the river. He didn't know what river he was on, but knew that eventually he would come out on the Yukon. He loaded the two hindquarters of the cow onto the raft, sitting more or less comfortably on them as he handled his clumsy craft by means of a long sweep.

In a surprisingly short time he came out on the Yukon to find a man camped on a flat, in the shadow of a mountain.

"What are you doing here?" he asked when he had landed his raft. "How far is it to Fortymile? And give me a pipe of tobacco."

"Larue's the name—Joe Larue," the man replied, handing over his pouch of tobacco. "I'm layin' me out a townsite. Me an' Art Harper figures to open up a tradin' post. There's a Siwash village four, five mile below. We fetched some trade goods down from Selkirk. It's only about forty or fifty mile down to Fortymile."

"Figuring on inducing the Siwashes to quit their village and come up here an' pay fancy prices for your town lots?" Til asked with a grin as he filled his pipe and returned the pouch.

"No. The Siwashes won't buy no lots. But they'll trade with us. It's white men'll buy them lots. I've got faith in this upper country. This here's the best townsite on the river—an' I'm bettin' that there'll be a strike made up the Klondike before long."

"Yeah?" Til drawled. "Most of the old-timers say it isn't so good."

"They don't know everything. 'Gold's where you find it,' an' I'm bettin' you'll see a stampede up the Klondike inside of a year. An' when it comes, we'll be settin' pretty with a townsite right here. But—where you ben? An' what you doin' here if you believe what everyone says about the upper country?"

"I hit out about a year ago, went up the Stewart, and came back across country."

"Didn't strike nothin', eh?"

"Well—maybe. Give me another pipe of tobacco. I haven't had a smoke for a month. What are you getting apiece for your lots?"

Larue grinned and tossed his pouch over. "Keep it," he said. "I've got more. Ain't set no figger on lots yet. Tell you what I'll do—jest to git started. I'll give you two lots—a corner one an' an inside one—for them two quarters of moose. You couldn't git no more'n fifty cents a pound fer 'em in Fortymile—an' they might spile on you besides."

Til shook his head. "No, Larue. You gave me some tobacco. I'll do better than that by you. I made a strike—and a good one. I'll let you in on it. Give me one corner lot and I'll tell you where you can sock your stakes right in the middle of a million dollars in gold!"

"Wher's that?" asked Larue without enthusiasm.

"It's up a flat crick only a little way above here. She don't look like a gold crick—half a mile or more between the rims —but she's lousy with gold."

Larue laughed. "What the hell have you an' Carmack got on?" he asked. "What's the big idea? I know that crick— Rabbit Crick, we've called it—but Carmack, he's changed the name to Bonanza. No one but a damn fool would look twicet at it. What's the sell? I wouldn't give you the insidest lot I got in my townsite fer the whole damn crick. But tell you what I will do—I'll make it two corner lots fer them two quarters of meat."

"You're on, Larue," said Til gravely. "But when the stampede comes through to Bonanza, you better climb on it!"

"Not me," Larue replied. "I'll be busy gittin' up the

tradin' post before snow flies. If you kin start a stampede, though, mebbe I'll git a little trade till she busts. Carmack an' Skookum Jim was through here about ten days ago, an' they tried to throw the same guff into me, about this here Rabbit Crick. You fellows got a townsite up there?"

"No, Larue—not any townsite—only claims. Well, so long. I feel like seeing some lights that aren't made by a wood fire or a candle."

XVII

In Bergman's Saloon

In Bergman's saloon they were talking about Carmack's gold—a group of the old-timers of Fortymile. Old Bettles, dean of the sourdoughs, was denouncing it.

"There ain't no such a strike upriver—an' we know it. I've ben upriver till hell won't have it, an' I never found no gold to speak of. So've we all—McQuesten, an' Swiftwater Bill, an' a lot more."

Moosehide Charlie fingered his drink. "Well," he admitted, "we've ben upriver. But mebbe we ain't seen it all. They ort to be a hell of a lot of country, take it on both sides of the river—an' as fer back as it stretches. Mebbe Carmack did make a strike on some side crick."

"Naw—there ain't nothin' to it," Bergman opined. "Hell-fire! If anyone was to make a strike in the upper country, it wouldn't be no damn squaw man, an' a Siwash, would it? It don't stand to reason. What do they know about prospectin'? An' they wouldn't make no strike on no flat like Carmack told about, would they? From what he says about this here crick he calls Bonanza, it ain't nothin' but that damn moose pasture of a Rabbit Crick that comes in a little ways up the Klondike. I've ben the hull len'th of it, an' so's a lot of you boys. No one with any sense would even stop to spit in it!"

Moosehide persisted: "I'm like Bettles, I don't favor the upper country neither. But 'Gold's where you find it,' the sayin' is—an', by God, it ain't partic'lar who finds it. It might be a Siwash, an' it might be the King of England."

"Yeah—an' it's jest as liable to be one as tother. But when the big strike comes, she's comin' down-river, or up Birch Crick or the Fortymile. An' it ain't goin' to be no king, nor no Siwash, nor no squaw man that locates it. It's goin' to be some sourdough that knows where to hunt fer it. Ain't that so, Camillo?"

Camillo Bill nodded judicially. "Stands to reason. But, at that, a Siwash might find gold. I seen one that had a meteor oncet."

"Yeah," Bettles scoffed, "an' I've seen a hell of a lot of 'em that had the itch, too—but what did that git 'em? I'm talkin' about gold. An' believe me, I've prospected clean up the Koyukuk an' back down it agin, an' on down through Alasky to here—an' up the Yukon an' back down it—an' this here camp looks good to me. Course I ain't takin' out no hell of a lot of dust right now—but I'm eatin' when I feel like it, an' I'm buyin' a drink now an' then—an' I'm satisfied."

Camillo Bill chuckled. "Now an' then, Bettles! Hell, you've ben histin' a drink every ten minutes ever since I've know'd you—an' that's ten year!"

"Well," asked old Bettles, "ain't that now an' then? Now is now—an' when we git another—that's then. An' that reminds me, these glasses has got a mean look about 'em—they're empty."

Camillo Bill bought another round, and the old-timers who were better qualified to talk about gold than any men on the Yukon talked. "I kind of hold with Bettles too," Jack McQuesten said. "I believe Carmack's strike is a plant. I don't think there's any gold to speak of upriver."

"By God!" exclaimed Moosehide, more for the sake of argument than from any conviction of the squaw man's integrity. "Carmack's got gold, ain't he? He's spendin' it. He was dead broke a month ago. Where the hell would he git it?"

"Listen," confided old Bettles. "Bob Henderson's upriver somewheres. So's Art Harper an' Joe Larue——"

"Yeah," seconded Camillo Bill, "an' young Til Carter's up there somewheres too. He pulled out a year ago. I seen Bob Henderson when he was down fer supplies in June, an' he told me he run onto Til along on the edge of winter headin' up the Stewart with an outfit of Siwash dogs. Til told him he figgered on prospectin' the back country up agin the mountains—an' he ain't ben seen nor heard tell of sence."

"Chances is he won't be, neither," foreboded Swiftwater Bill. "I liked that young feller. He'd of made a sourdough, instead of which, he won't listen to us but goes kihootin' off to hell an' gone to git himself bushed in a country where they ain't no gold—an' never was. The Fireweed told him he was a fool to hit out upriver alone—but he done it anyhow. How do you figger, Bettles? You know him better'n what we do."

"Yeah, I know him. Found him in St. Michael holed up with an Eskimo after knockin' hell out of a whalin' captain on his own deck an' then swimmin' through half a mile of ice water to shore. He's got guts. Him an' I wintered on Jim River. He was a chechako when I run onto him—but he ain't a chechako now—he might make a strike."

Moosehide Charlie shook his head. "A year's a hell of a while. I'm bettin' he's bushed."

Camillo Bill grinned. "You done consid'ble kihootin' yerself, an' you ain't bushed," he reminded.

"Yeah, but I most generally had a pardner," replied Moosehide, becoming more and more argumentative as his drinks took hold. "If there was two or three of 'em, I'd say he'd come back. Or if he was one of us old he-wolves. But take Til—accordin' to Bettles, he'd work like hell, but he liked his drinks an' a game of stud jest like any reasonable man would. He ain't a day over twenty-four—an' it don't stand to reason that any young feller like that's goin' to stick out in the back country fer a hull year.''

"But what's Henderson an' Larue an' Harper bein' upriver got to do with Carmack's gold?" persisted Bergman, eying Bettles.

"Like this," Bettles explained. "There was some Siwashes down here about a week before Carmack showed up, an' they said how Harper an' Larue was goin' to build a tradin' post at the mouth of the Klondike, an' how they was stakin' out that flat fer a townsite. This here Rabbit Crick comes in jest above there, an' if Larue an' Harper could git a stampede started, they'd make a cleanup sellin' supplies till she petered out. They might even sell some lots, too, 'cause, with a tradin' post, some part of the stampeders would locate up there an' prospect all the feeders an' dry washes in the country.

"So Harper an' Larue stake Carmack an' Skookum Jim to a poke of dust apiece an' send 'em down here, an' mebbe on to Circle City, to start a stampede by recordin' a couple of claims an' throwin' the dust around like they had a-plenty."

"Sounds reasonable," admitted Camillo Bill. "Joe Larue, he's smart."

"Here's Carmack now!" exclaimed Moosehide. "He's ben down to Circle, an' he's pretty well oiled." He motioned to a man who had entered the door, followed by an Indian. "Come over here, Carmack, an' belly up! We-all heard how you'd made a strike, an' we ben down to the recorder's an' looked up the record—an' we ain't none het up about it, neither."

Carmack joined the others at the bar and filled his glass. "I sure struck her at last, boys," he said with a slight hiccough. "Yes sir—right in the grass ruts! Me an' Skookum Jim, here. Skookum turns up the first pan, an' then I goes to it. Coarse gold, boys—right in the grass ruts. I'm tellin' you —an' if you had any sense, you'd be loadin' yer outfits into polin' boats an' hittin' upriver right now!"

The sourdoughs at the bar were joined by a dozen others who had been halfheartedly playing the wheel or sitting in a game of stud. All had heard of Carmack's alleged strike, but none had taken it seriously. But here was Carmack himself. After recording his location, the man had gone down to Circle City and begun spending his gold. Evidently the men of Circle were no more impressed by his strike than were the sourdoughs of Fortymile.

"Mebbe you run onto the tailin's of some brass factory," suggested Burr MacShane with elaborate sarcasm.

The crowd laughed, and Carmack, swallowing his drink, tossed a pouch onto the bar. "There she is—part of her—I've got more, an' so's Skookum. An' God knows how much in the gravel. I'm tellin' you, she's the big strike that everyone's ben sayin' fer years would come sometime." He turned to the bartender. "Fill 'em up!" he ordered.

Carmack had been a wageworker and a hunter of meat— a furtive, inconsequential man who had married a squaw. No man had ever before seen him toss a gold sack onto the bar and order a round of drinks for the house. The drinking he had done had been done alone, or back in the bush with his wife's Indian relatives. Here was a different Carmack— but the men were unimpressed.

"How come you staked a moose pasture an' expected to start a stampede?" asked Camillo Bill.

" 'Cause that's wher' I made my strike," insisted Carmack. "Right at the bottom of a birch tree on the bank of the crick —three, four dollars a pan, right in the grass ruts, I'm tellin' you!"

Old Bettles laughed in tipsy derision. "We was down to the recorder's an' looked at the record. You'd ort to picked you out a crick that looked reasonable. This here Bonanza, as you recorded it, ain't nothin' but Rabbit Crick—an' you changed the name so's we wouldn't git onto it till we'd got up there. We seen somethin' else down to the recorder's, too. We seen where Larue an' Harper has filed 'em a townsite on the flat at the mouth of the Klondike. Come on, Carmack, tell us how much they're payin' you to start a stampede? We don't give a damn, so long as it didn't work. Go on back down to Circle City—mebbe you kin fool them birds with yer upriver gold!"

"But I ain't tryin' to fool no one! You'll know who's the fools by spring, when it's too late to git in on Bonanza!"

"I suppose you never seen Harper an' Larue on that flat," grinned Camillo.

"Sure, I seen Larue. Harper's on the mountain gittin' out logs fer the tradin' post. I told Larue about my strike—an' he jest laffed, like you fellers."

"So then he seen where he could make a little stake fer hisself an' give you the gold to blow in down here to prove you'd made a strike," said Bettles.

"He never give me no gold! I showed him my dust, an' he wanted to sell me some lots in his townsite. But I told him to hell with 'em. I ain't goin' to have no time to fool with no townsite."

Toward the end of the bar, Moosehide Charlie had reached for the scales into which the bartender had dribbled the dust from Carmack's sack to pay for the round of drinks. For long moments he stared owlishly at the coarse gold. "Boys," he announced solemnly, "this here's different dust. She's lighter'n what ourn is—lighter'n coarser."

Shouts of laughter greeted the announcement. Old Bettles led the attack on the unfortunate Moosehide. "Haw, haw, haw! Drink up, Moosehide, an' have another! Couple more drinks, an' she'll look pink! Then we'll all be follerin' upriver after Carmack. God—a man would go anywheres after pink gold—even to a moose pasture!"

"But I'm tellin' you," persisted Moosehide, "this here gold looks different."

"Sure," railed Camillo Bill. "Every time you take a drink everything looks different! I've got me a lib'ral edgucation jest a-studyin' the things I've saw by takin' drinks—an' old Bettles, here—no wonder he's counted the smartest man on the Yukon! He must of saw everything I've missed!"

Bettles laughed in tipsy appreciation. "Tha's right. No question 'bout it—an' jes' to prove it, I'll sing you lil song:

> "In the days of old,
> In the days of gold,
> In the days of 'forty-nine——"

Which is as far as old Bettles ever got with his favorite ditty.

XVIII

The Sourdoughs Pull Off a Funeral

Moosehide Charlie turned to Carmack. "Listen, you," he said loud enough to be heard by all. "If you made a strike like you said, on this here Rabbit Crick, you was a fool not to buy you some lots in Larue's townsite. 'Cause when the stampede goes in, them lots is goin' to be worth what a man'll pay fer 'em! It might be I'll be polin' upriver myself."

Roars of laughter, from the now thoroughly tipsy crowd, drowned the man's voice, and once more old Bettles led the raillery against his friend. "When you buy out Larue's townsite, Moosehide, give me a option on the town pump, an' the cemetery! 'Cause if Carmack's made a strike up there, I might start in drinkin' water—an' then I wouldn't live long—er wouldn't want to! But speakin' of cemeteries, I ben thinkin' of pore Til Carter! An' him prob'ly layin' up some draw, er on the bottom of some river, deader'n hell, where he prob'ly won't never be found to be give no decent funeral to."

"Who said Til was dead?" asked a man from the crowd.

"Me," replied Bettles, wiping his eyes on the back of his hand. "He was a damn fine boy—could drink more'n any of you! An' now he's gone! Pore ol' Til! But we'll show him he ain't fergot! Yes sir! With coffins only five ounces apiece, by God, we'll give him a decent an' Christian funeral—with singin', an' candles, an' pallbearers, an' all. An' we'll plant him proper in the cemetery. An' when I git my own cemetery up on Larue's flat, I'll have him moved up there so's he'll be nearer the boys—an' I'll send back down to where I come from an' git some of these here erysipelas trees an' plant 'em there——"

"You mean willers, don't you, Bettles?" interrupted Moosehide. "Them's all that would grow on them flats."

"Hell—no!" answered Camillo Bill gravely. "He means umphas trees—which they plant 'em upside down in graveyards so the folks in under 'em kin see the leaves an' branches instead of the roots."

"But who the hell we goin' to bury," queried a man when the laughter had subsided, "if Til ain't ben found?"

"What difference does that make? Some Siwash'll do," announced Bettles.

Skookum Jim, the only Indian in the room, slipped quietly and unobtrusively out the back door.

"Don't have to have no reg'lar corp," opined Moosehide. "We kin rig up a dummy out of old clothes an' stuff. Til, he'll never know the difference."

"That's right," agreed Camillo. "We'd ort to save a Siwash, when practical."

"How about a parson? Can't have no proper funeral without no parson."

"There's Father Judge," Swiftwater Bill said.

Bettles shook his head. "No. Father Judge is a fine man. But he might think it was sort of frivolous—pullin' off a funeral without no reg'lar corpse."

"I read a piece in a book oncet about 'em tryin' a man *in absentia* fer somethin' he done. He wasn't there, but they tried him anyhow. What I claim, if they can try a man *in absentia*, why can't we bury one *in absentia?*"

"They bury folks in graves where I come from," Moosehide said.

"We could use a synthetic parson," Swiftwater Bill suggested.

"What kind is that?" Moosehide asked. "Father Judge is Catholic."

"Synthetic," explained Swiftwater gravely, "is where you call somethin' sumpthin' else which it ain't."

"The idee sounds reasonable," announced Bettles. "I'll appint Carmack fer the parson. He'd ort to make a good one. Didn't he convert Moosehide to upriver gold, an' Larue's townsite?" He turned gravely to the squaw man. "An' if you do it all right an' proper, Carmack, I'll recommend you to the reverend up to the Mission, so if yer strike should peter out on you, he'll prob'ly give you a job missionaryin' amongst the Siwashes. You talk their lingo, an' he could start you on wages, er mebbe only commission, an' give you a box of these here brimstone matches fer samples of hell—an' I'll bet you could have every damn Siwash in the hills scairt Christian in a couple of months. Anyhow, you'd have an ace in the hole if yer broke."

"Who'll dig the grave?" asked a voice from the crowd.

"We don't have to worry about no grave till the funeral's over," replied Bettles. "We'll play showdown to see who gits stuck fer that later. First off we got to git the coffin. The A.C. got four in on the boat. They're five ounces apiece. I priced 'em 'cause I figgered on gittin' one fer a sled box—but the lid ain't right."

"What's the use in blowin' in five ounces fer a coffin?" someone asked. "Five ounces would buy a hell of a lot of drinks. We could work it like they do over in Chiny er India, er some sech place. They git a big pile of wood an' lay the corpse on top of it an' set fire to it an' stand around an' watch him burn. I read about it one time. There's plenty of wood in that jam pile there in the bend of the crick—an' it won't cost nothin'. A funeral pyre, they call it."

Moosehide eyed the speaker contemptuously. "Fire, you damn fool—not pyre. You must be drunk."

Bettles vetoed the proposition. "Sech doin's is onseemly an' onchristian. Them folks is heathens over there. An' besides," he added, "a fire at a funeral would have a sort of forebodin' or prophetic slant that would be downright disturbin' fer most of us. So four of you fellers hit out an' fetch the coffin, an' a couple more rustle some old clothes an' somethin' to stuff 'em with—an' I'll take up a collection to pay fer the coffin an' the necessary refreshments durin' the festivities."

"Obscenities, you mean," corrected Moosehide Charlie. "I seen the word in a paper."

"The word is obskiskies," announced Ear Bitin' Finley, who had showed up in Fortymile during the previous winter. "I hearn the preacher say it when my little brother died, eighteen year ago," and thereupon he began to blubber aloud and gouge at his eyes with his sleeve.

"What the hell difference does it make? It ain't only a word!" broke in Bettles impatiently. "We got to be pickin' out the music. Here, you, Finley, dry up an' run down to the dance hall an' fetch Horse Face Joe up here. Tell him to fetch his fiddle. Now, what songs should we sing—there's 'The Days of Gold'——"

"Hell, that ain't no funeral piece!" cut in Camillo. "An' besides, it depends on what Horse Face kin fiddle."

"He gits off 'Buffalo Gals,' an' 'Turkey in the Straw,' an' 'Arkansaw Traveler' damn good an' lively," volunteered a man.

"Cripes," howled Bettles, "where was you raised? You want somethin' sad to a funeral. Now there's 'Nearer, By God, to Thee.' That's spoke well of, if anyone knows it. An' 'When You an' I Was Young, Maggie.' An' another piece named 'Lead, Kind of Lights'—them's the kind of things fer funerals—not no jig tunes!"

"I use to could speak off *The Face on the Bar-Room Floor*," volunteered a voice from the crowd.

Another interrupted: "Then there's 'The Dyin' Cowboy,' an' 'The Cowboy's Lament.' An' 'Frankie an' Johnnie's' a sad one, if you look at it that way."

"Sure," agreed Bettles, "them kind is more like it. Well, here comes the coffin. Roll out a couple of them kags to set her on, an' then we'll rig up the corpse. But first off we got to all drink formal—to Til Carter!"

They drank, and as many as could crowded about the casket and set to work with several armfuls of discarded clothing that had been collected in various deserted cabins of the camp. Within a half hour the casket contained a very fair replica of a dead man. Someone with a flair for pencil work had even sketched a passable likeness of Til's features upon an oval of paper that was arranged between shirt collar and cap. Candles were placed at the foot and head, and all once again adjourned to the bar, where several rounds of drinks were had as the men of Fortymile admired their handiwork.

"It don't hardly seem right to buryin' no one—an' him not here," said a man. "Til would got a kick outa this."

"Who in hell could git a kick outa his own funeral?" objected Bettles. "Can't you git it through yer skull that we're buryin' him by proxy? A vicarious funeral, the lawyers would call it—an' by God, that gives me an idee. I'll write up a eppygrapht fer his slab! Give me a drink, an' a pencil, an' some paper!" The articles were produced, and while the others talked, old Bettles labored mightily with pencil and paper. At the end of five minutes he handed the paper to Camillo Bill, who read:

"IN MEMORY OF
PROXY VICARIOUS SYNTHETIC
TIL CARTER.

Pore Til ain't here—only his dummy:
Jist a bunch of old clothes—an' them was crummy."

Shouts of acclaim greeted the epitaph, and other drinks were had. "Hell, I didn't know you could write po'try, Bettles," said Moosehide admiringly. "That's damn good po'try, an' it states the case."

"A man kin do anything he's got to do," replied Bettles deprecatingly.

At the bar half a dozen men were sobbing aloud, while others were furtively wiping their eyes. "God, I feel sad!" exclaimed a man brokenly. "An' say, B-Bettles—you write me one—when I'm gone—boo-hoo-hoo!"

"An' me too! An' me!" A chorus of demands, mostly accompanied by sobbing and sniveling.

"Sure," promised Bettles, wiping at his own eyes, "I won't never go back on you, boys! Bein' the only poet in the camp, I'll write a piece over every damn one of you that dies! I figger it's my duty—an' I'll see her through!"

Camillo Bill stepped up to Bettles and grasped his hand. "We take that kind of you, old-timer—you bet. 'Hill,' you know, that rhymes with Bill—an' the cemetery bein' on the hill, you might say somethin' like this on mine:

> "Pore Camillo Bill
> Has went up the hill."

"I could think up a better one if yer name was Dell," Bettles chuckled.

"God, a man hates to think he might of got buried without nothin' on his slab but jest his name if we hadn't found out you was a poet!" Camillo Bill said. "An' say, while I was thinkin', I heerd a song, 'way back when I was a kid. It's a song that's jest made to order, if anyone knows it, fer this here funeral—it goes: 'God be with you, Til! We meet agin!' It sounds real pretty if it's sung right."

"Jest the ticket! We'll save it fer the last one. But come on—let's git a-goin'."

Moosehide Charlie began to sob aloud. "Them po'ms is

145

all right fer you fellas on yer slab—but me, boo-hoo—I'm in a hell of a fix. They ain't no word rhymes with Moosehide!"

"Hell!" cried a horrified voice from the crowd. "We fergot the flowers!"

"Git some fireweed," suggested a man. "There's a big patch jest back of the camp."

"There's the Fireweed herself!" exclaimed another, and pointed toward the open door of the saloon, where Julie Condon, her flaming red hair seemingly ablaze in the sunlight, stood gazing in, wide-eyed.

"Who's dead?" she demanded, her eyes narrowing. "And what are you having his funeral in a saloon for? Shame on you—when you know you could have come to the restaurant! Who is it?"

Old Bettles explained: "It's Til Carter——"

"*Til Carter!*" For an instant the girl's face seemed perceptibly to pale. Then it resumed its color, and her voice was perfectly steady as she asked, "When did it happen—and how?"

"Well," began Bettles, pausing to clear his throat, "you see, Miss Julie, it ain't really Til—that is—not what you might say Til himself, you know—in person. It's like this: Til, he's ben gone a year—an' we figger, if he wasn't dead, he'd be back, 'cause he liked—that is, he had too much fun when he'd hit camp to stay away that long. An' so we figgered it would be a good an' a—a—kind of a pious thing to have a reg'lar funeral about it—that is, in case he was dead. If he ain't, we could dig up the coffin agin an' lay the head slab by till he does die——"

The girl snorted contemptuously. "You're all drunk!" she snapped, and disappeared from the doorway.

"Now what do you think of that?" mourned Camillo Bill. "An' jest when we was feelin' so nice an' sad! She claimed we're drunk—ain't that hell?"

"She's too damn sassy fer her britches," opined Bettles.

146

"She'd ort to be spanked! I knowed her when she was borned on the Koyukuk."

Moosehide chuckled. "I'd like to see someone try spankin' her. Them redheads is hell on wheels oncet they git started."

From the end of the bar Ear Bitin' Finley scowled darkly. He had picked Julie Condon for his own—Julie Condon, the Fireweed, as she was affectionately called by the bearded men of Fortymile, who worshiped her, though she scored them one and all for their shortcomings. Her father had died six months before, and the girl had taken over the management of the restaurant. Let a man be sick or in trouble, and Julie Condon would be found at his side, encouraging, aiding him, physically and spiritually, to the last ditch. She knew these men—understood their virtues and their foibles —and she loved them, even as they loved her. Ever since she could remember, they had constituted her entire world of men; her world of women had been even more restricted, yet in times of sickness or distress many a girl of the brothels and dance halls had felt the better for the warm, friendly clasp of her hand and the whispered words of comfort. Julie Condon was the good angel of Fortymile.

But since spring the old-timers had worried. Ear Bitin' Finley, a huge bully of a man, had been spending too much time in the company of Julie Condon. This was, in the opinion of the old sourdoughs, not as it should be. They knew little of Ear Bitin' Finley except that he had appeared and had staked a claim up near the famous "Kink" of Fortymile Creek—that he was truculent and cantankerous when drinking, and always spoiling for a fight. They knew, also, that at one time he had been on the Koyukuk, that far northern gold river that had also once been the stamping ground of old Bettles, and Tim Condon, and Burr MacShane. This much the men of Fortymile knew—and it had not made for their liking, especially as Bettles had more than once hinted that, in his opinion, Ear Bitin' Finley could tell the whole story of the disappearance of Davey Condon on Jim River. When Finley had first showed up in Forty-mile, Bettles had questioned him at length about Davey's disappearance, but the man denied any knowledge of it. Said he had never been on the Jim River and insisted he had been in Coldfoot in search of Harmon.

Three or four men entered the saloon, their arms laden with fireweed, which was arranged on and about the casket. The intrusion of Julie Condon was forgotten as a few more drinks were had, and Horse Face Joe succeeded in restoring the delicious sadness of the occasion by a squeaky rendition of "Nearer, My God, To Thee," accompanied by the vocal effort of half the house.

"Now, then, Carmack," said old Bettles, "git busy. You're the parson." He paused and, from an inside pocket of his faded blanket coat, drew a dilapidated Book of Common Prayer and, wetting his thumb, began to turn its pages. "A parson over in Alasky name of Hudson Stuck give me this book a hell of a while ago, an' I ben carryin' it ever since. There's some damn good readin' in it—but the print's too fine. Personal, I never did hold much with religion, except to funerals—but some likes it. Here you be, Carmack—Burial of the Dead. Git a-goin', now—an' don't mumble yer words." He paused and glared at the assembled men. "An' they won't be no talkin' nor drinkin' till he gits through. It'll take about a half an hour—accordin' to how fast Carmack kin read. Then we'll have a couple of drinks, an' sing us some more songs, an' carry the coffin up the hill."

Carmack took the book hesitatingly. "I can't read so good, Bettles," he apologized. "It's a hell of a while sinct I learnt."

"Well, what do you think about me? I learnt long before you did! Go ahead, an' skip the words you don't know—that's the way I do. If you git four out of five, it'll be pretty good. Some of them is hard words."

Carmack's halting voice droned on and on, while the men stood at respectful attention. By adroitly turning two pages at a time of the eight pages of the service, he shortened the ordeal by half, without anyone noticing it. As he handed the book back, Bettles consulted his huge silver watch. "Good work," he commented, pocketing the book. "You beat that parson at it by damn near fifteen minutes. I heard him read it once when a feller broke his neck in the Ramparts. All right, boys, belly up, an' we'll hist a couple 'fore we git to work at the singin'."

XIX

Til Carter Returns

Drifting down the Yukon on his raft, Til Carter laid his plans. As he neared Fortymile his eyes restlessly sought the margin of the mighty river for sight of the poling boats that must surely be pushing upriver at the news of Carmack's strike. Carmack and Skookum Jim must have recorded their claims—and they must have talked and showed their gold. That they had gold Til was certain, for he had seen their workings near the foot of the birch tree.

But where were the stampeders from Fortymile? At last, with the camp in sight, he began working his unwieldy craft toward the bank and, landing at the rude dock, stepped ashore with his packsack and hurried to the recorder's. Sure enough, there were the entries of Carmack and Skookum Jim. He recorded his own location, stepped from the office, and allowed his eyes to stray from old Tim Condon's Aurora Borealis restaurant to Bergman's saloon, where he knew some of the sourdoughs, in from the creeks, would be forgathered.

He must find Tim Condon and slip the old man the word of his strike, so he could get up to Bonanza and stake his claim. The chances were that old Tim would be at the saloon with the boys. Anyway, as long as the entries of Carmack and Skookum Jim had not stirred up any stampede, he might as well slip over to Bergman's first and heel himself with a couple of drinks. He would say nothing about his own strike until old Tim was safely on his way to Bonanza with a sure-thing start. Then he'd break the news and let the rest of the camp in.

Pausing for a moment in the doorway, Til stared in astonishment. Lining the bar were the backs of many men, evidently engaged in the serious act of drinking. In the center of the room, between the row of backs and himself, a casket, piled with fireweed, rested on a couple of kegs. Candles burned at the foot and head of the casket. Stepping swiftly to the bier, Til glanced downward to stare at what appeared to be the body of a man. But the man had a paper face!

"What the hell's coming off here?" he roared in a voice that brought the line of earnest drinkers to a rightabout-face. The next instant a most amazing thing happened. Amid a bedlam of frightened oaths, shrill cries, and inarticulate exclamations, the crowd bolted to a man for the back door, where they wedged and struggled in a frantic effort to make an exit. Only Bergman remained at his post as his widening eyes seemed to protrude from their sockets like china marbles. "My God, he's come to!" he yelled, and white apron tails flying, he, too, dashed for the back door, dived head foremost over the struggling mass in the doorway, and brought up in a heap amid a litter of empty bottles and rusty tin cans.

The doorway finally cleared, and Til found himself alone in the saloon. Strolling to the bar, he poured himself a drink and tossed it off. Then he poured another. He examined his features in the mirror behind the bar but could find nothing terrifying in his appearance.

"Well, what the hell?" he muttered with a puzzled grin.

"Has the whole camp gone crazy? Guess I'll just stick around and see. Someone's bound to come back sometime—er else I've fallen heir to a saloon."

Finally Bergman thrust his face around the jamb of the door. "That—that you, Til?" he inquired fearfully.

Til could see other faces peering in from the background. "Sure it's me! Who the hell do you suppose it is? And what's the matter with you-all, anyhow?"

Bergman hesitated and, turning, addressed old Bettles. "It's him, all right!" he said. "He come to. It might of ben that Bible readin' done it."

"How the hell could he?" queried Bettles. "It wasn't him to start with. Go on in, you damn fool!"

"You come too, then," insisted Bergman.

"Hell—let's all go," replied Bettles, beckoning to the others. "If it's Til, he ain't goin' to hurt us none. An' if it ain't—who the hell would it be?" he added lamely.

Til grinned broadly as the men of Fortymile came trooping back single file, led by the redoubtable Bergman, closely followed by old Bettles. "Hellò, Til," greeted that worthy. "We—we're glad to see you back."

"Yeah? You sure looked like it, the way you stampeded for that door! I don't know when I was ever greeted so cordially. But—let me in on it. What's the joke?"

"I got to have four drinks first," said Bettles, "an' then I kin talk. Damn you, Til—you scairt me plumb sober!"

Rounds of drinks were had, and old Bettles explained: "We was holdin' yer funeral, Til."

"*My* funeral! What the hell you talking about?"

"Yeah—yourn," Camillo Bill explained. "You see, you'd ben gone so long we figgered you must be dead, so we had you a funeral. An' it was a damn good funeral, too! Come on over an' meet yer corp. Bettles even writ you out a eppygraft fer yer board. He's got it there in his pocket." Solemnly Bettles produced the paper and handed it to Til, who read it with a roar of laughter.

"Fine!" he said. "It's too bad I came along and spoilt the fun."

"Fun—hell!" exclaimed Camillo Bill. "It wasn't no fun. We was plumb, an' honest-to-God, sad. Cripes—half of us was bellerin'.'"

"It's good for a man to know he's appreciated," grinned Til. "Very few men walk in on their own funeral. But I'm not dead yet, by a damn sight. Come on—drink up and have one on me."

"Did you do any good in the upper country?" asked Bettles, eying the sack Til tossed onto the bar.

"There's what I panned out in twelve months," he answered truthfully. "I figure it about sixty ounces. But I saw a hell of a lot of country."

"Yeah," chipped in Mooshide, "a man could, in twelve months. But he sure pays fer it."

Til grinned. "Sixty ounces'll buy a hell of a lot of drinks and dances."

"Yeah," admitted Camillo Bill. "But it ain't no hell of a stake in a stud game."

"We'll see," laughed Til. "I feel lucky. Drink up, and you fellows get a game going and I'll be back. I'm goin' over to the restaurant an' see old Tim. Funny he isn't here."

"Not so funny," answered Moosehide Charlie. "He's ben dead fer six months. Pneumony. Got sweated up one day over the stove an' went outside to cool off. Old Doc Pettus done what he could—which didn't 'mount to much more'n clawin' his whiskers an' shakin' his head—an' Tim died three days later. February, it was—an' God, the ground was froze hard! Tim would of laughed to see us burnin' in fer to git him down six foot—but we done 'er."

"Old Tim dead!" exclaimed Til, his face becoming suddenly grave. "What's become of Julie—the Pest—the Fire-weed?"

"She's runnin' the restaurant—an' doin' a damn good job."

"What—that kid!" cried Til. "Running the restaurant

alone! But I'll bet she could do it, at that. She took me on my first caribou hunt up on the Koyukuk. And just before I pulled out last summer she called me a fool for going. Just when I didn't want to be raised hell with—that's when she did it. Bettles used to call her the Pest, and sometimes I agreed with him."

Old Bettles chuckled. "You ain't saw her fer a year. She's a woman now. An' the purtiest woman that ever hit the Yukon—an' all the side cricks! If I remember right, you was all caked in on her up there on the Koyukuk. But she wasn't nothin' then to what she is now—you wait an' see."

"I won't wait long. I'm heading for the restaurant right now," answered Til. "Get your game going. I'll be back."

"Better have another drink 'fore you go—an' give her somethin' to rib you about. She jest give us all hell fer bein' drunk—which we ain't."

Ear Bitin' Finley edged his way over to Til's side. "You stay away from the Rory Bory—if you know what's good fer you, young feller," he said truculently. "The Fireweed's my gal, an' I got a date with her right pronto. If yer hell-bent fer eatin', they's the Midnight Sun restaurant. You kin eat there—see?"

Til Carter flushed to the hair roots as he gazed into the narrowed eyes of the larger man. "No," he answered in a cold, level voice, "I don't see. Who the hell are you to tell me where to keep away from and where to eat?"

"I'm Ear Bitin' Finley!" announced the man in a tone that carried to the farthest reach of the room. "I kin lick any man that ever stood on two legs! When a man fights me he kin kiss his ears good-by! I chaw 'em off an' eat 'em raw! I'm hell on wheels—an' the outfightenest son of a she-wolf that ever come up the river!"

"Son of a bitch-wolf is the word," answered Til in the same level voice. "An' in your case, Mr. Lop Eared Finney, or whatever you call yourself, you could leave off the 'wolf' —the name would fit better. In the meantime try that on

154

your piano!" With incredible swiftness Til struck—a blow that was not telegraphed by any foot-shifting, yet one that started low and landed high—squarely against the pugnaciously outthrust jaw of Ear Bitin' Finley.

The sourdoughs whooped with delight as the huge bully, stunned by the blow, staggered backward, clawing aimlessly at the air and shaking his head, as though to rid himself of some clinging thing. For only a moment he continued so—then his brain cleared, and balancing himself, he sprang straight at Til with a roar like the bellow of a bull. But Til was ready, expecting just that move, and dropping to one knee, he tackled the huge man above the knees, heaved upward with all his strength, and sprang free.

Ear Bitin' Finley's feet flew higher than the bar, and in falling his head hit the iron pipe that took the place of the time-honored brass rail in front of the bar with a thud that jarred the house. He struggled to rise, spitting blood as two teeth clicked on the floor. The next instant Til was upon him, punching, jabbing, hooking to the face, in a rain of blows that closed the man's eyes and caused the blood to spurt from nose and battered lips. Only when the other went limp did Til cease to pound, and batter, and thump. Then he rose to his feet and administered a contemptuous kick in the ribs to the inert form. "If he starts hunting me before I get back," he said, "you can tell him I'm down at the Aurora Borealis. I've got to go down an' tell the Fireweed I messed up her boy friend. That'll give her somethin' to talk about."

"With all his brag, he never hit a lick!" exclaimed Camillo Bill. "God, Til, you're fast!"

"Well—hell! You couldn't expect a man to stand around and let his ears get gnawed, could you?"

When Til had passed out the door, Moosehide Charlie glanced down at the man on the floor. "Say, fellers, mebbe we better do somethin'. Old Hell on Wheels, here, is bleedin' like a stuck moose."

"I am goin' to do somethin'," answered Bettles. "An' I'm goin' to do it now. I'm goin' to let him bleed—an' if he dreens plumb dry, I won't shed a tear. An' what's more, we could have a funeral in spite of Til bein' alive. It ain't no ways fittin' a cuss like him should be buzzin' around the Fireweed."

In the doorway of the restaurant Til Carter stopped dead to stare at the girl who sat at a desk in a recess near the end of the lunch counter, apparently engrossed in a column of figures. On the Koyukuk he had admired her for her wiry strength, her capability. Last year here in Fortymile, during the short interview he had with her, he had noted that she had developed from gangling girlhood into budding womanhood—she had gained a certain poise. He had never thought of her as beautiful. So he was entirely unprepared for this vision of feminine loveliness that met his eyes as a beam of sunlight fell aslant the hair which seemed to blaze with a living flame. Julie Condon—the Fireweed—the Pest—had bloomed into radiant womanhood.

The girl raised her head. Her deep blue eyes widened perceptibly as they met Til's steady gaze. Then the red lips smiled slightly, and she greeted him as casually as though he had stepped from the room an hour before. "Hello, Til. Where you been?"

Hat in hand, Til advanced awkwardly to the desk. "Over at Bergman's," he said.

The blue eyes chilled. "I see. Just as you did last year when you came up on the *Arctic*. You went to Bergman's first."

"No. First I went to the recorder's and then to Bergman's."

"It's a wonder you could tear yourself away from there. I looked in the door a while ago, and your little playmates were having lots of fun. They were holding your funeral—celebrating it would be the better word. Even Uncle Gordon—and he's old enough to know better. They ought to be ashamed of themselves—but men never grow up—they're like a lot of little boys!"

"But women do," replied Til seriously. "You've changed a lot in a year, Julie."

"Why not 'Pest'?" she flashed maliciously. "You haven't changed any that I can see. Make for the saloon as soon as you hit camp. Been down to the dance hall yet? Or are you saving that for tonight? And how long a spree is it going to take to clean you out this time?"

"Couldn't say," answered Til, flushing slightly. "I went over to Bergman's because I thought maybe Tim—your dad —might be there. You see, Julie, I've ben way back in the hills. I didn't know."

For the moment the girl dropped her raillery. "No—you couldn't have known. Bring a chair over from one of the tables, Til. There's no sense in your standing up."

"I won't be bothering you long," he answered stiffly. "I hear you've got a date."

"You must have been talking to Finley."

"Yeah, I talked with him some," answered the man in a hard, dry tone as he carried a chair to the desk and placed it close to the girl's. "I—I'm awfully sorry about Tim, Julie. I liked him."

The girl nodded thoughtfully, her eyes on the far hills that showed green and red through the window. "Most people did—that knew him," she answered. "He liked you, too. But the Lord knows why—men are funny."

Til ignored the jibe. "You said 'most' people, Julie. I guess everyone that knew him liked him."

The girl shook her head. "No. There's one man that didn't," she answered, her eyes hardening.

"Who's that? An' why didn't he like Tim?"

"I don't know why—but I will know someday. It don't make any difference who he is—at least not for the present."

"I thought maybe I could help you," answered Til.

157

The girl changed the subject. "You said you went over to Bergman's to see Daddy," she reminded. "I don't more than half believe that, but I'll give you the benefit of the doubt. I think you went for a drink—and took several. You smell like a brewery."

"I'm not one, though—and I couldn't smell like one either. I drank no beer. Whisky is made in distilleries."

The girl sniffed. "You ought to know. It must take several of 'em to keep you going. But what did you want to see Daddy about?"

Til glanced carefully about the room and, intercepting the glance, the girl reassured him. "The Chink is in the kitchen. He don't savvy much English, anyhow. And the waitress is off duty."

"Well, then," Til began, lowering his voice and edging his chair an inch closer, "it's like this. Your dad grubstaked me for my trip upriver——"

"Yes, I know," interrupted the girl. "He wouldn't have had to if you'd had sense enough not to blow in your dust as soon as you got it. But go ahead. You haven't told me any secrets yet."

"I'll tell you one now, though," Til said. "I made a strike —an' a whopping big one!"

The girl's eyes lighted. "Where?" she asked.

"On Bonanza—just above Carmack's an' Skookum Jim's Discovery. I recorded No. 1 Above."

The light in the girl's eyes changed to a glint of derision. She threw back her head and laughed, disclosing two rows of pearly teeth. "And are you working for Harper and Larue too?" she taunted.

"Listen," said Til, flushing, "Harper knows nothing about this—and Larue don't believe it! What are you driving at, anyhow?"

"Oh, don't play me for a fool, Til! Come on, get it over with. What do you want to do, sell me a lot in Larue's townsite? Or a claim? Most of the real sourdoughs eat in here, and I've heard 'em talk—Uncle Gordon, and Camillo Bill, and Moosehide, and a lot more. And ever since Carmack and Skookum Jim came down and recorded their claims on that flat moose pasture the old-timers—the men that know gold—have been kidding about it. They figure it's a scheme of Larue's to start a stampede and sell lots in his townsite and goods in his trading post. And, you bet, the sourdoughs are right! You can't fool men like that by locating claims in moose pastures!"

"So that's why there was no stampede when Carmack and Skookum Jim recorded, eh? I wondered, all the time I was floating down the river on a raft, why I wasn't meeting poling boats. But the sourdoughs are fooled this time—and badly fooled! I tell you, Julie, it's the biggest strike ever made! I took out better than sixty ounces in less than three days, with nothing but a shovel and a pan. And that's more than Bettles and I ever took out on the Jim River in two weeks' time."

"Did you tell 'em about it in Bergman's?" she asked. "About this wonderful strike of yours?"

Once again Til flushed at the sarcasm in the girl's voice. "No," he said, "I didn't. Tim Condon staked me—and when I found out he was dead, it was up to me to come here and tell you before I tipped the strike off to anyone. They asked me if I had done any good, and I tossed a sixty-ounce sack on the bar and told 'em it was what I'd panned in twelve months of prospecting—and it was the truth. I didn't show 'em the green hide pouch I had in my pack, with more than that in it that I panned in two days an' a half on Bonanza. After you've staked an' recorded, I'll let the others in on it."

The girl's eyes narrowed. "I don't see your game, Til. Daddy grubstaked you and filed his power of attorney with the recorder that allowed you to stake and record for him. Now why should I have to stake a claim? Didn't you stake one for Daddy? I'm his sole heir—I'll inherit Daddy's claim."

Til smiled. "You don't savvy the law, Julie. If I'd staked

my claim on any river or creek on which I'd made a discovery, I could have filed a claim for your dad. But I didn't make the discovery on Bonanza! Carmack an' Skookum Jim made the discovery and had already recorded it. I staked a creek that had already ben filed on—and therefore any claim, besides my own, that I staked would be null an' void. That's the law. Go ask the recorder. Even if I could have legally filed for Tim, you'd have to go and stake your own claim. I didn't know it, but Tim had been dead for months before I ever saw Bonanza."

Again the girl laughed. "It isn't worth going across the street to ask the recorder about—if that's where you staked. I've heard what the sourdoughs say about this Bonanza. And one thing they say is that its real name is Rabbit Creek and Carmack changed it to Bonanza so the old-timers would be fooled and not find out about it till they had hit Larue's."

"I don't know why Carmack changed the name," answered Til with a show of impatience, "and I don't give a damn! What I'm telling you is that you've got to get up there an' file as quick as the Lord will let you! The old-timers have made a bum guess this time—show 'em you've got more sense than they have!"

"Sure," sneered the girl. "Show men that were here in the North when I was born that I've got more sense than they have! Show 'em that—because you say so! You know mighty well, Til Carter, that I was born in the North—and way north of here. I was born on the Koyukuk! And I've lived in mining camps and on the creeks all my life. After Daddy lost his leg we both knew that his prospecting days were over, so we came down here where we could make a living. How long have you lived in the North? And you're asking me to take your word against my own judgment and the judgment of the real sourdoughs!"

Til Carter rose from his chair and faced the girl with narrowed eyes. "As you well know, I've ben in the North for two years. One year with Bettles on the Jim River—and a year upriver on my own. And it seems that maybe I've learnt more than some of the sourdoughs that have been here for forty years. They all say that 'gold's where you find it'—and not a damn one of 'em has sense enough to believe what they all say! But you're going up there and file, whether you want to or not! Oh yes—and I'd almost forgotten it—it was so easy—I punched hell out of your boy friend a few minutes ago over at Bergman's."

"My boy friend! What do you mean, Til Carter? Are you crazy—or just drunk?"

"Neither one. When I told 'em I was coming over here, up steps a large gent who announced that his name is Ear Bitin' Finley. He warns me to keep away from here—asserting that you were his gal and advising me that if I was hungry I could eat at the other restaurant. He backed up his remarks with a lot of brag, which I interrupted with physical violence to the extent that I left him asleep and bleeding on the saloon floor."

The blue eyes widened. "Til! You didn't kill him, did you?"

The man noted the real concern in her voice and turned away. "No—he's not dead. So long, Pest. You seem to have even less sense about men than you have about gold!"

XX

Til Sets His Stage

Back in Bergman's, Til joined the old-timers at the bar. "Where's the bitch-wolf's pup?" he asked, eying the pool of blood beneath the iron footrail.

"Oh, he come to an' snuck out the back way a while ago," answered Camillo Bill. "I expect he's gone to his shack to think him up a new brag. The one he used wasn't so good—seems like."

"What became of the stud game you-all were going to start?"

"Seems like we ain't honin' fer stud this afternoon. We'll git us up a game tonight, mebbe," answered Bettles. "Come on, drink up an' have another. D'ye see the Fireweed?"

"Yeah," replied Til indifferently. "I saw her. She was adding up figures. Seems to be making a go of old Tim's restaurant."

"I'll tell a hand she is!" Swiftwater Bill exclaimed. "An' she's doin' better with it than Tim ever done. Barrin' right around mealtimes, Tim warn't hardly ever there. He liked to loaf over here an' have a few drinks with the boys. An' he liked him a game of stud, persistent. Which ain't nothin' agin Tim, mind you, but it was hard on the restaurant. Tim was a damn good feller, an' he's missed accordin'. But, an' however, as the feller says, the Fireweed, she don't drink none, an' she don't play no stud, which leaves time hangin' heavy on her hands, so she puts it in on the restaurant. She's on the job reg'lar from ten in the mornin' till one at night. Then she goes home an' ketches her some sleep till next mornin'—onlest there's someone that's sick or needin' help. She'll quit her bed, er the restaurant, any time of day or night to go an' nurse someone's that's sick er hurt, er show some klooch how to pin a didie on her new baby."

"Living where she and Tim did last summer, I suppose, in the cabin back of the restaurant."

"Yeah, an' she's fixed it all up—knocked out a partition so they's only two rooms now—one big un, an' her bedroom. She don't need no kitchen, 'cause she eats at the restaurant. She had a fireplace built in, an' it looks nice of an evenin' to see the wood fire burnin'. You see, every Thursday night she has what she calls a 'Public Forum,' which means that us old-timers has got to go over there an' set around an' talk. First fifteen minutes we got to talk about the good of the camp. If any regulatin's got to be done—like Siwashes bein' sold hooch to, er dumpin' tin cans an' rubbish in the street—a committee's appinted to see about it—an' by God, it's saw about, too! Then, if she's dug up anyone needin' help, we got to chip in an' fix that—like buyin' grub, or medicine, an' suchlike. The next half an hour she reads to us. If the boat's ben in, they's noospapers, from the outside to read up on—an' if not, they's magazines. Then fer the next hour er so we talk about anythin' we want to. Like next Thursday—that's day after tomorrow—we'll prob'ly talk about this here Carmack strike. He'll be asked to give his side of it—an' then we'll auger it, pro an' con, as the sayin' is —an' we'll show how he couldn't of made no strike where he claimed he done. You kin smoke but you can't chaw—she won't have no spitoons, an' she barred spittin' at the fireplace, after a fair trial. We didn't take to these meetin's first off, but she kep' at us, an' now we wouldn't miss one fer nothin'. Believe me, the Fireweed's all right! They ain't a man in the camp that wouldn't go to hell fer her!"

"But when you come in here we was debatin' what to do with this here coffin. Some was fer rafflin' it off, an' some was——"

"Hold on!" interrupted Til with a grin. "That's my coffin!"

"Yourn?"

"Sure, mine! It was my funeral you were celebrating, wasn't it?"

"That's right," agreed Bettles amid general laughter. "But what the hell do you want with a coffin?"

"Put runners under her, maybe, and use her for a stampeding sled next winter. Those fancy handles would sure come in handy on a rough trail. Anyway, she's mine. A coffin is a handy thing to have around. I threw my packsack in that empty shack between the dock and the Siwash camp. I aim to live there while I'm in camp. When we go to supper I'll thank three, four of you to help me pack my coffin down there. It's liable to get knocked off an' broken if we leave it on those kegs—an' besides, it's in the way." Til paused to appeal to the bartender. "Ain't it, Bergman?"

"Yeah—git the damn thing outa here! It gives me the creeps."

Drinks were had, and rough horseplay engaged in for an hour or so, when Bettles consulted his watch. "Hell, boys, it's five minutes to six! One more round, an' we got to git a-goin' if we aim to help Til down to his shack with his coffin."

He turned to Til. "You see, she likes us to git to meals on time. Used to be, when Tim run the place, we'd go an' eat, one or two to a time, whenever we got hungry. But she claims that ain't no way to do. She claims that onreg'lar eatin's onhealthy fer us—an' makes a damn sight more work fer her. So we kind of got in the habit of goin' reg'lar. The onhealthy part is the bunk—but we don't aim to make it no harder fer her. Course, if anyone's got a reason why he can't git there on time, he kin git anythin' he wants when he does go. But she don't hold that a general drinkin' bout is a reasonable excuse fer bein' late. It's ben tried—but it ain't ben got away with. Ruther'n to have her light in on us—she don't never raise no hell, but she kin think of things to say, sweet, an' sarcastic, like, that makes us feel like a lot of damn fools—we try to git there on time."

"Come on," cried Camillo Bill impatiently, "hist this un an' then grab aholt of them handles. We ain't got time to take Til's dummy out. Cripes, we'll be late!"

So with Horse Face Joe, playing his conception of a funeral march on his fiddle, leading the procession, followed by the pallbearers carrying the casket, the tipsy sourdoughs of Fortymile fell in behind and solemnly paraded down past the Aurora Borealis to the shack by the river. There they dumped the casket unceremoniously onto the floor and stampeded for the-restaurant.

As they passed the door on the way to the shack, the Fire-weed, hearing the fiddling, looked out upon the procession. "The darn fools!" she exclaimed, and then, with a smile that nobody saw, she muttered words that nobody heard: "But they work hard when they work, and they've got to have their fun. I—I love 'em all, and sometimes I wish I could play with 'em!"

When they arrived, more or less out of breath, the girl greeted them with a smile. "Pretty good, boys—you're only ten minutes late."

"Ten minutes late!" cried Bettles, producing his huge silver watch which he had deftly turned back twelve minutes as he ran. "Why, shame on you, Julie—we're a minute ahead! Look, an' see fer yerself!"

The smile widened. "That's the second time that's happened in a month, Uncle Gordon. You'll have to send your watch outside to a jeweler. It's gaining time."

"We was holdin' a political caucus," explained Camillo Bill with a grin. "I'm thinkin' of runnin' fer mayor."

"Carcass, you mean, don't you?" laughed the girl. "I saw the parade go by. And I think you're a lot of darned old fools!"

After supper Til turned toward his shack.

"Hey," called Bettles, "where the hell you goin'? How about that stud game?"

"I'll be over there directly. I'm going down first and jump in the river, an' change my clothes. I've been sweating, and I need a bath."

Stepping into the shack, Til made sure that he was not followed and then, slipping out the back door, proceeded hastily to the Indian camp near the Mission. At the door of the first shack he came to—a low log hut—he paused and knocked. The door opened, and an old Indian eyed him expectantly. "W'at you want?" he asked abruptly.

"Is your name Mathew?" Til asked.

"Yes. Me Mat'ew."

"Til Carter's my name. I know your wife's brother, Kootlak. He lives down at St. Michael and he did me a good turn last year when I deserted from a whaler. I——"

The Indian thrust out his hand. "You Til Carter, you damn good mans. You gave Kootlak baby two hundred and fifty dolla."

"I gave the money to the baby because Kootlak wouldn't take any money for what he did for me."

"No tak money for let col' man git warm—for let hongre man eat."

"Okay," Til said. "But now I need help again, and I'm wondering if you will help me?"

The Indian nodded vigorously. "Yes, me help you. You good mans."

"I've made a big strike upriver——"

"Dat dam' good t'ing. I'm lak I'm see you mak' de beeg strike. Ba goss, you de good mans! You geeve de baby two hundred and fifty dolla."

"You can forget that," said Til gruffly. "But here's something you must not forget—I won't lie to you. Everything I tell you will be the truth. Will you believe me, now—no matter what I tell you?"

"Yes."

"And will you help me—no matter what I ask you to do?"

"Yes," came the unhesitating reply. "You de good mans."

"Well, then, listen. Carmack and Skookum Jim made a strike upriver—and a damn good one."

The Indian nodded. "Skookum Jim tell me. I'm goin' oop dere w'en I git outfit."

"I'll give you the outfit—an' see that you get staked on a good claim. You and one other Siwash. But you got to start tonight—midnight—see?"

"Een de canoe?"

"No—poling boat."

"Me, I'm ain' got polin' boat."

"I'll get the poling boat, and I'll buy the grub at the A.C., right now. You find another Siwash you can trust, and pack that grub from the store and load the poling boat—right here in front of your shack—and then you do as I say— savvy?"

"Yes."

"Do you know who's got a poling boat to sell?"

"Mike Two Bear got good polin' boat, lak for sell."

"All right, I'll buy it. You know that shack by the dock— well, my pack's in there. You put my pack in the boat too— an' a coffin you'll find in the shack."

"Coffin? Who dead?"

"No one's dead, and no one's going to be dead. But I'm taking the coffin along. Load the stuff so that coffin will sit level on top of the load." Til paused and glanced about the hut. "Where's your woman?" he asked.

"She gone' Mike Two Bear house. Back pret' queek."

"You have this loading done by midnight. Then you go to the Aurora Borealis restaurant an' tell the Fireweed that your woman is sick and you want her to come down here with you. Tell her you've sent another Siwash after Doc Pettus."

Til was aware that the man was regarding him shrewdly. "My 'oman ain' seek. Me, I'm ain' lak' I'm fool de Fireweed. She com' wan tam an' mak' de 'oman git well."

Til nodded. "The Fireweed's the best damn woman in the North!" he said. "It's like this, Mathew—her dad, old Tim, grubstaked me for my prospecting trip. So I owe him a good location. But he's dead. I made a strike on Bonanza and located just above Carmack an' Skookum Jim. The men here in Fortymile don't believe they made any strike. You know that—or they'd have stampeded up there. All right—she hears the sourdoughs talk in the restaurant, and she don't believe it either. I told her I've made a strike, but she won't believe me. So she won't go up there and locate a claim. She thinks Carmack and Skookum Jim and I are lying. But we're not lying. We're telling the truth. It's the biggest strike ever made. So I'm going to make her go! I'm going to kidnap her, and take her upriver, and show her the gold in the gravel! Then she'll believe it, and file. She's got it coming —this gold—and she's going to have it! It's the only way to make her believe me. She'll thank me for it in the long run —but she's going to be God-almighty mad first. You get her down here, and I'll grab her and gag her, and we'll shove her in that coffin, where she can rest comfortably. You an' this other Siwash will be along every minute. But you wouldn't have to be, at that. I wouldn't hurt her. My God, someday I'm going to marry her! Only she don't know that—yet."

The old Indian smiled a slow smile. "Me—I'm b'lieve w'at you say. I'm gon' do lak you tall me. Me an' you—we tak good car' de Fireweed—you bet!"

"Who'll you get to help with the poling?"

"Bum Eye Bob—he dam' good mans. He go."

"All right, then—come on, we'll go buy the poling boat, then you get Bum Eyed Bob and work her up to here, and then hustle the stuff down from my shack and the store. And be damn sure you have her loaded by midnight, and go at exactly twelve o'clock to the restaurant and hustle the Fireweed down here, I'll be waiting—and we'll get going."

XXI

At Larue's Townsite

The purchase of the poling boat and the grub at the A.C. store emptied the green moosehide sack of the dust Til had panned on Bonanza. He did not stock heavily, as he knew that Larue and Harper would have their trading post on the flat finished by the time snow would fly.

When he showed up at Bergman's the stud game was already in session.

"What the hell's ben keepin' you?" queried Moosehide Charlie, looking up from careful scrutiny of his hole card.

"He's ben takin' him a bath," chuckled old Bettles, folding his hand as Camillo Bill shoved in a stack of chips. "God! He looks quite a bit slimmer, at that!"

Til grinned and tossed his smoke-tanned pouch onto the bar. "Weigh her in, Bergman, and give me the chips."

Bergman weighed the dust that Til had collected during the eleven months of toil in the far hills. "She figgers fifty-seven an' a quarter ounces," he announced. "That's nine hundred an' sixteen dollars. You want it all in chips?"

"Sure," answered Til. "I'm playing the poke—an' chips are good for drinks, if I want to use 'em that way."

Room was made at the table, and Til Carter sat down to the most peculiar game of stud poker he was ever to play. He was playing to go broke—and to go broke at exactly a quarter to twelve—else how could he explain his abrupt departure from the game at that hour? For stud games in Fortymile were all-night affairs. Only a good excuse would permit a man to quit without suffering merciless kidding and chaffing—and going broke was the best excuse of all. Thinking of the gold in the gravel of his claim, Til grinned. Two days—with a pan!

It was eight-fifteen when Til sat in the game. The cards were running slow, and the play was desultory for an hour. New decks were introduced without result. The cards would not warm up. Then after a red deck had been run in at Camillo Bill's earnest solicitation, Til found himself with a pair of tens, back to back. Camillo, having the deck, flamboyantly bet his exposed king. Bettles, Moosehide Charlie, and Burr MacShane saw the bet. Til raised it twenty. Camillo raised forty. The game was warming up. Bettles tilted the edge of his hole card and raised another forty. Moosehide trailed, and MacShane folded. Til raised a hundred on his pair of tens. Camillo Bill trailed. Bettles studied his hole card. He had a seven up. He slipped the chips into the pot, not happily. On the next round Camillo dealt himself an ace, Bettles a trey, Moosehide a queen, and Til a queen. Camillo led with a bet of a hundred. Bettles called, Moosehide quit, and Til raised a hundred. Camillo saw the raise, so did Bettles. On the next deal Camillo dealt himself another king, Bettles a four, and Til a ten-spot. With two kings showing, Camillo bet two hundred. Bettles dropped out, and Til raised two hundred. Camillo called. The next deal gave Camillo a six and Til an ace. Camillo bet three hundred, and Til doubled it. Camillo called, and lost to Til's three tens.

From that deal the game warmed up. Hardly a hand was played with less than a thousand in the pot—and Til was winning his share. At eleven-thirty he measured his chips.

He had twenty-seven hundred and thirty dollars in front of him. He bought a round of drinks. At twenty minutes to twelve it was twenty-two hundred and sixty. Five minutes to play—now was his time to lose!

It was his own deal. He found an exposed ace, and a four in the hole. Bettles led with a bet of a hundred on an exposed jack, Moosehide dropped, and MacShane stayed. Til raised it five hundred. Camillo folded, and Bettles saw the raise. So did MacShane. Til dealt again, and Bettles paired his jack, face up. He bet a thousand. MacShane quit, and Til promptly raised him the six hundred and sixty he had left. Bettles saw the raise—the deal proceeded to a showdown. Bettles won. Til rose from the table with a laugh. "I'm cleaned. But I'll get you some other time. I'm going out and dig some more gold."

Old Bettles protested: "Hell, Til, yer finger bet's good in this game fer all you want!"

"I don't make finger bets. Thanks just the same. Next time I play I'll even up the score—and I'll have the dust in my poke to back it."

"But where you goin'?" asked Camillo Bill. "Hell, you jest come in off a damn long trail. Ain't you goin' to prod around none? We'll bust this game up an' go over to the dance hall."

Til shook his head. "I'm broke, and I'm tired. I know you-all would stake me for a frolic—but I'm not in the mood for a frolic tonight. I've got to catch some sleep. So long. I'll be seeing you directly—and then we'll cut loose for fair."

"Now what do you think of that?" asked old Bettles as Til went out the door. "I never seen him like that before! He ain't feelin' fer a frolic—an' him out in the hills fer a whole damn year! Hell-fire! He'd ort to be jest gittin' steamed up! An' he ain't even ben over to the dance hall!"

Camillo Bill grinned sagely. "Yeah—but he's ben an' talked with the Fireweed. You mebbe didn't notice that when he come back from there he was lookin' kind of glum. But I did. She prob'ly took him over the jumps. I'll bet he told her about knockin' hell out of Ear Bitin' Finley. An', believe me, she might give him hell fer doin' it—but she's no fool —she's tickled to death he's back here an' done it!"

Moosehide Charlie frowned. "I ain't so shore about her bein' tickled if Finley got licked. Seems like he's ben buzzin' around her pretty thick. I come by the restaurant yesterday an' looked through the winder an' seen her an' Finley talkin' together there by the counter. I know the Fireweed ain't no fool. Most ways she's smart as hell. But lots of wimmin is fools when it comes to a man—look at the sons-of-bitches some of 'em marry."

"She might of rode Til fer fightin' with Finley," Camillo said, "an' she might of smelt likker on his breath an' raised hell about that. But I'll lay a bet right here—someday she'll marry him—he's got guts! An' it's his guts that's keepin' him away from the dance hall, an' from us fellers tonight. God— whether she liked it er not, he sure poured Ear Bitin' Finley back in the jug!"

Til Carter made his way swiftly from the saloon to the shack of Mathew, the Indian. The hut was dark. He felt his way to the riverbank and found the poling boat tied up, and loaded as he had ordered. The casket lay carefully nested on top of the load. He was about to turn back to Mathew's cabin when rough hands seized him from behind and he was thrown violently to the ground. "W'at you do?" hissed a voice in his ear. "W'at you wan' here?"

Til struggled against the arms that held him pinioned. "Who the hell are you?" he gasped. "Where's Mathew?"

The arms relaxed a bit. "Who you?"

"I'm Til Carter. I'm looking for Mathew."

The arms relaxed altogether, and a strong arm was helping him to his feet. "Me—Bum Eye Bob. I ain't know you. Mat'ew tell me watch de pole boat—no let no wan com'. He say Til Carter good mans. I excuse."

"You're all right, Bob. Where's Mathew?"

"Heem gon' for git de Fireweed. Dey com' now pret' queek." The powerful Indian squared himself in the darkness before Til, and through the dark Til could see gleaming black eyes. "By Goddam, you ain' hurt de Fireweed! Me—I'm go 'long. I ain' know you. I know de Fireweed. Mat'ew say you good mans. Dat good. Mat'ew good mans too. Fireweed, she mak my lil boy for walk. Heem leg she drag—now she go long lak' me! You steal Fireweed—giv' um good claim—dat good. You steal Fireweed—sump'n else— Goddam! Me—Bum Eye Bob—go 'long!"

"Fine, Bob," said Til. "We think jest alike. Come on, let's get up here in the dark of Mathew's shack, where we can grab her when she comes along. You get her arms—an' I'll gag her. If she'd yell, she'd lose a million!"

Together the two slipped into the shadow of the hut—and none too soon. Footsteps sounded from the direction of the camp, and then words were audible: "What are the symptoms, Mathew—what——"

"Ain' got sim'tim—my 'oman—she seek——" A dark form passed Til, who crouched against the wall of the hut—and another smaller form—the Fireweed! There was a blur of motion in the dark. A great shape shot from the deep shadow. The Fireweed gasped, struggled for a second, as Til threw a thick woolen muffler about her lips and tightened it. Bum Eyed Bob held her in a grip of iron. Her frantic struggles were as the wriggling of a babe in his mighty arms. She tried to scream, but the sound, through the thick woolen muffler, scarcely reached the ears of her captors.

Making the muffler fast, Til motioned Bum Eyed Bob to pick the girl up and led the way to the poling boat. Despite desperate struggling, during which Til had to grasp her flailing legs and hold them together, she was forced into the casket, the upper part of the lid of which he had hacked off with his ax. The remainder of the lid was then secured with a few wraps of babiche line.

The poling boat immediately got under way. Hour after hour the three shoved upriver, keeping in the shallows at the edge of the mighty stream, taking advantage of the eddies that at times pushed them upstream at a faster rate than the main current coursed downstream. That's the Yukon.

Dawn found them fourteen miles upriver from Fortymile. Til motioned the Indians to keep poling. Relinquishing his own pole, he crept over the litter of duffel to the casket, from which two deep blue eyes blazed up into his own with a light that reminded him of the unholy fire of an opal. Gravely he undid the thick woolen muffler. "You can yell all you want to now," he said.

The deep blue eyes still blazed. "It's much nicer without the gag, Til," the Fireweed said with ominous calm. "Thank you for taking it off. I'm not going to yell—and your coffin makes a really comfortable bed."

Til bent closer, a hopeful gleam in his eyes. "Then you understand, Julie! You know why I'm taking you upriver!"

The hopeful gleam faded at her words. "Oh yes—I understand. You rotter! You bribed Siwashes that I've befriended to take me upriver. You think that because you're the youngest man that's counted a sourdough you'll get me —and the restaurant business along with me. It's a good business, Til—but you'll never get it! You want me to think you're taking me upriver for my own good! You're a bigger fool than I thought you were if you think you can get away with it! Look at this boat—what would happen to me, fastened in this coffin, if we'd hit a sweeper, or a planter, or a deadhead? I'd drown like a rat in a trap, and you'd probably get ashore!"

Til grinned. "Nope, Julie, you wouldn't drown. I could kind of swim alongside of you an' steer you to shore—or else maybe I could get straddle of the coffin and paddle us on upriver—to our gold. It's a good coffin, Julie—it won't leak."

"You think you're a hell of a man, Til Carter! And that you've pulled a great stunt! But let me tell you—when the real sourdoughs of Fortymile find I'm gone, they'll tear up the Yukon to find me! And when they find me, where will you and your Siwashes be?"

Til smiled down into the outraged face. "I reckon I'll be right with you, Julie—right there on our two claims on Bonanza. The sourdoughs are your friends. They're mine too. And by the time they overtake us you'll know that I'm the best friend you ever had, Julie. You don't know it now—but you will. And the two Siwashes I've got with me are your good friends too—you've helped 'em both out of troubles. Good God, if I wasn't figgering to be square with you, I wouldn't of picked those two Siwashes, would I? I had to do this, Julie. It was the only way I could get you up to the location. Damn it! You know gold! If you don't, you're a fool—you've lived all your life with gold!"

The blue eyes in the casket softened. "Will you raise the lid, Til?" she asked. "I'd like to stretch my legs." As he complied she heaved herself erect. "You told me," she said, "that I'm going up there and file whether I want to or not. All right, I'll go. I'm not afraid of you, Til—in the way I'd be afraid of some men. You're a sourdough at heart. But God forgive you if I'm wrong in my estimate of you. As I told you, when they find I'm gone, the men of Fortymile will hunt me—and they'll find me—you bet!"

Til's eyes narrowed and his voice sounded hard, gritty. "And by God, the quicker they find you, the better I'll like it—Pest! We've got a good start of 'em—we'll stake your claim, in spite of you, and then they can take you off my hands!"

The girl stretched a leg out of the casket, swung the other out, stood up, and stretched herself. "Got another pole?" she asked. "And isn't it about time we were landing for breakfast?"

Til motioned the Indians to beach the boat. They complied and made a fire. Knowing that the eyes of the girl were upon them, they moved awkwardly, as though half afraid.

Til glanced at the girl. "If you don't mind," he said, "I'll sleep while you eat. Wake me up when you're ready to start. There'll be no sense in trying to make these Siwashes pull out on me. Mathew believes me. He knows why you are here."

"Sleep, by all means," urged the girl. "And if it will make your sleep any easier, I promise not to try to escape."

"It will make it easier. I'm dead tired. Give me an hour."

It is possible that a white woman interrogated an Indian about the motive or intent of a white man. If so, Til Carter never knew. He slept.

Awakened at the end of his hour by the sound of a soft voice, he heard the girl say: "It's time to get up, Til. Here's a cup of tea—and some bannocks the Siwashes cooked. I recommend the tea."

His eyes opened to meet the deep blue eyes above him. "Yeah, I'll get up," he said. "Where's the tea?"

She brought him the tea and watched him drink it in gulps.

"Let's get going," he said. "We don't want those Forty-milers on our tail till you get located on the best claim you ever heard of."

On the boat, poling up the river, the girl made her way to Til's side. "You dared a lot—for me," she said. "If you've really made a strike."

Til continued to pole the boat. "For you? Hell, forget that! It's for old Tim Condon—your dad! He grubstaked me! I had to make good. An' the only way to make good was to kidnap you, because you didn't have sense enough to believe me."

The girl edged closer. "Then you don't care for me at all, Til?"

"Hell, no! Why should I? God knows you've made me trouble enough—what with having to pull out of Fortymile

177

almost as soon as I got there. I had to get this outfit together —Siwashes and all—and kidnap you and pull out in middle of the night. You're just like Bettles claimed you always were—the Pest! But I owe it to old Tim. I'll file you on a million-dollar claim—and then—to hell with you!"

"Do you want me to crawl back into my coffin, or can I sit around?"

"You can sit around any damn place you like, just so you don't pester me. Go pester the Siwashes—they're paid for it."

The girl made her way to the after end of the boat, where she sat gazing pensively into the water.

Late that evening they landed at Larue's flat. Before they landed Til edged over to the girl, who sat beside old Mathew. "We're going to camp on Larue's townsite to-night," he explained. "Are you going to raise hell, or aren't you? I guess we've seen enough of each other to know both of us are honest."

The deep blue eyes stabbed Til's gaze. "Yes," the girl said, "I think we have. I won't raise hell."

Til smiled grimly. "You're all right, Pest. I hate you for what you've put me through, but——"

The words were taken out of his teeth. "You hate me! Why, you—you chechako! What do I give a damn whether you hate me or not? I know Joe Larue—and Harper. A word from me and they'd do just what any other sourdough would do—kill you!"

"Yeah," grinned Til. "Maybe. But killing works both ways. Anyhow, I'm not worrying. You've given me your word—and that's plenty for me."

Together they walked up to the trading post that was less than half completed. Joe Larue met them before a fire of brightly burning jackpine. "Well, damn if it ain't the Fireweed! An' Til Carter too! What did you do, Til—persuade her that you got a strike on Rabbit Crick?"

Before Til could open his mouth, the girl answered: "Yes, Joe, he did. I want to buy a lot on your townsite to build a restaurant on. What have you got?" Til stared at her, open-mouthed, as Larue beamed.

"I'll tell you, Miss—er—Fireweed——"

"You can forget the 'Miss' part of it, Joe—don't be a fool just because you want to sell a lot."

"But—I don't want to sell none! That's what I was gittin' at. Wait till I git the plat—it come sence Til was down here —an' he's got two corner lots to locate. I want you to pick you out the best lot in the hull outfit—if Til will hold off locatin' hisn till you do—an' I'll give you a deed to it."

The girl smiled. "But why should you do that, Joe? Townsite lots are to sell—not to give away."

"Yeah—but you're different! It's a cinch that if Til hadn't made no strike, you wouldn't be comin' up here with him. Why the rest of 'em ain't here ain't none of my lookout— they'll be along, if you come! An', believe me, I'm goin' up along with you in the mornin' an' git in on it too! But with a strike on Rabbit Crick, my lots is goin' hell a-whoopin'. So I want to git you in on a good un!"

"But I'll buy a lot, Joe——"

"No you won't—not on my townsite, you won't! God A'mighty, it would make the place if you'd come! Start a Public Forsome—er whatever you call it—like you've got down there. I'll put up the buildin' fer you, with a big room fer the meetin's an' another fer the restaurant. An' it won't cost you a damn ounce—'cause if you're here, all Fortymile will be here—an' don't you fergit it! Here's the plat—pick you out a lot!"

The girl turned to Til. "It's your turn to pick first. Joe said you had two corner lots coming."

Til grinned. "Go ahead and take your pick—I'll take the next two." The girl selected a corner. Til located his lots and followed Larue to his tent.

"What makes you think there's a stampede coming through?" he asked.

"Christ—the Fireweed's here, along of you, ain't she? You can't fool her! She's jest about a jump an' a half ahead of all the rest of Fortymile—an' if *she's* come upriver, by God, they'll all come, an' we're made! I didn't put no faith in you claimin' you'd made a strike on Rabbit Crick when you come through here—nor I didn't believe Carmack neither, but if the Fireweed believes you, by God, it must be so!"

XXII

The Fireweed Stakes a Claim

The following morning, with Larue accompanying them, they pushed the poling boat up the Klondike to the mouth of Bonanza. The creek was too small to allow its ascent with the heavy poling boat, so they walked up the valley toward location.

Larue was still frankly skeptical. "It don't stand to reason there's gold on this here bottom," he said, indicating the wide sweep of the valley with a wave of the arm. "No one but a Godam klooch tamer would figger there was. It's them fast-runnin' gravelly cricks in the hills where the gold is. Carmack's a damn fool if he thinks the sourdoughs is goin' to stampede to a moose pasture."

The man paused and glanced at Julie. "But you're a sourdough, Fireweed, an' a damn sight smarter'n most of them old-timers—an' you're stampedin' up here. Howcome you fell fer this here strike Til claims he made on Rabbit Crick? I shore didn't when he told me about it—him an' Carmack both."

Julie laughed and slanted a glance at Til. "I didn't believe him at first either. But he put up a mighty strong argument, so I came along."

They were then possibly a mile and a half above the mouth of the creek.

Til grinned. "I didn't do any panning this low down," he said. "But I'll bet you ten ounces against another lot in your townsite that if you'd bust the sod right where you're standing, and fill a pan, you'll pan a dollar."

"You're on!" laughed Larue. "An' if I pan fifty cents, I'll give you the lot! An' if I pan a dollar in the grass roots, you all can go on up to where you're goin'—that'll be good enough for me—I'll locate right here!"

Larue filled his pan, and all walked to the river and watched as he rotated the water and flirted out the dross. The Fireweed, her dark blue eyes alight with excitement, was the first to see the color as Larue raked the coarse gravel out with his fingers.

"Oh!" she cried, dancing up and down and clapping her hands. "It's there! It's there!"

Larue's hands were trembling with excitement as he removed the last of the gravel and all stood looking down at the yellow gold. "What'll she go?" asked Til with a grin.

"Two dollars, if there's a grain!" cried the girl. "I'm going to locate here too."

Larue looked up, white-faced. "You can have it, Miss—er —Fireweed. I'll file either up or down."

"No—what do you take me for? This is yours! I'll go up or down!"

Til slipped a strong hand under the girl's arm. "You'll go up," he said in a voice that reached only her ears. "With me. Your location is Number 2 above. Mine's Number 1. I brought you this far, Pest—why not go to the end of the trail?"

The firm white chin flew up, and eyes of deepest blue focused on the steel-gray eyes of the speaker. The red lips parted for a quick retort, but the retort did not come. For long moments their glances held. Til felt the firm young muscles of the girl's arm stiffen, even as the girl felt the firmer grip of strong fingers. Then the muscles of the arm relaxed, the blue eyes lowered, and a wondrous smile curved the imperious red lips. "To the end of the trail, Til? Do you mean—to the end of the trail?"

The Indians were humped with Larue over the pan with its yellow bottom. "*Pest!*" whispered the man, white-lipped. "Come on—let's go!" He turned to the others. "Mathew, you and Bob better locate in next to Larue. It's good stuff. The Fireweed and I are going on up the crick."

Bum Eyed Bob looked from one to the other, his dark eyes coming to rest on the face of the Fireweed. "W'at you t'ink?" he asked bluntly.

The girl laughed lightly—a laugh that was altogether good to hear. It held a note that caused Larue to look up sharply from his pan. He grinned knowingly.

"By God, you'll be a pair to draw to!" he said, and his eyes returned to the gold.

The girl answered the Indian. "Til and I are going on up the creek. You heard what he said. Wait for us here."

Bum Eyed Bob nodded and pointed a thick finger at Til. "Heem Godam good mans. You go. Dat Bite Ear Finley— by Godams, he no good!"

The two walked on almost in silence. Once Til paused to point out the form of a cow moose, dimly visible through the yellowing leaves of a birch copse; and again, at a spring, they stopped to drink. Abruptly the girl spoke, her eyes on the lean form stretched for the moment on the sod:

"You're so fine, Til—when you're out of a camp."

"Yeah?" he questioned with a smile. "Well, there's times for this—an' times for that."

"Do you want to be just like all the other old-timers?"

"They're good men, aren't they?" came the quick retort.

The girl answered nothing, and they pushed on.

An hour later Til paused and pointed to a lone birch tree that showed far ahead. "There's Discovery," he said. "That's where Carmack and Skookum Jim made their strike. My stakes are in just above—and yours will be next to mine. Take a good look at the valley—as she is. She'll never look the same again. In a few years, when we pull out of here, she'll look like a gravel dump. We've walked over millions in gold."

Arriving at the location, Til proceeded to wash pan after pan from the girl's claim. Going only into the grass roots, he took out, from widely separated spots on both sides of the creek, a total of seven ounces, which he presented to her with a flourish. "There you are—the tangible evidence of your million!"

The girl stood fondling the blue cotton bandanna that held the gold as she stared at the man who stood smiling before her. "Oh, Til!" she cried, her eyes flashing. "This is it! This is the big strike the old-timers said was sure to come! Oh, I'm—I'm so proud of you!"

"You called me a fool for hitting out upriver alone," he reminded her. "And when I got back to Fortymile and told you about this strike, you accused me of being either drunk or crazy."

The girl nodded, and her eyes dropped to the blue bandanna that was heavy with gold in her hand. "I was the fool, Til," she said. "But don't rub it in—please."

"I won't. You don't need to worry. I'm going to get busy and pan about a hundred ounces out of my claim here, and hit back to Fortymile and pull off the doggonedest jamboree I ever had. The sourdoughs know I was broke when I walked out of Bergman's the other night. I didn't mention this strike then—I couldn't until I'd seen your stake planted on this location. I owed that to old Tim. But I can tell 'em now—and when I show 'em the gold they'll believe me. We'll pull off one hell of an orgy—drink up Bergman's liquor and swing the dance gals high!"

"Can't you ever be serious?"

"I'll try sometime and see. In fact, I'll try right now! We've got a job to do. I'll get out your stakes and shape 'em up and dig the holes—but you've got to plant 'em. If I help, that's no one's business but ours. Anyhow, the law don't say you can't be helped."

In a nearby thicket Til found and shaped two stakes to conform to the legal requirements. He dug the holes, and the girl set them while he tamped the ground at their bases.

"Now," he said when the stakes were in place, "we'll mark 'em. I named my claim the Moosehorn. You don't have to name yours if you don't want to. You can jest call it Number 2."

The girl was gazing pensively at the far hills. "I think I'll name mine the Coffin," she said.

Til laughed. "Fine! And I'll bring the coffin up an' set it on your claim! It'll make a handy box to keep your tools in!"

"I was wondering," the Fireweed said, her unsmiling eyes still on the hills, "whether this spot might not be the grave of high hopes."

"Hell—no!" cried Til exuberantly. "You'll take out a million—maybe two or three! If she's like this in the grass roots, what'll she be on bedrock? Pest—we'll see a hundred dollars washed out of a pan!"

"I wasn't thinking of the gold," answered the girl, balancing the bandanna in her hand. "Gold isn't everything," she added wistfully.

"It's what we're up here for," retorted the man gruffly. "I've paid my debt to Tim Condon."

"Yes," answered the girl. "You're square, Til. Squarer than most men would have been—the way I've treated you. But—how about Tim's daughter?"

"That's what I want to know," rasped the man. "What you trying to do—play both ends against the middle?"

"What do you mean?" cried the girl, hot blood flooding her cheeks as her eyes met his burning gaze.

"I'll tell you what I mean—if you don't know! I mean I love you! There hasn't ben a single day nor a single night of the year I spent out in the hills that I didn't think about you and try to figure how you'd look, and what you'd be like when you really grew up. And my wildest guess never come anywhere near the truth. When I stood in the restaurant door the other day and saw you sitting there at your desk, I knew I was looking at the most beautiful woman in the world. Back in Bergman's I didn't believe Ear Bitin' Finley when he said you were his girl—an' that he had a date with you. But when I told you I wouldn't bother you long because I heard you had a date, and you said I must have been talking to Finley, I knew it was true.

"It hurt like hell, Julie—to find that out. But hurt or no hurt, I still owed my debt to Tim Condon. And I paid it the only way I could pay it, when you wouldn't listen to me—I kidnaped you an' brought you up here and planted you on top of a fortune.

"Now the debt's paid. A woman's got the right to pick the man she wants. An' if you and he mind your own business, I won't be bothering you any more—and you're not to bother me any more, either."

The girl's face was partly turned from him, her eyes on the rimrocks. "What do you mean—bother you?" she asked in a low, peculiar voice.

"You know what I mean! Like back there before we left Larue and the Siwashes—you asked me if I meant 'to the end of the trail.' And when we were resting there at the spring you said I was so fine when I was away from the camps. And a few minutes ago, when you said, 'Gold isn't everything'—and asked me 'how about Tim's daughter?' It isn't just the words—it's the way you say 'em, and the look in your eyes, and all. It's enough to drive a man crazy—a man that cares! It's too damn bad Tim Condon couldn't have lived a little longer! Tim had sense, and he'd have killed Ear Bitin' Finley before he'd had him hangin' around you! The sourdoughs all claim you're smart. But I'm telling you you're a damn fool!"

The girl laughed—a silvery, ringing peal of laughter that was caught up by the far rims. "You're a wonderful lover,

Til! I wonder if any woman ever had love growled at her before? But I accept—dear. We'll be married as soon as you can find time to come down to the Mission."

"No, we won't! I'm not playing second fiddle to Ear Bitin' Finley!"

"Just a little boy—and such a bad little boy, who drinks whisky and gambles, and jumps to conclusions, and does things little boys ought not to do."

"What do you mean—jumps to conclusions? He told me you were his girl, and he warned me to keep away from the restaurant. You had a date with him, didn't you? And the only reason he didn't keep it was because I mussed up his map so his own mother couldn't have told him from a link of boloney. And when I told you about doing it, there wasn't anything casual or disinterested in the way you asked me if I'd killed him—not by a long shot there wasn't! Your voice and the look in your eyes told me that you were mighty interested in the welfare of Ear Bitin' Finley. It's all right with me. But don't you think for a minute that just because I've planted my stakes on a million-dollar claim you can throw him over and take up with me just to get in on the million! My debt to Tim Condon is paid. And there's plenty of gold between those stakes of yours for you and Finley both. If there isn't, there's nothing to prevent him from locating another claim on the crick. There's plenty of room here yet—if you tell him to hurry."

The girl faced him, her cheeks flaming and her blue eyes flashing fire. "Til Carter, you're a damn fool! And it would serve you right if I never married you—after that! But I'm going to—so there! You've had your say. Now you sit down there with your back against that stake while I have mine. And don't you interrupt me till I'm through, either! It's true that I did have a date with Finley that afternoon. I hoped I could get him to admit that he murdered my brother. He believes I have a secret that he wants—the location of the gold cache on the Jim River claim. I've let him think so—

kept stringing him along, hoping to get the evidence against him that will hang him.

"As you know, I was living in Bettles with the Kempers while Daddy and Davey worked the Jim River claim. Finley and Harmon had a claim on a crick just a little way out from Bettles. I detested Finley. He spent most of his time hanging around the Swede's. He was always drunk, or half drunk, and when I'd meet him sometimes on my way to or from school he would leer at me in a way that sent cold shivers shooting along my spine.

"Just a short time before you and Uncle Gordon came up on the *North Star*, Daddy came down to Bettles to see how I was getting along. He and Uncle Gordon were old friends, so when Uncle Gordon stepped off the steamboat they hit for the Swede's." The girl paused and smiled. "That's the first time I ever saw you, and I thought you were horrid—to laugh as you did when I dropped that sack of flour."

Til grinned. "And you called me a chechako and wouldn't let me help you hoist it back onto your shoulders."

"And you called me a redhead!"

"Well, I was right, wasn't I?"

"Anyhow," the girl continued, "Finley was in the saloon at the time, and he heard Daddy tell Uncle Gordon that he and Davey had a thousand ounces cached on the Jim River claim.

"Before he left the claim Daddy told Davey to move the cache after he had gone. He knew he'd do considerable drinking with the boys in Bettles, and he was afraid he might get to talking too much and reveal the location of the cache. Daddy told me later that he remembered that while he and Uncle Gordon sat at a table talking in the saloon that day, Finley lay sprawled over a nearby table, apparently dead drunk. He didn't believe that Finley could have overheard their conversation. But after Daddy died, Finley showed up in Fortymile and he told me he did hear what Daddy said about having a thousand ounces cached on the claim, but didn't pay much attention to it. He told me that when he went back to his claim that evening he casually mentioned the thousand-ounce cache to Harmon—and the next morning Harmon was gone. Finley said that he took out after him, figuring that Harmon had hit for Jim River to rob that cache. He changed his story later, as you'll see.

"You know more than I do about what happened up there on the Jim River—about finding Harmon dying on the floor of the cabin with his head bashed in, about you and Uncle Gordon taking him down to the doctor, and his dying before you got him there—about Daddy's unsuccessful search for Davey, and how you and Uncle Gordon found him with his leg smashed among the rocks where he had shot that bear.

"Daddy said that you three saw Finley in Coldfoot when you were on your way up to the claim, and that Crim said that Finley told him he was hunting for Harmon, who, he claimed, had robbed their cache down near Bettles and pulled out. Daddy died believing that Harmon had tried to rob the Jim River cache and that Davey had bashed his head in and then pulled out, thinking he had killed Harmon. Daddy thought that Davey had intended to hide out until he returned from Bettles and that he had met with an accident that killed him."

Til nodded. "Yes—and it was better that way. Here's something you don't know, because neither Bettles nor I ever told Tim. Soon after we found Harmon unconscious on the floor of the cabin, Tim went out to feed the dogs. Bettles managed to pour some whisky down Harmon's throat, and he come to for just a few seconds—long enough to mutter that Finley was burning Davey with a candle, and that he, Harmon, tried to stop him. Then he passed out and never uttered another word.

"Bettles and I agreed never to let Tim know of this, because he would then realize that Finley had heard him mention the cache that day in the Swede's place and would always blame himself for Davey's torture.

"As a matter of fact, Bettles believes that Finley did overhear everything Tim said there in the saloon—that he wasn't near as drunk as he pretended to be." He paused and regarded the girl with a puzzled glance. "But what I can't see is why Finley should think that you know the location of the Jim River cache."

"I'm coming to that," the girl said, drying the tears that had welled from her eyes at mention of Davey's torture. "As I told you, a month or so after Daddy died, Finley showed up in Fortymile. I knew that both he and Harmon had disappeared from Bettles about the time you and Daddy and Uncle Gordon hit out for the Jim River. And later, when Daddy mentioned seeing Finley in Coldfoot, I figured right then that he and not Harmon was at the bottom of Davey's disappearance. I knew Harmon as a sort of non-entity—a shiftless sort of chechako who was completely dominated by Finley. So when Finley stepped into the restaurant that day, I had all I could do to keep from shooting him on the spot. I could have done it, too. I always keep a loaded revolver under the counter. But I got hold of myself.

"Finley located a claim up near the Kink, but spent most of his time hanging around Bergman's saloon. He ate at the restaurant, coming in at odd hours when no one else was around. I wondered at that—decided there must be some reason for it—so I encouraged him by talking with him, hoping that he might let slip something that would give me a clue to Davey's disappearance. He didn't suspect that I believed that he had done away with Davey. He told me that he figured that Harmon had gone to the Jim River claim and tried to make Davey tell where the cache was, and that they had a fight and that Davey killed Harmon.

"He said that he hung around the Coldfoot country and ran onto a prospector named Pete Jones who had a claim on the Jim River above Daddy's claim, and that this Jones told him that a short time before Daddy returned from Bettles, Davey had given him a letter to post at Coldfoot. That the letter was addressed to me, and that Davey told him it contained the description of the location of the new cache.

"Then in the spring, when Davey didn't show up and Daddy sold out to Crim and went on down to Bettles, Finley says he hung around to see if Daddy would come back or send someone after the gold in the cache. He brazenly admitted that he had intended to rob whoever got the gold. Then when he heard of Daddy's death he came to Fortymile to make a deal with me. He proposed that I tell him where the cache was and he would get the gold and divide it with me. I asked him why he could expect me to trust him to bring the gold back and divide it, after he'd told me he had intended to rob whoever went up there after the gold, and he replied that if he'd have pulled off that robbery, no one would have known who did it—but in this case I would know that he was the only one who could have the gold, and if he didn't show up with it, I could notify the United States marshal. I pretended to be dumb enough to accept his explanation, and kept stalling him along, not letting him know that I knew no more about the location of the cache than he did—always hoping that he would say something that would incriminate him.

"He became impatient and offered to go and get the gold for a quarter, and finally even a fifth, of it. He even proposed that I go up there with him after the gold—even offered to marry me and take me up there. I kept stalling him off—and the more I stalled, the more impatient he got. It seemed to be his one obsession—to go up to the Jim River and get that thousand ounces of gold.

"Just the day before you came back I figured he might be gold-crazy enough to admit killing Davey. So I told him that I was too busy to go up to the Jim River—that I wasn't much interested in that gold anyway, as I was making good money right there in the restaurant. I told him that I wasn't satisfied with his story that Davey killed Harmon—that I suspected that he, Finley, had killed them both.

"At first he swore and blustered around and denied that he knew anything about the killings. I just shrugged and told him I didn't believe a word he said. That I knew he was lying about a letter this man Jones was supposed to have posted in Coldfoot, because I knew that Davey wouldn't have been fool enough to tell Jones that the letter described the location of the new cache. I told him that the only way he could possibly know that Davey had written me about the cache would be for Davey himself to have told him when he was trying to make him tell where the cache was. I told him that the uncertainty of Davey's death weighed heavily on my mind, night and day, and that if I could only know for a certainty about it, so far as I was concerned he could have all the gold in the cache.

"He seemed to be considering what I said, when a couple of customers came in and took seats at a table. As the girl took their order Finley leaned close and whispered that I couldn't do a damn thing about it if there were no witnesses to hear what he had to say. He said he'd tell me all about it if I'd tell him where to find the cache. I agreed to give him every bit of information I had about the cache—which, of course, is exactly nothing, as I never got any letter from Davey about it.

"But I insisted that he tell me about Davey first. I pointed out that he could depend on me keeping my word, but that I certainly couldn't depend on him. Other customers began to drift in for supper, and he told me that if I'd be alone in the restaurant the following afternoon, he'd come in and tell me the whole story. I knew then that I had hit the nail on the head—that Davey had lied to Finley about writing me the location of the cache, hoping that if Finley knew the robbery could be checked he might not try to pull it off.

"That evening I slipped over to the detachment and talked to Corporal Downey. You noticed that my desk stands close to the lunch counter. Well, there are two wide shelves under the counter, where we keep the dishes. When you came in that day, I was expecting Finley any moment. Corporal Downey was lying flat on one of those shelves, behind the curtain. And Constable Peters was in the cellar with his ear glued to a hole we had bored through the floor just behind the desk. They heard all you said—but, of course, Finley never showed up."

As the girl concluded, Til Carter was on his feet, his arms about her shoulders, drawing her close against his chest. Their lips met in a long, lingering kiss.

"I was a damn fool, Julie," he murmured as he gazed down into the eyes of deepest blue. "I ought to have known you'd never fall for a big fourflusher like Finley. But you sure had me seeing red. Ear Bitin' Finley murdered Davey, all right. You leave him to me."

The girl wriggled free. "No, no! Don't kill him, Til! It would be murder—and they'd hang you! Then where would I be?"

"They won't hang me. I'm not going to commit a murder. But I've got a hunch that Ear Bitin' Finley's going to meet up with hard luck. Come on. What's the date? We've got to burn the location on these stakes. And I haven't got anything to burn in with but my knife. That'll cost you a new knife, Pest—because it'll take all the temper out."

Til built a little fire and, heating his knife blade time and time again, burned in the inscription:

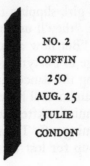

NO. 2
COFFIN
250
AUG. 25
JULIE
CONDON

When it was completed, they stood together and took one last, long look around. "You're going back to Fortymile, Julie," Til said. "I'm staying on here. I've got a lot of stuff to pack up from the poling boat, and a winter camp to make. We'll build our cabin right here where the two claims join. We'll go on back to the mouth of the crick now and unload the boat, then you and the Siwashes can go back in her. Wait a minute, though, till I scratch a note to old Bettles. I told the boys that I only panned out sixty ounces in twelve months—which was true. I couldn't say anything about the sixty or seventy ounces I panned here in two days and a half —or they'd all have been up here and beat you to location. I owed my debt to Tim. But now I want 'em all to come boiling in! It won't be a long note I'm going to scratch—just this." He took a pencil from his pocket, and on a scrap of birch bark he wrote:

> *Bettles, Fortymile:*
> *The Fireweed will tell you.*
>
> *Til Carter*

"You slip that to old Bettles when you get back to Fortymile—and tell him the dope. Tell him and Camillo and Moosehide and Swiftwater and Burr MacShane to pass up the lower stretch and file up here above us. The gravel's better and we'll all be together. They'll know why I didn't let 'em in on it. I couldn't—with you having to run a restaurant for your living. I'd have died first. They'll understand."

"Yes," answered the girl, slipping the bit of bark beneath the bosom of her shirt, "they'll understand." Then she shot him a sidewise glance. "But how about that grand jamboree you were going to stage in Fortymile—drink up all of Bergman's whisky and swing the dance girls high?"

Til grinned. "That jamboree'll have to wait, Pest. I've got other things on my mind. After we're married, maybe, you'll give me an evening off. Then I'll get the boys together an' we'll make up for lost time."

The girl giggled. "Okay, Til. Only you've got to promise to give me fair warning, so I can have the rolling pin ready when you come home."

They walked back, passing the new locations of Larue and the two Indians. Almost at the junction of the rivers, the girl halted. She had pulled the tam from her head, and Til had been watching the play of the westerly sunlight in the red hair. She faced about. "Til," she said, "when are we going to be married?"

Til smiled and rumpled the flaming curls with his fingers. "Just as soon as I can get the shack up. We've got to have some place to live. We'll be married at Larue's new town-site—all the boys will be up here, an' they'll want to be in on it. Father Judge will be up there too—because when the sour-doughs hear what you have to tell 'em, there won't be any more Fortymile."

They found Larue and the Indians waiting at the boat. Til's outfit was piled on the bank. Larue spoke:

"Say, Til—if you're figgerin' to stay here, why not all drop down to my place tonight an' let the Fireweed go back with the Siwashes?"

"That," said Til, "is what I figured on doing."

"But," cried the girl, "I won't take your poling boat! You'll need it!"

"Ain't no need to," said Larue. "I kin git you a canoe. An' you kin make better time down-river than you could in a polin' boat. 'Tain't only forty, fifty mile."

The rest of the day was spent in planning the combined restaurant and community house—and in arranging with Larue for its building. And early the following morning the girl headed down-river in the canoe, with the two Indians paddling.

XXIII

The Stampede Is On

Ear Bitin' Finley awoke from a long sleep. He wondered vaguely where he was. He couldn't see. Try as he might, he couldn't open his eyes. Yet he sensed it was daylight. He must have got awful drunk. He remembered taking many drinks in Bergman's saloon. Prying an eyelid apart with his fingers, he looked at his watch. It was nine-thirty.

He lay back on the half-empty duffel bag that served as a pillow and strove to recall yesterday's happenings. He remembered being in Bergman's saloon and taking numerous drinks. Then—he had a fight. Gradually his benumbed brain began to function. There was some guy named Til. They were having his funeral—only it wasn't a regular funeral—and then the guy came to and everyone beat it. They went back, and this guy said he was going to see the Fireweed, and he had jumped him about it—had warned him to stay away from the Fireweed. And then—— Who the hell was this Til Carter, anyhow? He had never heard of him. He himself was Ear Bitin' Finley—known from the Koyukuk to Fortymile as a bad man. What had happened? His mouth hurt, and his exploratory finger found the vacancy left by two missing front teeth. He knew then that he had been licked in a fight—and properly licked—but who was Til Carter? Some punk he had never even heard of until yesterday. But the sourdoughs seemed to know him. They were holding his funeral—but hell—Til Carter wasn't dead.

Ear Bitin' Finley had swung his brag wide in Fortymile. He knew that none of the sourdoughs would call his bluff—except for cause. He had been careful to give them no cause—so he was tolerated in the Fortymile camp. And the Fireweed knew this Til Carter. He remembered the look in her eyes when she stood in the doorway of the saloon and Bettles told her they were holding his funeral. This Carter looked like a kid. It had looked like a cinch to make his bluff good. But it hadn't worked out—and Ear Bitin' Finley mumbled an oath from between his puffed lips.

To hell with his claim up at the Kink! That had been filed as a blind. But—where did he stand now? He knew that Tim Condon had never returned to Jim River after losing his leg and selling his claim to Crim. But the cache was there—the Fireweed knew where it was. Davey had told him, just before he died, about mailing her the new location of the cache. She had offered to tell him all she knew about it if he would tell about the killing of Davey. Well—why not? She couldn't do a damn thing about it if he did tell her. It would be her word against his—and he could tell 'em he never told her he killed her brother—it don't stand to reason a man would tell it around if he'd murdered a man. The police wouldn't believe her—and they couldn't prove it, if they did. A thousand ounces of dust—that's sixteen thousand dollars! It's easy to get the best of a woman! She was to tell him about the cache yesterday. But this Til Carter had come along and spilt the beans. Well—she could tell him today as well as yesterday—if he could catch her alone.

The man got up, pried his eyes apart, and dressed. He elaborately patched and crisscrossed his face with tape, till he looked like a hospital case. Then he went down to the

Aurora Borealis restaurant. The Chink took his order. He ate slowly, deliberately, awaiting the time the Fireweed would appear. Ten o'clock passed. She was ordinarily as regular as the clock. This day she didn't come. The Chink went to her cabin to waken her. He came back wide-eyed. She wasn't there!

Guarded questioning on the part of Ear Bitin' Finley brought out the fact that an Indian had come to the restaurant at midnight, telling the girl that his wife was sick, and she had immediately left with him. She hadn't returned.

Ear Bitin' Finley finished his breakfast and sauntered down to the Indian village. "The damn klootch must be pretty sick to keep her this long," he muttered.

An Indian was twining a net on the riverbank. Ear Bitin' Finley approached him. "What house sick woman in?" he asked, his eyes traveling over the hotchpotch of shacks, cabins, and tepees that was the Indian village.

The Indian shook his head. "No seek 'oman," he said.

"Wasn't there a sick woman here in the Siwash town last night?"

"I ain' know 'bout no seek 'oman."

"Some Siwash come up to the restaurant at midnight an' got the Fireweed fer to tend some sick woman. What do you know about that?"

The Indian laid his twine aside and considered. "Sump'n fonny. Las' night w'ite mans buy my pole boat. Pay dus'. Mat'ew an' Bum Eye Bob tak' boat to Mat'ew house." He paused and indicated a hut on the riverbank a short distance away. "Tie boat oop an' load plent' grub—load w'ite man packsack—an' coffin. Me—I'm t'ink dat dam' fonny—w'ite mans tak' coffin 'long in pole boat. I'm lay in de weeds an' watch. Bum Eye Bob stay by de boat. By-m-by, w'ite mans com' 'long w'at buy my pole boat. Bum Eye Bob grab um, t'row um down. Den dey git oop. Pret' queek Mat'ew com' an' Fireweed 'long wit'. Bum Eye Bob grab Fireweed. W'ite mans fix muffler on Fireweed face so can't holler. She fight lak hell—but dat don' do no good. Tak' her down to pole boat. Put een de coffin. Gon' 'way, upriv'—w'ite mans, Fireweed, Mat'ew, Bum Eye Bob."

"What fer lookin' was this white man?" asked Ear Bitin' Finley.

"Yong mans—beeg tall—no w'iskers on de face—no fat on de belly. Mat'ew call 'Til', w'en buy my pole boat."

Ear Bitin' Finley turned away, walked a few steps, and faced about. "You stay where yer at," he ordered. "They'll be more white men down here, d'reckly, askin' you about this here night's work! Hell's goin' to be poppin' in Fortymile when I git to Bergman's! It looks like this here Til Carter's earnt hisself a lynchin'!"

Ear Bitin' Finley proceeded at once to Bergman's saloon. It was nearly noon, and half a dozen of the sourdoughs were standing at the bar.

All glanced up at his approach, but nobody commented upon his patched appearance—black eyes, swollen lips, and tape-bridged nose.

"Drink up, an' have one," he invited, tossing a gold sack onto the bar. "It looks like this here Til Carter give me a trimmin' yesterday."

"You wouldn't have no trouble makin' a jury believe it," grinned old Bettles. "Til's fast! We-all didn't know he could fight."

"He kin fight, all right," scowled Ear Bitin' Finley. "An' that ain't all he kin do."

"Meanin'?" asked Camillo Bill.

"Meanin' he kin kidnap women."

"What did he do now?" asked Bettles, chuckling. "Go down to the dance hall an' grab him off a cabinful?"

"He's stole the Fireweed an' headed upriver with a couple of Siwashes an' a polin' boat."

"Stole the Fireweed!" cried Moosehide Charlie. "Yer crazy as hell! No one could steal the Fireweed!"

"If them two's gone off upriver together," opined Bettles,

"it's because she wanted to go. An' fer one—I'm damn glad of it! Them two'd ort to hit it off right lively."

"Is that so?" asked Ear Bitin' Finley, a sneer in his voice. "Well, put this in yer pipe an' smoke it—a Siwash comes down to the restaurant las' night an' tells the Fireweed his woman's sick. The Fireweed goes with him, an' when they git to the Siwash camp, she's grabbed off by a big Siwash, an' Til Carter gags her with a muffler, so she can't yell, an' they chuck her in that there coffin, which it's loaded into a polin' boat with a lot of grub—an' with the two Siwashes— the one that went an' fetched her an' the one that grabbed her—they all pull out upriver."

Camillo Bill grinned. "Sounds reasonable an' natural," he said with elaborate sarcasm. "Did you stand around an' look on while it was comin' off, er jest dream it?"

"I didn't do neither one!" cried Ear Bitin' Finley, so vehemently that, despite the apparent absurdity of the yarn, the sourdoughs were half convinced. "A Siwash that seen the whole play told me—an' he's the one offen which Til Carter boughten the polin' boat. He thought things looked funny, an' he laid in the weeds an' watched. He's down by the river right now makin' a net."

The sourdoughs eyed one another. "What in hell would Til be hittin' back upriver fer?" speculated Camillo Bill. "He jest come down from there, an' he only panned sixty ounces in a year."

"An' what the hell would he want of the Fireweed—if she didn't want to go along?" asked Moosehide. "If a man's huntin' trouble, all he's got to do is take a woman where she don't want to be at—an' the Fireweed—my God!"

"By Christ," vociferated Burr MacShane, "if he's gone an' stole the Fireweed, it's goin' to be jest too damn bad fer him! She's never reniged on helpin' anyone out—white, red, or yaller—when they needed it! She gives us hell sometimes —but mebbe we got it comin'! Tellin' you about me—I'm hittin' their trail! An' if things ain't right, Til's goin' to damn well need that coffin! 'Cause there's goin' to be a real funeral somewheres upriver—an' Til Carter'll be in on it—in the 'title role,' as them show bills down to Seattle used to say! Who's goin' along?" MacShane challenged the sourdoughs with his eyes.

"Hell, yes! I'll go!" cried a voice from the group that had been augmented by new arrivals.

"Yer dam' whistlin'!" cried Moosehide. "We'll all go!"

Camillo Bill nodded thoughtfully and eyed old Bettles. "Looks like we got to go," he said.

Bettles poured himself a drink and motioned for the others to do likewise. "There ain't no use of gettin' het up," he opined. "Either this here thing happened er it didn't. If Til loaded a polin' boat with grub, an' his coffin, an' the Fireweed, an' a couple of Siwashes, an' went upriver, we kin easy find it out. He had to git the grub at the A.C. There'll be two Siwashes missin' from the village. Him, an' his pack, an' his coffin will be gone from his shack. The Fireweed will be missin'. An' there's a polin' boat to be accounted fer.

"If he went back upriver, he went fer a purpose. That wouldn't be nothin' else than gold. He told us he didn't do so good. We're friends of his—an' he knows it. I figure he's square. I know him better'n any of you. I wintered with him on the Jim River. If he ain't square, we'll damn soon know.

"We'll git busy an' git the facts in the case. Finley, you go to the river an' fetch that Siwash up here that you claim told you this here yarn. Moosehide, you go to the A.C. an' find out if Til Carter bought an outfit of grub. Camillo, you go down to the recorder's an' find out if Til filed him a location anywheres. Burr, you go down to Til's shack an' see if him an' his coffin is gone. An' I'll go over to the restaurant an' talk to the Chink. Let's git a-goin'."

A half hour later they once more assembled at Bergman's bar. Each man reported, and the evidence substantiated Ear

Bitin' Finley's story to a dot. Mike Two Bear reiterated what he had told Ear Bitin' Finley, and old Bettles summed up:

"It's a cinch we was wrong when we misdoubted Carmack an' Skookum Jim. They made a strike—or Til Carter wouldn't never of filed on Rabbit Crick. 'Gold's where you find it' has ben said all along—but we-all didn't heed the sayin', on account, mebbe, of Carmack bein' a squaw man an' not of no repute.

"Til Carter's filed Number One above Carmack's Discovery claim. He told us he'd panned out sixty ounces in twelve months in the hills—an' fer one, I believe him. He didn't say nothin' about Bonanza, er Rabbit Crick, whichever you want to call it. When a man don't let his friends in on a good thing, there's a reason. Either he's a son-of-a-bitch er he ain't. I don't figger Til Carter fer no son-of-a-bitch. So there must be a reason. I've ben doin' some figgerin'. We know Til was broke when he hit out into the hills a year ago. He blowed in all he had. How'd he git heeled fer that year-long trip upriver? Mebbe, I thinks, Tim Condon grubstaked him. So when I left the restaurant I goes down to the recorder's an' sees if there's a grubstake affydavit on file. There is. All right—Til could of filed fer Tim if he made a discovery strike—which he didn't—him comin' onto Rabbit Crick after Carmack had filed. So he couldn't file fer Tim—but he come down to slip the word to Tim to go on up an' file fer hisself. But Tim's dead—so he slips the Fireweed the word—an' she don't believe him, 'cause she's heard us pannin' Carmack fer a fool. An' she'd believe us! Of course she would! God, we're her men! We know Til went down an' had a talk with the Fireweed an' come back here kind of low in his mind. That was because she wouldn't believe he'd made a strike. So he done the only thing a man with his kind of guts could think of doin'—he kidnaped the Fireweed an' took her up to show her the gold in the gravel! An' I kin see now that his goin' broke in the stud game last

202

night was part of his scheme. Til's no damn fool. An' he plays a good game of stud. But he played that last deal of stud last night like a damn fool. He played it like that a-purpose to go broke—so he'd have an excuse fer quittin'."

Bettles paused and glanced into the tense faces about him. "Mebbe I'm wrong—but I've got a hundred ounces that says I'm right! There's a stampede headin' upriver today—an' by God, I'm on the head of it! It ain't only forty mile er so to the Klondike, an' only a little ways above the mouth to Rabbit Crick! An' here's another bet—I'll bet that before we git there we'll meet a Siwash comin' down with word fer us fellers to come on up an' git in on it! Boys, if I'm right, Til Carter done a man's job—an' a damn good man! Jesus! Kidnapin' the Fireweed!"

Ear Bitin' Finley had listened to the discourse with growing disapprobation. He wanted Til Carter out of the picture —and the farther out, the better. His acquaintance with the Fireweed told him that no man could thwart her to the extent of kidnaping her and get away with it. He counted on her for an ally. Hadn't she played up to him all summer? Though not once had she ever been alone with him. She knew what he wanted to know, and when he got that out of her—to hell with her! Then she and the damned Forty-mile sourdoughs could go to hell! He'd go back on the Koyukuk and get the thousand ounces out of Condon's cache and sit pretty.

He voiced disapproval. "What I claim," he vociferated, "this here Til Carter grabs off the pick of Fortymile 'cause he wanted him a woman!"

Camillo Bill slanted him a bleak grin. "Be you in on the stampede?" he asked. "If so, you'll have a chanct to tell that to Til Carter."

"Yer damn right I'm in on it!" announced Ear Bitin' Finley, a sudden thought coming into his mind. "I've got my own polin' boat—an' I'll hire me some Siwashes!" He turned to Mike Two Bear. "An ounce a day, damn you! An' the same to another one—to shove me up to the Klondike! An' another ounce on top of it if you git me there first!"

Mike Two Bear grinned. "W'ere you boat?" he asked. "You git de grub—I'm be dere."

Hell broke loose in Fortymile. The news spread to the dance hall—to the remotest cabin—a stampede was on! Poling boats became worth what a man would pay for them. Canoes were loaded with grub and headed upriver. Anything that could be made to float was heaped with grub and bedding and manned by wild-eyed stampeders.

On the river old Bettles drew a quart bottle from his pocket, popped the cork out by banging its bottom against his tightly rolled bed, and took a long drink. Then he passed the bottle back to Camillo Bill and Moosehide Charlie, who with one Siwash made up the crew of the poling boat that was forging steadily upriver. "Give her hell, boys!" he encouraged. "We're on the head of her now! I claimed I'd take a drink when we passed that damn Ear Bitin' Finley! Trouble with all the rest of 'em is they didn't stop to think that Harper an' Larue has a tradin' post stocked up on the flat—so they loaded their boats down with grub! Look at 'em!" He waved an arm down-river, where the Fortymile stampede was strung out in a long, thin line. "They'll git there—but, by God, when they do they'll find us staked alongside Til Carter an' the Fireweed! God! The guts of a man that would kidnap the Fireweed!"

"This Ear Bitin' Finley," said Camillo Bill casually, "he's got a bulge in the front of his shirt."

"Meanin'," asked Bettles, "that he's packin' a short-gun?"

"Well," said Camillo, "I don't figger it's his belly button!"

"My God," exclaimed Bettles, "he don't wear his shirt no closter to his belly than what I do!" and proceeded to dig into his pack.

"Me neither," said Moosehide Charlie.

"Nor me," agreed Camillo Bill. "What's the damn country comin' to when you got to dig out yer six-guns on stampedes?"

Long shadows stretched like reaching hands across the surface of the mighty river. Then the sun sank behind the high hills—and there were no shadows.

"Look ahead!" exclaimed Bettles. "Here comes a canoe! They see us! They're headin' in! I'm bettin' it's Til Carter's Siwashes tellin' us to come on up!"

"Yeah," agreed Camillo Bill, dryly lowering a glass from his eyes. "An' the Fireweed's with 'em. Shove in to shore, Moosehide. We'll be hearin' us an earful!"

They pushed in to the bank, and the other boats from Fortymile, sighting the approaching canoe and seeing Bettles's boat put ashore, followed.

The upriver canoe grounded on the shingle. Old Bettles reached for the Fireweed's hand. "It's good to see you, Pest," he said. "We figgered you was stole."

The girl smiled radiantly as the Fortymilers crowded around. "You're right for once in your long life, Uncle Gordon—I was! And hustled upriver in a coffin!"

"You don't look none the worst fer it," grinned Bettles.

The girl laughed. "The worse for it! I'm a million dollars better off for it! And you-all better hustle up there and get your stakes in. Bonanza's rotten with gold right in the grass roots! But—what started the stampede? I expected to do that when I hit Fortymile. Here's a note for you from Til Carter." Adjusting his steel-rimmed spectacles, Bettles read the words scrolled on the bit of bark. He handed it to Camillo, and so it passed from hand to hand of the crowding Fortymilers.

"Well, Julie, I guess you've told us all we need to know," grinned Bettles. "What started the stampede was that Ear Bitin' Finley, here, got worried when you didn't show up this mornin' at the restaurant, an' started huntin' you. A Siwash told him you'd be'n toled off an' stole forcible, an' he come up to Bergman's an' told us, an' we done some nosin' around an' found out that Til had located him a claim in next to Carmack an' Skookum Jim.

"It's one thing fer a squaw man an' a Siwash to locate claims—an' another thing when Til Carter locates one! So we hit out hell-a-whoopin'. Wait till I see that doggone coot —fer not lettin' us in on it!"

The girl laid a restraining hand on old Bettles's arm. "Til couldn't let you in. He had to look out for me first," she said earnestly. "Daddy had grubstaked him! He let you-all in as soon as he located me on a claim. He had to kidnap me to do it, because I wouldn't believe him when he told me Carmack had made a real strike on Bonanza. He did it for Daddy."

"Yeah?" grinned Camillo Bill. "His duty sure weighs heavy on him."

Old Bettles regarded the girl gravely. "Yer comin' on back up as quick as you record yer location, ain't you, Julie? If this here's a real strike, Fortymile is dead as hell right now. I seen the police inspector before we started, an' he's sendin' Corporal Downey up to see if this strike is as good as Carmack claims. An' if it is, they'll be movin' the detachment. The only thing that will be left in Fortymile will be the Mission. Bergman is packin' up his stuff right now. We'll have us a saloon handy inside a week! Better jest lock up yer restaurant—she won't make you an ounce a week no more. But you don't have to fool with a restaurant if this strike pans out."

"Lock up my restaurant!" cried the girl. "And let you boys eat greasy stews, and soggy bread, and anything they want to shove in front of you when you're in camp! Not by a long shot! I've bought a lot in Larue's townsite, and a restaurant is being built on it right now! There won't be any town on Bonanza—it'll be right where Larue figured it —on the flat beside the big river, where the steamboats can bring the freight right to the camp. Listen to me! Larue's townsite won't be a camp very long—it'll be a town—and then a city! Bonanza isn't the only creek up there—by a long shot! Circle City, Eagle, and Fort Yukon will be piling in on us—and when the news reaches the outside, there'll be the biggest stampede the world ever saw! Buy lots in Larue's townsite—buy claims on the creeks—buy anything anyone will sell! I can see it coming! I'll hire men to work my claim —and I'll run a good restaurant and let Til boss the work on the claims! I'm right now hitting back to arrange for the transportation of my dishes, and stove, and furniture."

"Mebbe yer right, Julie. I hope to God you be. But you better git goin', now, an' record yer location. Us fellers'll go on up an' git staked."

The girl drew the old man aside and whispered in his ear: "Til said to tell you and Camillo and Moosehide and Burr MacShane and Swiftwater to pass up the lower stretch and file above us. The gravel's better up there—and we'll all be together."

Ear Bitin' Finley pushed his way to the girl's side. "It was me that got worried when you didn't show up this mornin', Fireweed. If yer passin' out any inside dope, I'd ort to be in on it. Anyhow, us Koyukukers ort to stick together."

The girl smiled sweetly on the battered man. "I was delivering a message from Til Carter. It was to Uncle Gordon. Surely you remember Til Carter, Finley. I believe you met him a couple of days ago in Bergman's saloon," she said with a glance at his battered face.

XXIV

The End of Ear Bitin' Finley

Most of the Fortymilers called it a day, and camped. Bettles, Moosehide, and Camillo Bill pushed on. MacShane and Swiftwater Bill, with three Indians poling, followed. So did Ear Bitin' Finley and half a dozen other boats. At early daylight Joe Larue stood on the bank and waved his hat as the little flotilla turned up the Klondike and passed his townsite.

The stampeders found Til Carter putting his straps on a pack at the mouth of Bonanza, where he had left his poling boat.

He greeted them with a yell. "Come on, you sourdoughs! File on a moose pasture—an' tell 'em you like it! 'Gold's where you find it,' you know—an', by God, she's here!"

The five old-timers, Bettles, Camillo, Swiftwater Bill, Moosehide, and MacShane, grinned and tossed stakes out of their poling boat. A legal stake is not just a piece of wood driven into the ground. It must conform to specifications. It must have a diameter throughout of not less than five inches, must stand not less than four feet above the ground, must be flatted on two sides at least one foot from the top, each flatted side must measure at least four inches across the face, and there must be a stake at each end of a claim. They had fashioned their stakes as they poled upriver.

Each man shouldered his two stakes.

"Where do we go from here, Til?" asked Bettles.

Til eyed the four with the heavy green jackpine stakes over their shoulders. He grinned. "Drop 'em," he said, "an' I'll tell you!"

Ear Bitin' Finley, with a dozen men following, moved off up the creek, carrying grub packs.

The three cast their stakes onto the ground. "What the hell?" asked Camillo. "You don't want to git us beat by them, do you?" He indicated the vanishing backs.

Removing his straps from his pack, Til grinned. "Not any," he replied. "They'll stake when they run onto Larue's location. He and Mathew and Bum Eyed Bob staked just a little piece above here. We're going further up, where the Fireweed and I are located on Numbers One and Two above Carmack's Discovery claim. It's all good—the whole damn crick—but up there it's better. And we'll all be together."

"Suits me," said Bettles. "But why shuck our stakes?"

Til laughed and pointed to the casket. "Put 'em in there," he said, "and we can use those imitation-silver handles and all take a hand. I'll tell you, boys, there's nothing handier than a coffin! The Fireweed and I are going to use it for a toolbox! Grab onto those fancy handles—and let's mush!"

Hours later, with the stakes in, the five sat down to a meal that Til prepared from the contents of a pack he had carried up the evening before. Each had panned a single pan out of grass roots.

"Buy every damn claim you kin buy," advised Bettles. "That's what the Fireweed told us. An', you bet, she had the dope—she's smart! Me—I'm goin' to prospect the next crick—an' the next. This is the big strike, Til, that I told you was comin'—but who in the hell would of figgered it would come upriver!"

They camped that night in their blankets, and the following day, while Til felled spruce logs for his cabin on the rim slope, the five sourdoughs test-panned their claims. And in every pan, from gravel taken right out of the grass roots, they washed gold.

"Hadn't you fellows better hit out for Fortymile and record your locations?" asked Til the following morning.

Bettles shook his head. "I'm staked in next above Julie, an' Camillo above me, an' Moosehide above him, an' MacShane next, an' then Swiftwater. You're in below her. We're all right here in a pod. You got shells fer your rifle?" he asked.

"A full box," answered Til. "I only had one shell left when I hit Fortymile."

Bettles drew a six-gun from the front of his shirt and examined it carefully. "It's a hell of a while sence I've packed one of these on me," he said. "Not sence the early days on the Koyukuk. But comin' upriver, we noticed that besides his rifle Ear Bitin' Finley had a bulge inunder his shirt which wasn't ice cream he et fer breakfast. So we dug into our packs fer our authority. I don't reckon we'll have any trouble about bein' jumped. I kind of wish we would. I reckon we'll stick around a few days. Julie's movin' her restaurant up to Larue's townsite, an' Bergman's movin' his bar an' his likker, an' they'll be movin' the police detachment an' the recorder's office." He paused and grinned. "Here's one time I ain't bustin' a gut to hit for the recorder's. By God, I'm waitin' till the recorder comes to me! An' while I'm waitin' I'd like to see some son-of-a-bitch sink his stakes in alongside of mine—not mentionin' no names! But I seen Finley prowlin' around here last evenin', kind of lookin' things over. Mebbe he didn't locate down below."

The rabble of Fortymile had, as Til had predicted, staked the lower reach of the creek. There were still long reaches unstaked, for the simple reason that not enough men had come onto the creek to cover it. There was no crowding. Circle City and Eagle had not yet believed in the strike—

and as for the outside world, it would wait nearly two years!

On the morning of the first of September, Til stepped from his tent to see a new stake set beside the Fireweed's stake at each end of her location. He walked over and read the inscription. He read both inscriptions—they were side by side.

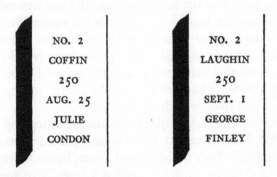

NO. 2	NO. 2
COFFIN	LAUGHIN
250	250
AUG. 25	SEPT. 1
JULIE	GEORGE
CONDON	FINLEY

Then he shouted for Bettles.

The old sourdough appeared, his fingers firmly grasping the neck of a bottle of whisky. "Christ, can't you let a man finish his breakfast?"

"Come over here and look at these stakes!" answered Til. "Now what the hell do you make of that? The Fireweed's ben down to Fortymile an' filed two, three days ago. What does Finley figure that play will get him?"

Old Bettles scratched his head, running gnarled fingers through long hair.

"When I called him a son-of-a-bitch a day or so ago, I onderstated the case. I'm jest rememberin' what I'd ort to re-membered a while back. Julie Condon ain't eighteen till the third of September. Cripes, I ort to know! I ben givin' her birthday presents sence they was pinnin' 'em on her three-cornered! I was up on the Koyukuk when she was born. Ear Bitin' Finley was up there too. An' he'd remember about it, because they always throwed a hell of a celebration on her birthday on account she was the first white baby to be born on the Koyukuk. Till day after tomorrow she can't file no legal claim!"

Til Carter waited to hear no more. Ducking into his tent, he came out with a rifle. "I don't know how much start he's got, Bettles," he said. "I hope it isn't too much. If Ear Bitin' Finley's jumped her claim—and got away with it—it's just too God-damn bad for him, that's all! If I can overtake him before he hits the recorder's, so much the better. But if he's already recorded her location in his name—you promise me to see that she gets my claim, when they hang me. So long."

"An' about this here date on her stakes," said Bettles. "I'll fix it up a little. It had ort to read the fourth of September instead of the twenty-fifth of August."

Til burned the trail to the Klondike and, stepping into a canoe, hit down-river. At the townsite Joe Larue told him that Ear Bitin' Finley had passed three hours before in a canoe. "An' he was a-goin'," added Larue, "like somethin' was after him."

Pushing out into the Yukon, Til headed downstream and, with his rifle placed conveniently in front of him, bent to his paddle. He knew Finley for a powerful man, and one whose long experience in the North had doubtless made him proficient in handling a canoe. Therefore he had small hope of overtaking the man before he reached Fortymile. However, there was a chance. Accidents happen, even to the best of canoemen—a broken paddle—a deadhead just below the surface—a sweeper. In his haste to reach the recorder, Finley might snap his paddle or drive the canoe onto a snag.

As Til paddled furiously downstream he formulated his plans. Should he overtake Finley on the river, it would merely be a question of shooting it out with him. Should the man succeed in reaching Fortymile and recording the claim that the Fireweed had innocently recorded illegally, he would hunt him up and, at the point of his rifle, force him to relinquish the claim so that the girl could legally file.

Should Finley refuse—well, the gun would go off, and the police would bury Finley.

Believing, as he did, that Finley had not only tortured the girl's brother in his cabin on Jim River but had murdered him and his own partner in crime in cold blood, Til felt not the slightest compunction in shooting him down like the dog he was. What would happen to himself as the result of the shooting Til refused to consider, dismissing the thought with a shrug.

His eyes sweeping the river ahead, Til held well inshore, just outside the eddies, so as to take advantage of a broader sweep of view with a water background. Rounding a bend some six or eight miles below Larue's, he checked his flying canoe by deftly swerving it into an eddy. Holding the light craft in the backwater, he fixed his gaze on a dark object that showed a quarter of a mile ahead. It was a canoe, drawn half clear of the water on a low jutting point of coarse gravel. Had Finley broken a paddle and been forced to land? If so, he could slant across the river and, keeping well out of range of Finley's rifle, could slip on down to Forty-mile in plenty of time to warn the girl to refile her claim.

"Nose her ashore, an' don't reach fer yer rifle!" Til Carter whirled at the short, clipped words of the command, to stare directly into the muzzle of Ear Bitin' Finley's rifle. Scarcely ten yards away, the man stood, head and shoulders above the rock fragment that had concealed him, the rifle sighted at point-blank range. For an instant Til hesitated as wild ideas flashed into his brain—a swift grab for his own rifle—the sudden overturning of the canoe—but—either would be suicide! Finley could not miss at that range. The canoe was swinging slowly at the outer edge of the eddy. "Come on, er I'll drill you!" grated the voice from the shore. "This trigger's set light, an' I'm gittin' nervous."

With a twist of the paddle, Til shot the light craft shoreward, and as the bow grated against the steep-pitched rocky shore, Finley reached down and, picking up Til's gun, hurled it into the river. Behind the cocked rifle, the face of Ear Bitin' Finley grinned malevolently. "Climb out. An' never mind yer pack. You won't be needin' it no more."

"What's the big idea?" asked Til, summoning a grin as the man stepped back to give room for the canoe to be drawn half clear of the water.

"I've got a lot of big idees," answered Finley, his eyes glittering with an insane hate. "The main one of 'em is that you've jest made yer last landin'!"

"Yeah? Figgerin' on knocking me off, eh? Well, it looks like you've got the time, the place, an' the weapon. Why the delay?"

"Quick killin's too good fer you, after the way you done me there in Bergman's," growled the man, his hatred spurred by the devil-may-care attitude of the younger man. "Them two teeth you broke off agin the bar rail has ben givin' me hell till I can't sleep of nights."

"And you're not as pretty as you used to be, either," grinned Til. "Have you looked in the glass lately?"

"Damn you! You think I'm bluffin'! But I hain't! You'll have plenty time to wisht to God you hadn't of broke them teeth off!"

"Goin' to tie me up and work on me with a hot gun barrel? Or have you got a candle in your pocket, so you can torture me like you did Davey Condon, up there on Jim River? When you get through you'd better make a good job of it and not leave me alive like you did Harmon, or I might squeal on you, like he did."

The insane glitter heightened at the words till it seemed the man's eyes spat flickering flame. "It's a God-damn lie! I did kill Harmon—left him layin' there on the floor—dead as Davey! I hain't afraid to tell you! You hain't goin' no place from here! What d'you mean—left him alive?"

"Just another way of sayin' he wasn't dead when you left him. He was still alive when Tim Condon and Bettles and I found him lying there on the cabin floor. Bettles and

I took him to the doctor in Coldfoot. He died on the way down—but not before he talked—and believe me, he told us plenty!"

"It's a damn lie!" The man fairly shouted the words.

"Yeah," grinned Til. "Then how do you suppose some folks know that you tortured Davey with a candle, and slugged Harmon with a blackjack because he tried to stop you?"

"Yer a damn liar! No one knows that!"

"No? I just dreamt it, I suppose? But it's just exactly what came off up there on Jim River, isn't it, Finley? You ought to know. But if you think you're the only one that knows, you're a damn fool. But come on—get to work tying me up. I won't promise to lie still while you're working on my hands and feet with your candle."

"Yeah?" taunted the man. "Smart as hell, hain't you? Figgerin' on my gittin' clost enough so's you kin jump in between me an' the end of my gun. Well, it wouldn't work, even if I figgered on tyin' you up." As he spoke the man loosened the buttons of his shirt front and, drawing a forty-four revolver, cocked it and returned it beneath his shirt. "I've got this baby handy, jest in case. Turn around, now, an' climb up the bank a ways till you come to a flat place. An' don't try no monkey business like runnin' off er grabbin' up a rock, er I'll fill you as full of holes as a rocker bottom."

Til ascended the short, steep slope with Finley at his heels, rifle a-cock. On a narrow terrace, some twenty-five feet above the surface of the river, they halted, and Finley motioned toward a dead spruce.

"Break off some branches an' git a fire goin'," he ordered. "I hain't had no breakfast, an' I'm feelin' fer a bilin' of tea an some sowbelly. I filled the tea pail an' fryin' pan 'fore you come along. Didn't dast to build no fire, er you'd see the smoke. I figgered you'd hit out after me hell-bent when you seen them stakes of mine. An' I figgered you'd stop right here when you seen that canoe drawed up on the pint below. Figgered how I'd busted a paddle er somethin', an' you'd cut around an' beat me to the recorder's, didn't you? Well, anyone that outfiggers Ear Bitin' Finley's got to git up a damn sight earlier in the mornin' than what you're habited to. Come on, git to work on them sticks an' git that tea a-bilin'. You kin look on while I eat. Feeding you would be a waste of grub. A man can go to hell as easy on a empty stummick as a full one."

Til collected a pile of spruce branches, kindled a fire, nested the teapot and frying pan on it, and sat down on the rock-strewn terrace with a pile of broken branches at his side, from which he judiciously fed the little fire. Finley seated himself opposite, his finger crooked on the trigger of the cocked rifle that rested on his knees, its muzzle trained squarely upon the younger man's chest.

"They's worst kind of tortures than candles," confided Finley with a leer. "An' it saves tyin' a man up. Take like a man jest waitin' to be knocked off—when he knows he hain't got a chanct in the world. 'Special a young feller that's jest planted his stakes on top of a million-dollar claim. Look at the fun he could have—if only he could live. An' then think of the Fireweed. She fell fer you—an' fell hard—after you'd kidnaped her an' set her down on a million-dollar claim. I could tell that when she was talkin' to Bettles there on the bank of the river when she give him yer birch-bark note. You an' her figgered on goin' a long ways on yer gold, didn't you? Well, she's goin' a long ways—but not with you! It's me an' her that'll be spendin' that gold—along with the thousan' ounces that's in the Jim River cache. If you could kidnap her with Fortymile plumb full of sourdoughs, an' take her off upriver, by God, I kin kidnap her when they hain't hardly no one but Siwashes left in camp. Hell, the police will be outa there in a few days, an' then I'll grab her off an' take her down-river, an' up the Koyukuk, an' on up the Jim to the cache. An' by the time we come back to

Bonanza—to our claim—she'll be mine, all right—er she won't never come back! An' all the while you'll be layin' on the bottom of the river with enough rocks tied to you so you won't never come up. They'll find yer canoe millin' around in some eddy—an' mebbe they'll pull another funeral fer you sometime when they're drunk enough—only next time you won't be showin' up to bust no one's teeth out! How does that listen to you, eh?"

"Sounds kind of funny," answered Til, feeding some more little sticks to the flames that licked at the sides of the tea pail. "Did you dream it, or read it out of a book?"

"I didn't do neither one—an' if you think I hain't a-goin' to plug you right where you set, you're a damn fool."

"It would be surer if you plugged me through the heart, or the head," grinned Til. "Then I wouldn't live to talk—like Harmon did."

"You got guts," snarled the man, maddened by Til's seeming indifference to his fate. "But yer sufferin'—no man could help it. I know. Didn't I set for long days an' nights in the death house—back in the States—waitin' fer the mornin' they was goin' to hang me fer knockin' off a guy! God, it was hell! Worst, even, than these teeth!"

"Did they decide you weren't worth hanging?" asked Til.

"They'd of hung me, all right," growled the man. "Only the noospapers printed a lot about it, an' a lot of damn-fool women an' preachers an' such got up a partition an' tuk it to the governor, an' he didn't dast do nothin' but change my sentence to life, 'cause 'lection was comin' on an' he figgered he might git beat if he didn't. Couple of years later four of us knocks a guard on the head, an' rushes the warden in his office, an' gits the key to the gun room, an' shoots our way out through the gate, killin' two more guards. They ketched the other three an' hung 'em—but I was too smart fer 'em. Don't tell me you ain't sufferin'! By God, I know! An' they ain't no noospapers, an' women, an' preachers up here—an' no governor to sign you off on account of 'lection!"

"You've lived a noble life, haven't you, Finley?" taunted Til, feeding more sticks to the little flames. "But, with all the unstaked ground on Bonanza, I don't see yet why you bothered to jump the Fireweed's claim instead of filing one of your own. I think you'll find that was a blunder."

"The hell you say! Well, I hain't no fool! I wasn't made in a minute! Don't you s'pose I knowed that you'd set her stakes into the best claim on the creek, outside of yer own? An' don't I know that if a man files on a crick, he can't file another claim on that crick inside of sixty days? If I'd located me a claim somewheres elst on the crick, I couldn't of sunk my stakes on hern, could I? What the hell! A man would be a damn fool to stake a claim that mightn't never pay wages, an' pass up one he knowed was rich, wouldn't he? I know the law. I know no one can't record no legal location till they're eighteen—an' I knowed the Fireweed wouldn't be eighteen till the third, an' that's the day after tomorrow. Hell—I was on the Koyukuk when they use' to celebrate her birthday!"

"You've got a good memory for birthdays, haven't you, Finley?" observed Til, adding a few little sticks to the fire.

"No one on the Koyukuk could fergit hern. She was the first white kid borned there, an' every year we use' to make a kind of hollerday out of her birthday—like the Fourth of July in the States. Everything would close up but the saloons, an' we'd go to it. Everyone would kick in with some kind of a present or other fer the kid, an' we'd have us a kind of jamboree."

Ear Bitin' Finley shifted his position slightly to ease a cramped leg, and Til noted that the slight shifting threw the gun muzzle just out of line with his chest. Very casually he added a stick or two to the blaze as Finley, evidently enjoying the exposition of his own acumen, launched into philosophy. "A man can't never know too much," he asserted ponderously. "Take me, now—I never figgered that knowin' about her birthday, that-a-way, would ever set me on top of a million-dollar claim. But it done so. An' knowin' men like I do made it a cinch fer me to trap you like I done this mornin'—I knowed you'd hit out after me, an' I knowed you'd slack up right about here to study that there canoe."

"Yeah," admitted Til, "but, knowing men like you do, it looks to me like you're overlooking one hell of a bet. Bettles was on the Koyukuk when the Fireweed was born, an' for a long time afterward. He's known her longer than you have—and he likes her. And all the rest of the sourdoughs that are up here on Bonanza like her too. A man that'll jump a claim isn't looked on with favor—and especially a man that would jump a woman's claim—and, more especially, the Fireweed's claim. Knowing men like you do, it seems funny that you'd think the sourdoughs are going to sit around and let you get away with it."

Finley laughed, exposing behind his ragged mustache the gaping aperture where two front teeth should have been and inadvertently shifting the rifle muzzle a bit more out of line. "Like I told you, me an' the Fireweed's goin' to hit the long trail to Jim River. What happens about that claim's up to her. A man should ort to have a woman—an' she'd be as good as any other. If she's got as much sense as I think she's got, she'll marry me over there in Alasky somewheres. An' when we come back from the Jim River cache with them thousan' ounces, an' hit fer our claim on Bonanza, everything'll be all jake. The sourdoughs hain't goin' to start no trouble betwixt a man an' his woman.

"If she ain't got no sense, an' don't throw in with me, she's goin' to Jim River jest the same—an' before I'm through with her she'll come acrost with that cache, too. She knows where it's at. Davey told me he writ out its location an' mailed it down to her after old Tim pulled out fer Bettles. Then it's up to her—if she don't throw in with me, she'll go the same road you an' Davey an' Harmon went—it's all the same to me. Only in sech case I don't go back to Bonanza. The claim on Bonanza's mine, my legal stakes bein' in beside her onlegal ones. I'll lay up at Eagle, er Star, er Circle on the American side, an' sell out a half interest to a couple of workin' pardners, an' set back an' take it easy. What with half that comes out of the claim, an' the thousan' ounces from Jim River, I'll be settin' pretty. An' there won't be a damn thing on me, 'cause there won't no one know I kidnaped the Fireweed. An' they can't no one prove I knocked off Davey an' Harmon. All I got to do is keep out of the way of the sourdoughs that might pot me jist out of spite fer jumpin' the Fireweed's claim."

Til listened intently, his eyes on the simmering tea pail. He leaned forward, with a handful of little sticks, just as the reddish-brown surface of the liquid broke into a seething boil. It was the moment for which he had been waiting. Quick as a flash, he dropped the sticks and, heedless of the blistering heat, grasped the pail by its rim and dashed its boiling contents squarely into the face of Ear Bitin' Finley. The rifle went off with a deafening roar, almost in Til's face, and the air was filled with agonized shrieks of pain as Ear Bitin' Finley leaped to his feet, clawing wildly at his tortured face.

Half bewildered himself, Til sprang forward across the fire, with the idea of throwing the man down, when a misstep on a loose stone threw him violently against the screaming man. Instantly huge arms encircled him in a viselike grip, and despite his frantic struggles to free himself, he was drawn with crushing force against the writhing body. For a single instant Til gazed into the lobster-red face, and in that instant the scalded eyelids parted to disclose horrible sightless eyeballs, flaming red, in which no trace of iris or pupil showed.

Redoubling his efforts, Til strove to reach the screaming throat with his fingers, but his arms were pinioned to his sides in an ever-tightening death grip that seemed to be crushing the very life from his body. For several moments they weaved on the brink of the steep, rock-rubbled bank of the river. Then Til tripped the other, and together they crashed to the ground and the next instant were rolling down the steep declivity locked together by the mighty grip of Finley's arms, every revolution bringing torturing stabs of pain as Til's body or his head came into violent contact with the protruding rocks of the slope. As they struck the water Til filled his lungs with a great gasp of air, while Finley, whose sightless eyes gave him no warning of the water, struck it with a scream of pain that ended in a blubbering, bubbly sound, followed by profound silence, as the two sank struggling to the bottom.

The shock of the cold water caused Til to forget his burned fingers and bruise-tortured body, and revived him to redouble his frantic struggles to free himself from the grip that must soon prove the death grip for both. Til's lungs seemed bursting, and the pressure of the water set up a ringing in his throbbing ears.

In the grip of the current, the two forms scraped and bumped along the rock-strewn floor of the river. Til's upper arms, locked fast to his sides, allowed action only from the elbows down. And he frantically punched and gouged and tore at the other's belly. He was becoming dizzy, and great swirling red shapes seemed writhing before his eyes. Suddenly, just as it seemed that he must expel the pent-up air from his bursting lungs, his hand slipped inside Finley's shirt and clutched the butt of the cocked revolver. Wrenching it about so as to bring the muzzle against the man's naked belly, he pulled the trigger. There was a convulsive spasm of writhing muscles, which suddenly went limp and flaccid, and the next moment Til Carter felt himself rising slowly to the surface. He opened his eyes, and through the murky water saw the daylight above him. Fighting for consciousness, he paddled furiously, and a moment later his head broke the surface and he was pumping the life-giving air into his lungs in great, sobbing gasps. Summoning his last atom of strength, he struck out for the shore, only a few feet distant, and succeeded in pulling himself half clear of the water at a point a few yards upriver, where the current of the eddy had carried him. Then the world went black.

How long he lay there, Til Carter never knew. When consciousness returned, he was numb from the hips downward, and it was with the greatest difficulty that he succeeded in drawing himself clear. A half hour later he regained the little terrace and rekindled the fire of dry spruce twigs. Removing his clothing, he wrung out the water and took stock of his bruises, which, though superficial, were numerous and painful, as were the seared and scalded fingers with which he had seized the pail of boiling tea.

Making his way to the canoe, he recovered his pack and, returning to the fire, proceeded to prepare and eat a liberal breakfast, washing it down with great draughts of scalding-hot tea.

In another hour, save for the aches and pains of his bruises, he was fit as ever. And it was with a light heart and a sense of grim duty well done that he stepped into his canoe and shoved off into the current. "She won't need to bother about gitting evidence against Ear Bitin' Finley now," he muttered to himself as the canoe floated lazily toward Fortymile. "The way he got his was a damn sight worse than hanging —and he didn't get any more than was coming to him, at that. She'll have to file over again tomorrow, to make it legal —and then—well, I'll be down there—and—and Father Judge is still at the Mission. We'll move the restaurant fixtures up to Larue's townsite. And by that time Bergman will have his saloon going. We'll be married in the new forum room, and believe me, that will be a wedding to figure dates by. The boys will celebrate for a week!"